NEVER SEND FLOWERS

by John Gardner

BERKLEY BOOKS, NEW YORK

NEVER SEND FLOWERS

A Berkley Book / published by arrangement with Glidrose Publications Ltd.

PRINTING HISTORY
G. P. Putnam's Sons edition / May 1993
Berkley edition / June 1994

ISBN: 0-425-14250-7

BERKLEY®
Berkley Books are published by
The Berkley Publishing Group, 200 Madison Avenue, New York, New York 10016.
BERKLEY and the "B" design are trademarks of Berkley Publishing Corporation

PRINTED IN THE UNITED STATES OF AMERICA

10 9 8 7 6 5 4

Acknowledgment

I must thank the Senior Vice-President and Board of EuroDisney SA for their cooperation in allowing me to use the wonderful EuroDisney facility as a backdrop to the final scenes in this book.

Particular thanks must go to my friend Jean Marie Gerbeaux, Vice-President, Communications, EuroDisney SA, for all his help in providing information.

For the purposes of a work of fiction, and for complete security, I have played a little with the security arrangements at EuroDisney. Only those who know will spot these alterations, which are minor, for this tremendous complex remains one of the best Disney facilities in the world.

JOHN GARDNER
Virginia 1992

For Bunny—My First Fan

Contents

Lay her i' the earth;
And from her fair and unpolluted flesh
May violets spring!

Hamlet: *William Shakespeare*

NEVER SEND FLOWERS

1

Week of the Assassins

Father Paolo Di Sio had been annoyed from the moment His Holiness had made his wishes clear. Di Sio had even argued with the Supreme Pontiff, not an unusual occurrence, for, as the Pope had been known to remark, "I seem to be a constant thorn in the side of my senior secretary."

Indeed, Father Di Sio was exceptionally anxious, and this was the final reason that only a very few members of His Holiness' entourage knew of the change of plan. For one day—in fact for slightly less than fifteen hours—the Pope would leave his lakeside summer residence at Castel Gandolfo, and travel back into the boiling cauldron that was Rome in the month of August.

The cause of Paolo Di Sio's annoyance was a combination of his devotion to the Pope and his feeling that the journey was quite unnecessary.

After all, the General could quite easily have come
to Castel Gandolfo for the audience. Instead, His
Holiness would be put under needless strain, and
all for the sake of a military man whose ego would
undoubtedly be greatly enlarged by the fact that
the Pope had honored him with a private audience
at the Vatican, in the dog days of summer.

His Holiness viewed the matter somewhat dif-
ferently. Generale Claudio Carrousso was not
simply a military man, for in the past year the
General had become arguably the most famous
soldier in the world—except for General Norman
Schwarzkopf.

Carrousso had served with great bravery during the Gulf War, gallantly leading one of Italy's
squadrons of Tornadoes on dangerous low-level
attacks against Iraqi targets.

On his return from the Gulf, the General had
requested a year's sabbatical during which he
wrote the book that was eventually to make
him a household name: *The Use of Air Power
for Peace.*

While the title was hardly the stuff of the
bestseller lists, Carrousso's talent as an author
was immediately apparent to military scholars
and laymen alike. His style was a subtle cross
between Tom Clancy and John le Carré, and book
reviewers were quick to point out that he had done
the impossible by bridging the gap between the
dust-dry stuff of strategy and the fast, grabbing
pace of a technothriller. Six months after its
appearance in the original Italian, *The Use of
Air Power for Peace* had been translated and
published in eleven languages, and was topping

the nonfiction lists in as many countries.

His Holiness recognized the General as a mover and shaker for world peace, and, as such, felt that the military man should be openly recognized by the Church as an exceptional power for good in this wicked world.

So it was, that, despite the scoldings of advisers, the Supreme Pontiff made the journey into Rome on a hot August morning, and met for a full hour with Generale Claudio Carrousso in the private Papal apartments in the Vatican.

It was a little after two-thirty in the afternoon that the General emerged from a private door in the heart of the Vatican City and joined his ADC and a Vatican security officer.

Purposely, the General's party had been led from a side door into the warren of streets behind St. Peter's, where only specifically authorized vehicles were allowed along the narrow road. Though the roar of Rome's normal snarl of traffic could be clearly heard as they waited for the General's car, they could have been in a different city, and at a different period of history. Within the walls of the Vatican, as Carrousso said, time seemed to stand still. So, as they waited in this strange time warp, the General spoke, in an awed voice, of the saintliness of the Pope, and his surprising knowledge of military matters.

The small group only vaguely heard the popping sound of the motor scooter, though the General himself glanced up and saw the slightly amusing sight of a nun, in full habit, approaching, sitting straight-backed on a puttering scooter, followed, at what seemed to be a respectful distance, by his own official car.

The General picked up his briefcase, looking past the nun toward his car with the red-and-blue pennants fluttering in the sun. For him, this had been a great and memorable experience.

Only the Vatican security officer stood frozen with a sudden concern, staring at the nun. Very few religious societies for women still wore the full-length black habits of their order, and the man realized just how much of an anachronism this figure really was, dressed in a style which had long disappeared as outmoded.

As his brain processed the information, he saw, with a sudden horror, that the nun on a motor scooter was certainly not what she seemed. Her robes were of the kind only seen nowadays in historical movies, or on actresses playing medieval nuns on the stage.

None of them saw the nun's face, though the security officer cried out a warning just as the scooter came abreast of the three men. The nun swiveled on the small saddle, the wicked snout of a machine pistol poking, almost invisible, from the folds of her habit.

Later, the forensic specialists would identify the weapon as a standard 9mm Uzi machine pistol, but by then it mattered little to the General. The nun fired three short, accurate, and deadly bursts, proving that she was a markswoman of great skill. The Uzi was fitted with some kind of noise-reduction system, so that its soft ripping noise was almost drowned by the popping of the motor scooter. By the time she had disappeared, the General lay dead, and his two companions writhed in agony from neatly placed flesh wounds, their blood soaking the pavement.

There was no doubt that the General had been the principal target, for it was no accident that his ADC and the Vatican security officer had simply been immobilized and not mortally wounded. In all, the killing of Generale Claudio Carrousso had been immaculately planned, and expertly carried out.

The newspapers, naturally, had a field day: MURDER IN THE VATICAN and GENERAL ASSASSINATED screamed from the front pages, while experts on terrorism named at least three possible pro-Iraqi terrorist groups as the most natural perpetrators.

The second assassination took place on the following day, in London.

The Honorable Archie Shaw MP was one of the country's favorite politicians, a possible reason why he had never attained any truly powerful government appointment. Certainly he was a member of the present Prime Minister's Cabinet, but only as Minister for the Arts, a job which kept him well clear of making life-or-death decisions for either his country's, or party's, home and foreign policies.

Nonetheless, Archie Shaw was a true lover of the Arts, and fought tooth and nail for larger government subsidies in matters which fell within his bailiwick: a fact which made him the particular darling of actors, directors, musicians, painters, and all others concerned with what they saw as the United Kingdom's primary export: theatre, music, ballet, opera, and the like.

On that August Monday, Archie Shaw lunched
at Le Chat Noir, his favorite restaurant in
Chelsea. With him were his wife, the dazzling
Angela Shaw, and two internationally famous
theatre directors. Later the public learned that
the conversation had concerned an attempt to
inject massive sums of money into the country's
now nonexistent movie industry. It was a scandal,
Archie had said toward the end of the meal, that
Britain, once a prime moviemaking country, had
been denuded of the facilities which at one time
had drawn directors and actors from all over the
world.

The lunch finished at exactly three o'clock.
Farewells were said on the pavement outside the
restaurant, and "The Archie and Angela Show"—
as they were commonly referred to in the press—
walked slowly to their car, which had been parked
in a side street some five minutes away. They
strolled, hand in hand like young lovers, he tall,
broad-shouldered with one of those patrician profiles which remind people of the lineations found
on coins of the great old Roman Empire; she petite,
snub-nosed, with blazing red shining hair falling
to her shoulders.

They reached the car, which Archie unlocked,
swiftly moving around the vehicle to open the
passenger-side door to see his wife safely in before
returning and settling himself into the driver's
seat. They planned to drive to their small country
cottage some ten miles south of Oxford.

Archie turned the key in the ignition, and
died, together with his wife and three innocent

bystanders. The explosion was heard over five miles away, as it ripped through the car, throwing shards of metal in every direction. One of the dead was a passing cabdriver whose passenger emerged without even a graze. "I saw this great blood-red gash of fire," this lucky man said to the television news cameras. "I can't recall even hearing the explosion, but the fire seems to have burned itself into my memory. I shall never forget it because I swear that I saw an arm come flying from the middle of the fire."

Later evidence showed that the bomb had been in place for almost forty-eight hours, controlled by an ingenious device which had allowed the vehicle to be started and driven eight times before the mercury switch was activated to detonate the twenty pounds of Semtex, wedged in a neat package directly behind the dashboard.

Nobody was surprised when the head of the Bomb Squad, a Metropolitan Police Commander, gave a press conference that evening, indicating that the explosive device bore all the hallmarks of the Irish Republican Army. There was much said about barbarity and a complete disregard for the sanctity of human life.

On the following morning the IRA vigorously denied having placed the bomb, and on that same Tuesday afternoon, a third assassination took place. This time in Paris.

Pavel Gruskochev was another household name. A survivor of the Cold War, he had come into prominence about the same time as another great Russian writer, Alexander Solzhenitsyn.

Gruskochev had fled to political asylum in the West as early as 1964, having had his great seminal work, *A Little Death,* banned from publication within the Soviet Union. Indeed, he only got out of Russia by the skin of his teeth, with the hounds of KGB baying at his heels.

The novel was published in London and Paris in 1965, and in the United States early in 1966. It was a vast and huge literary success, a triumph that would be repeated three years later with *After the Onion Skins.* Both of the books tore down the ragged canvas of Communism, using every device at the novelist's disposal—satire, romance, the shades of real history, fear, and wonderfully vivid narratives which blew away the cobwebs of the mind.

Now, on this Tuesday afternoon in August, the month when Parisians ritualistically leave their city to the tourists, Pavel Gruskochev announced a press conference. Every newspaper and magazine in the world had someone there, for the Russian was known for his lack of interest in the press and his almost hermitlike existence.

As well as the representatives of the press and TV, many of the author's devotees, hearing of the press conference, rushed to be present, so when the great man stepped up to the microphone-laden podium, in his French publishers' office, he blinked, surprised at the crowd packing the room.

His statement was short, terse, slightly emotional, and could quite easily have been sent out as a written document.

"I have asked you here because those who advise me feel it is necessary for me to say what I have to tell you, here in public, and not as a disembodied voice informing you on paper," he began in his halting, still highly accented English.

"This is, I think, a little like closing the door after the horse has bolted, for so many of my Russian friends have already returned to the place of their births. I have hesitated, and rightly so, for—until recently—I was still regarded officially as a nonperson, that strange term the old régime granted to people who told the truth. Well, I am no longer a nonperson." He held up a small slip of paper and a passport.

"This morning I was informed of my reinstatement as a Russian citizen, so, it is with immense pride and pleasure that tomorrow I shall return to the place of my birth, to my roots which, even in a long exile, have remained intact."

He went on a little longer, thanking people in France, Britain, and the United States for their friendship, help, and understanding during his years spent far from his homeland, then, as quickly as it had begun, the conference was over.

People pressed around him; reporters barraged him with questions, men and women thrust flowers into his hand, and one very tall woman, dark and wearing a broad, stylish hat that almost hid her face, handed him a wrapped package.

Later, those near to Pavel Gruskochev swore that the woman spoke to him in Russian, that he smiled at her and clutched the package to him as though it were something very precious. Certainly there was one photograph of the moment which showed him peering toward his benefactor with what appeared to be almost awe.

Ten minutes later, as he sat alone in the back of a taxi, the package exploded, leaving the great novelist as though he had never been, his driver severely injured, and the traffic around the Champs-Elysées clogged for several hours.

On Wednesday came the fourth assassination, though at that time nobody was linking any of these deaths one with another.

Twelve noon, Eastern Standard Time, Washington D.C.

Mark Fish was unknown to most people. Only insiders, and the political correspondents, knew him as well as they could know any man in his shoes. As Assistant to the Director of Central Intelligence, he was usually kept lurking in the background, for the Central Intelligence Agency is like an iceberg. Everyone knows it is there, but outsiders only see the tip, for the rest is cloaked and out of sight. Mark Fish was normally out of sight.

On this Wednesday, the DCI was out of the country, so it was Fish who made the trip from Langley, Virginia, to Pennsylvania Avenue and the White House to deliver the weekly personal briefing to the President. He had been called upon to do this on several previous occasions, so it was nothing out of the ordinary.

The briefing lasted a little longer than usual, and just before noon he returned to his car, was driven out of the side entrance, and then down onto Pennsylvania Avenue itself.

The driver had to wait for a matter of two minutes for a break in the traffic, so the car moved quite slowly into the right-hand lane. It was at this point that Mark Fish shifted his position, leaning toward the near-side window as though to get more light on the document he was studying.

Nobody either saw or heard the shot. The window fragmented and Fish was thrown against the back of his seat, the top of his head exploding, hurling bloody debris against the leather and glass, three Equalloy bullets smashing into his head. The Equalloy round, made in the United Kingdom, is now an almost redundant type of ammunition, but it is still available. A fourth-generation Accelerated Energy Transfer (AET) round, the Equalloy is designed to fragment on hitting its target. It also has all the necessary non-shoot-through requirements of present-day special forces, thereby minimizing the risk of killing bystanders. On its initial tests, the Equalloy penetrated only 2.5 inches of Swedish soap— the ammunition-designers' substitute for human tissue.

Later, the D.C. Police Department, aided by both the FBI and Secret Service, measured and calculated the trajectory of the bullets, thereby roughly approximating from where they had come.

Among the many bystanders was one tourist who had been taking photographs at the time. One frame from his 35mm camera yielded a small clue, for it showed an elderly man standing in

almost the precise spot from which they had esti-
mated the bullet had been fired.

He appeared to be a man in his late seventies
or early eighties, dressed in jeans, an L.L. Bean
checked shirt, and a blue, billed cap bearing the
legend *Toto, I don't think we're in Kansas anymore.* The Old Guy, as the investigators called
him, carried a thick walking cane with a duck's
head brass handle. At the moment the picture
had been taken, he had the cane raised, pointing
directly at Mark Fish's car. Once this photograph
had been enlarged and enhanced, there was little
doubt that the Old Guy had been the assassin,
and that his walking stick was in reality some
kind of deadly weapon.

Only a couple of international newspapers
picked up on the fact that three high-profile figures and one very senior intelligence officer had
been murdered in as many days, and in as many
countries, but no link was officially made by any of
the law-enforcement organizations involved. Yet
the truth was that, in less than one week, four
prominent victims had died in various ruthless,
brutal acts of violence. Though nobody linked the
deaths, one thing was certain: each of them had
been a target; each had been stalked, sought out,
and killed with some care and preparation; and,
while the specialists in terrorism had named possible groups as the perpetrators of these killings,
no organization had come forward to claim responsibility—an oddity that was the one constant in
the four deaths, for terrorist groups are rarely
slow in claiming success after a carefully planned
operation.

On Friday of the same week, another killing took place. This time it happened in Switzerland, and the victim could not by any stretch of the imagination be called high profile. In fact, she was just the opposite, and it was this fifth death which brought James Bond into the picture.

2

Gazing Down at the Jungfrau

She left her hotel in Interlaken at around ten-thirty in the morning. Switzerland's Bernese Oberland always had a calming effect on her, and Laura March needed peace and quiet more than ever before.

As a child, her parents had often brought her to this part of Switzerland and she remembered her father telling her, years ago, how therapeutic it was simply to sit and look at the mountains. She desperately needed to think, allow the pain to subside, and reassess her life.

It had rained on and off all the previous day, but this morning the sky was cloudless, the deep and perfect blue seen only at high altitudes. The mountains, with their constant caps of snow, were clear and sharp against the skyline and, in the distance, she could just see the great curve of rock

which looked like the breast of a young woman—
the reason they called that particular mountain
the Jungfrau.

At the Interlaken West station, Laura boarded
the train to Grindelwald. She was always amazed
that so little had changed here since her childhood.
Even her traveling companions seemed familiar to
her: a group of chattering young people on a day
trip, led by a solemn, plump woman, bossy and
arrogant; there was an unsmiling young man,
wearing stout walking boots, his rucksack on the
luggage rack, face buried in some guide book, out
for a day or two of serious walking; a middle-
aged couple, healthy and red-faced, dressed in
jeans and sweaters; and a dozen other people,
all remembered from the long-ago days when
she had gazed in wonder from the rattling train
window, clutching her father's hand.

Everything was familiar, from the long slanted
roofs of the chalets, to the splash of color in window
boxes, and the smell. All countries, she thought,
had a particular scent to them, retained in the
memory of visitors, and immediately recognizable on return. Her father had often said that he
remembered the smell of Switzerland, rather than
the views, and she had known what he meant. Her
mother used to say it was the smell of money, but
that was a family joke. The scent of Switzerland
was a kind of cleanliness found in so few places
these days.

At Grindelwald, she walked slowly up through
the village, dodging other tourists, strolling along
the crowded high pavements, pausing to look
into the shop windows: picture postcards, seeds

of mountain flowers, patches to sew onto jeans, little metal tags to attach to walking sticks, and mountains of food, the stores presided over by serious-looking men and women. For the Swiss, all business is serious, and Grindelwald is, rightly, a prosperous place, sitting as it does on the edge of the Glacier Gorge. For decades it has been a playground, in winter and summer, for climbers, sightseers, and long-distance skiers alike.

It was after eleven-thirty when she reached the chair lift, paying her few francs and swinging into the chair to be levitated almost noiselessly upward, above the bright lush green grass of the foothills, the flash of a trickling stream below as the cable swung her, rising up the long slope.

She disembarked at the lookout point they called First, that boasted only a large log cabin in which delicious food was served—crowded at this time of day, but the perfect place to sit and eat an omelet, fried potatoes, and crisp bread, washed down with a glass of *Apfelsaft*.

When she had eaten, Laura walked a little way up the slope and sat on the soft grass, looking out toward the Mittaghorn range, the dark brooding slopes of the Schwarz Mönch, the toy houses of Grindelwald far below, the contrast in color, greens, yellows, the seasoned blackish green of the pine trees, and the wonderful skyline of the Jungfrau, just visible off to her far right; the awesome Gletscherschlucht, the glacier itself, and the crowning glory in the distance—the summit of the Eiger.

The mountains, she thought, were like scale models made from cleverly folded gray paper, brushed at their peaks with white powder. David loved it here, but that was over and done with. This was a time of healing for her battered emotions. No more David, for that was finished and she had to resurrect herself from the small death which had come only a short time ago.

As she feasted on the view, it was as if, by some trick of time and light, she were being mentally enfolded by crags, peaks, fissures. Her father had been right, the grandeur and beauty of the view helped to put her own small concerns and pain as a human into perspective. It seemed as though this spot could magically sweep her small anguish into its proper place. The awesome wonder of the vast range of mountains was already doing its work.

When she felt the unexpected stab of pain in her neck, she thought, almost lazily, that she had been stung by a bee. She tried to put her hand up to trap the insect, and was puzzled when she could not get her arm above shoulder height.

She did not panic. It was as if she viewed her strange situation from very far away. The numbness seemed to spread from where she had been stung on the neck. First, her arms became immobile, then she experienced a not unpleasant sense of her entire body being invaded so that she could not move at all.

"This is a dream. I shall wake in a moment," she thought, trying unsuccessfully to smile, for there was her dead father waving, running up the flower-dotted slope toward her. Then the darkness smothered everything.

The people who ran the small restaurant found her body just before dusk.

The next morning, a Saturday, James Bond was finishing his last cup of breakfast coffee and contemplating a lazy weekend—which included a promising dinner that night with a young woman called Charlotte Helpful—when the telephone rang, banishing all plans for the next few weeks, let alone fun and games with Ms. Helpful.

"Before we begin, Captain Bond, I'd like you to take a look at this photograph." M slid a matt eight-by-ten, black-and-white print across his desk. His mood had been somber from the moment Bond had entered the room.

It had been Moneypenny, the Chief's secretary, who summoned Bond to the suite of offices occupied by M and his personal staff, on the ninth floor of the anonymous building overlooking Regent's Park.

"You're to go straight in, take no notice of *that.*" She had nodded toward the door, above which the familiar red DO-NOT-ENTER light flashed. As Bond took a pace forward, Moneypenny dropped her voice. "He's got a pair of our sisters in there." She gave him a quick little smile before looking away, a fierce blush scalding her cheeks. The torch she carried for James Bond was no secret to anyone in the building.

The "sisters" were a man and woman from the Security Service, MI5, introduced to Bond as Mr. Grant and Ms. Chantry—a portly man, dressed in the dark-suited Whitehall uniform, and a rather frumpish young woman, sitting to attention, inflexible, with her backside perched on the edge of her chair. Both of these officers looked uncomfortable, for members of the Security Service are seldom at ease when circumstances force them to ask favors of the Secret Intelligence Service. There was little doubt in Bond's mind that they were here to crave a boon from M.

He glanced at the photograph of a young woman, possibly in her early thirties, with light-blonde hair and a pixieish, pleasant face.

"Should I recognize her, sir?" Bond raised his eyebrows in query.

"Only you can answer that, Captain Bond." M remained unsmiling. "I am aware that there are occasional cross-fertilizations between our service and our sisters."

"She's one of yours?" Bond addressed Ms. Chantry.

"*Was* one of ours." Impatient, but somehow full of suspicion.

He thought he could also detect a tiny fleeting stab of pain in her voice, and saw it pass across her face, there one minute, gone the next. He turned back to his Chief. "No, sir. No, I don't recognize the young lady."

M nodded, then looked across at Grant. "Tell him what you've just told me." His tone was not unfriendly, but nobody could doubt that the Old Man was in one of his tough, all-business moods.

Grant, in his mid-forties, had a prissy mouth and a tendency to be fussy, his hands constantly straightening his tie or brushing imaginary lint from his trousers. Bond put him down as a deskman—personnel or accounts.

After clearing his throat a couple of times and fiddling with his cuff links, Grant began tentatively—"Her name is Laura March. Age thirty-five, been with our service for ten years. Worked five years with the Watcher Division, then moved on to Anti-Terrorist Intelligence. Mainly analysis of raw information. Very good record. Knew her stuff." For a second he paused as if treading on uncertain ground.

"And?" Bond gave him an encouraging smile. "She's disappeared with the family jewels?"

"She's dead." It came out flat and uneasy.

"Murdered, it would seem." M filled the gap.

"In Switzerland," Ms. Chantry supplied. "She was on leave."

"Ah." The truth was out, Bond thought. MI5's jurisdiction was effective only in the United Kingdom and its dependencies, a situation which often led to ill-feeling between the two organizations.

Grant sounded a shade petulant now. "That's why we need your help. She was staying in Interlaken—Switzerland . . ."

"I know where Interlaken is." This time Bond was neither encouraging nor smiling. "Switzerland. Little place with lots of lakes and mountains. Lots of banks and chocolate as well."

Grant frowned. "You're familiar with Interlaken?"

"I know it's a tourist center for the Bernese Oberland." Bond wanted to demagnetize the highly charged atmosphere, maybe even force a smile from this somewhat pompous man. So he half sang, " 'Gazing down on the Jungfrau, from our secret chalet for two.' *Kiss Me Kate* and all that."

"The only way you can gaze down at the Jungfrau is from a helicopter or an airplane." Grant looked puzzled.

"That's the whole point," Bond snorted. "Cole Porter wrote that song as a satire on the stupidity of some operettas. I—"

"Captain Bond," M snapped. "We do not require a lesson in musical comedies. This is a serious business. Let Mr. Grant give you the facts."

Bond, still a little irritated at having been called away from what was to have been a delightful weekend, and possibly two reckless nights with the nubile Ms. Helpful, knew how far he could go with M, and his Chief's voice had now hit what he liked to think of as the Mutiny on the Bounty level. He closed his mouth and nodded politely to Grant.

"It's a beautiful part of the world," Grant continued lamely. "And it appears that she was particularly fond of it. She had been there for two days, and yesterday morning she took the chair lift up to First, a very good viewing point above Grindelwald. Last night she was found dead, about half a mile from the chair-lift staging point."

"Dead as in natural causes, or the other kind?"

"It would seem the other kind."

"How?" Bond looked toward Ms. Chantry, who had gone pale, her eyes reflecting the anguish he had noted earlier.

"As you know, the Swiss authorities have a tendency to work by the book, Captain Bond. The police were called, treated the matter as a possible murder or suicide, did the usual things, and then moved the body to Interlaken. They did an autopsy in the early hours of this morning, and the results are both puzzling and unpleasant."

"I'm used to unpleasant matters." Bond had slipped into his own somber mode. If you cannot beat them, join them, he considered. "I've spent the past week looking at photographs and reading autopsy reports on four terrorist assassinations which might just impinge on matters of intelligence, so a fifth postmortem isn't going to make me queasy."

Grant nodded. "The only unusual mark they found on the body was an angry bruise on her neck, just below the right ear. The skin was broken and they recovered a tiny fragment of gelatin. Part of a capsule which had penetrated the skin."

"How?"

"We don't know. The Swiss won't commit themselves."

"So what was the cause of death?"

Grant frowned. "They're still doing tests. Nothing confirmed as yet except that whatever killed her almost certainly got into her via the capsule. I understand that they've now brought some specialist forensic doctor up from Bern."

"And this, having happened in Switzerland, brings you to the point of your visit to us?"

"We've been refused permission by both the Foreign Office and Swiss security to operate on their turf. They know of Ms. March's link with us, and they're fairly paranoid."

"Point is," M cut in, as though annoyed at Grant for taking too long to explain the full situation. "Point is that they will accept Scotland Yard or one representative from us."

"And we're not happy about Mr. Plod treading all over one of our own," Grant added.

"So I'm the lucky winner?" Bond's spirits rose slightly. An all-expenses-paid weekend in Switzerland—even on grim business—was relatively appealing.

"You fly out this afternoon." M did not even look at him. "They'll be holding the inquest on Monday, so you'll have plenty of time to go over the ground."

"Haven't we got anybody in Switzerland anymore, sir?"

"You know how it is, Bond. Cutbacks, reorganization. Yes, we have somebody in Geneva, at the embassy . . ."

"Well, can't—"

"No, he can't. He's on leave. In the old days we would have had him covered, but those luxuries are gone. You go out, flying the flag, to Bern this afternoon. They'll meet you at the airport and ferry you to Interlaken."

"Who's 'they'? The cops?"

"No. Swiss Intelligence. What used to be the old Defense Department 27—disbanded last January. They've reorganized like everybody else, and one of their people will meet your flight, take you around, show you the crime scene, fill you in and hold your hand at the inquest. Your job is simply to gather details and make sure the Swiss police have done a thorough job."

"They always do a thorough job," Grant muttered. "They're Swiss, and the Swiss bring a new meaning to the word brusque."

"You make sure they've done a thorough job."
M was not to be put off. "And you make certain
that their coroner releases the body to you."

"And I bring the unfortunate lady home?"

"That's about the size of it."

"And if I pick up any clues as to the circumstances of her death?"

"You report your findings to me." M made a
small dismissive gesture, indicating that as far
as he was concerned the meeting was over.

"Sir, might I ask some questions of our friends
here?" If he were going to be used as a detective,
he had to conduct himself as such.

"If you must."

Bond nodded, turning to face Grant and Chan-
try. "Ms. March worked in Terrorist Intelligence.
Was she involved in any particular operation?
Dealing with one particular group?"

Grant shifted in his chair, pausing just a fraction too long for Bond's comfort. "She worked the
whole spectrum," he said eventually. "And she
knew her business. Familiar with all the most
visible groups from the IRA to the Middle East."

"She had an incredible memory." Ms. Chantry
had a slightly husky voice, very attractive and,
Bond decided, very sexy. He took a closer look at
the young woman as she spoke. "Laura always
knew who, among known terrorists, was in the
United Kingdom at any given time."

"She knew those who had been spotted coming in," Grant interrupted quickly. "Yes, she did
retain the information from the daily reports—
the sightings by our people at airports and other
entry points."

Bond grunted. He was still appraising Ms. Chantry. At first sight she had appeared to look somewhat schoolmarmish, dark hair pulled straight back from a high forehead and fastened in a bun at the nape of her neck; granny glasses, and a severe lightweight suit that did nothing for her figure. Now that Bond looked closely, he saw clearly that Ms. Chantry seemed to be hiding her light under a bushel of little makeup and a lot of austerity. Her large brown eyes looked steadily into his, and the curve of her thighs and breasts under the forbidding suit gave the impression of an exceptional body. Under an astringent exterior, Ms. Chantry was probably all woman and then some.

"Ms. March? Was she concerned about anyone in particular? I mean any one known terrorist in the country at this time?" he asked.

The two MI5 officers both shook their heads.

"So, I presume," Bond continued, "that you both worked quite closely with her?"

"I am head of the Terrorist Intelligence Section." Grant sounded paradoxically superior and unhappy about revealing his exalted place in the scheme of the Security Service. "She reported directly to me. Ms. Chantry is my number two, so, as such, was in contact with her on a daily basis."

Bond's instinct still told him there was a great deal missing from the simple answers. "And what about the other side of the coin? To your knowledge did any of the terrorist groups know of her existence?"

"Who can tell?" Grant shrugged. "We like to think that we're invisible, but your own service has had problems with penetration in the past, Captain Bond. None of us can be one hundred percent certain that we are not compromised."

"If she *had* been compromised, is there any reason to believe that any one terrorist organization had a motive for taking her out?"

"No!" It was Ms. Chantry who replied, her voice rising, breaking, the single word coming out just a little too quickly. "No! No, I really think you can rule that out."

"What about her private life?"

"What about it?" Now Grant sounded almost aggressive, his forehead wrinkling belligerently.

"If she died an unnatural death, it could be of great importance."

"She kept herself to herself. Didn't talk much about her personal life," from Ms. Chantry, once more a shade fast and easy.

"What about positive vetting?" asked Bond, referring to the regular background checks on officers working in the twin labyrinths of intelligence and security. He cocked an eyebrow at Grant. "We still do positive vetting, even in this piping time of peace. You were her superior, Mr. Grant."

"Yes. Yes. Of course. Yes." This time Grant fussed with his tie. "I regularly saw the results of her positive vetting."

"Well?"

Grant spoke like a small man trying to pull himself up to his full height. "It would not be proper for me to divulge the results of a colleague's PV in the present company."

"Then just give us a pencil sketch."

"I don't—"

"Mr. Grant, I would suggest that you either allow Ms. Chantry to leave the room or get on with it," M growled. "We're all adults here. Do as Captain Bond suggests. A pencil sketch; outline map, eh?"

Grant gave a petulant sigh. "Very well." He did not actually speak through clenched teeth, but came within an ace of it. "Thirty-five years of age; entered the Service after taking the Diplomatic Corps examination at age twenty-five. A First in Modern Languages, Cambridge. No brothers or sisters. Both parents killed in that wretched PanAm bombing—going to spend Christmas with friends in New England. No overt political affiliations. Basically clean."

"Boyfriends?"

"Not currently, no."

"Girlfriends then?"

"She *was* heterosexual, Captain Bond, if that's what you're trying to ask."

"I wasn't, but it's as well to know. No boyfriends currently, you say. What's that mean exactly?"

Grant hesitated for just too long. "She was engaged. It was broken off a month or so ago."

"The fiancé, then. Clean?"

"Scrupulously."

"Service?"

"No. Neither ours nor yours."

"You want to tell me about him?"

"I think that would be unwise."

"Right. Thank you, Mr. Grant." Bond rose. "I think we've heard enough, and I suspect I've a lot to do before I leave for Bern."

M gestured for him to sit down again, then turned to Grant and Chantry. "You can tell your DG that the whole matter will be dealt with efficiently and discreetly." He made a gesture with his right hand leaving no doubt this time that the visiting firemen should go.

As he moved his arm, Moneypenny appeared in the doorway in response to some hidden signal activated by the Old Man.

"Moneypenny, our friends will be leaving now. Perhaps you'd have them escorted from the building."

Grant's face was a picture of barely controlled anger. Chantry, on the other hand, seemed to accept M's blatantly rude instructions as part of the normal cross she had to bear.

They had hardly left the office before M grunted a half-amused laugh. "I'm always amazed at our sister service, James." He now seemed almost amiable.

"Wouldn't trust Grant to mail a letter for me." Bond looked toward the door, his lips set in a curving cruel smile. "As for the Chantry girl, she's very upset about the death. Grant kept her on a short leash, and I suspect he'd rather have come on his own. There's something missing, sir."

"Just a lot, my boy. Just a lot. Never trust Greeks bearing gifts, nor Five coming for help. They can't bear telling the entire story, and there's something about the March girl that they've no intention of telling us. Just watch your back, James. It wouldn't surprise me if Grant put some kind of leech on you in Switzerland. So take care." He began to load his pipe, tamping

down the tobacco with near ferocity. "Couple of
things before you go. First, there's no convenient scheduled service to Bern, so you'll be going
out in the company jet, which is standing by at
Northolt." The so-called company jet was an aging
RAF-owned Hawker Siddley 125 Series 700, in
a white livery with the Transworld Consortium
logo on fuselage and tail. M, careful as he was,
used the aircraft only when absolutely necessary.
Ever since the retreat of the Russian threat, he
considered it far too high-profile. "Incidentally,
you're going out as a grieving relative. The
March girl only had one old aunt, living up in
Birmingham, so you've been dubbed as a second
cousin. Get back to me if you think Five've put
surveillance on you. They're like a barrel load of
monkeys when they become paranoid. Now . . ."
He began to give his agent some specific instructions regarding Switzerland.

At five o'clock Swiss time, that same afternoon,
the company jet taxied in, coming to a halt at the
main terminal of Bern International Airport, and
Bond walked quickly into the main building.

Immigration was, as always, dourly efficient,
and he emerged into the arrivals hall, carrying
his compact pigskin garment bag slung over his
shoulder, eyes rapidly taking in the array of written notice boards held by limousine drivers, looking for his name.

M had given him the name of his contact.
"Freddie von Grüsse. Never met the fellow, but
he's a von so probably an insufferable bore, and a
snob to boot. You know how the Swiss uppercrust
are, James."

There was no driver holding a card for Bond, so he walked further into the arrivals hall, and was about to approach the enquiry desk when a deep, pleasant female voice whispered at his ear, "James Bond?"

He caught the subtle scent of Chanel, turned, and found himself looking into a pair of wide, twinkling green eyes.

"Mr. Bond, I'm Freddie von Grüsse." Her hand was firm in his, and her elegance was of the kind rarely seen outside the pages of fashion magazines. "Fredericka von Grüsse actually, but my close friends call me Flicka."

"Can I be counted as a close friend?" It was a lame opening, but she had literally taken his breath away.

She laughed, and there seemed to be an almost tangible silver glitter in the air. "Oh, I think we will probably become very close friends, Mr. Bond, or may I call you James?"

"Call me anything you like." A couple of seconds later, he realized that he actually meant what he had said. She could have called him Dickbrain and he would still have smiled at her happily.

3

Flicka

She was tall, around five-eleven, which meant the full six feet plus in high heels. Tall and slender, though not what bad journalists would call willowy. One glance was enough to confirm athleticism in all senses of the word. She had the look of someone who worked out regularly, and took great care of her personal appearance. She also gave off that indefinable static, immediately recognizable in some women, which said she was a sexual knockout, but on her own terms. The kind of woman who got exactly what she wanted, when *she* wanted it.

She wore a white flared skirt, which ended just above the knee and swung around her thighs with every movement. A wide, studded black leather belt divided the skirt from her light-blue silk shirt, decorated at the throat by a loosely knotted

scarf. Her hair, black and shoulder length, had a
thick silky texture. The right-hand fall of hair—
cut longer than the left—tended to drop over one
eye, and she pushed it back, raking it with long
fine fingers, her head tilted, green eyes sparkling
in tune with her laugh. The body of hair fell back
into place as though she had never even touched
it. Flicka von Grüsse, Bond considered, would be
thoroughly disliked by most women.

"Come along, then, James. We've got a nice
drive ahead of us. You want to eat first or shall
we catch something on the way?" She was off,
striding a few paces ahead of him, and he saw
the ripple of her thighs and the firm movement of
her buttocks beneath the skirt. From long ago, he
recalled a partly remembered line of poetry: "then
(methinks) how sweetly flows; that liquefaction of
her clothes."

She paused, looking back over her right shoulder. "James, there are lots of better views where
we're going."

Bond walked a little faster, and with more
bounce to his step than he had felt for some time.
"Doubt it, but where are we going anyway?" He
felt their shoulders touch, and the merest hint of
mutual attraction sparking between them.

"Interlaken, of course. Where else?" The woman was a witch, moving their invisible emotions
close together with speed.

"Then, as you say, we'd better get moving. Can
we eat in Thun?"

"Naturally."

"Oh, just one thing." He placed a hand lightly
on her shoulder, feeling her flesh through the

silk, like static on his fingers.

"Yes?" She turned, slowing to a halt.

"I hate to do this to you, Flicka, but I need some ID. A man can't be too careful these days."

Once more the silver dust of her laugh spread around them. "Okay, James. I'll show you mine if you'll show me yours."

"Chance would be a fine thing." He flipped open his wallet to reveal his service ID, beneath its little laminated shield, and Flicka reached into a large leather shoulder bag, producing her own card. As she returned it, he caught a glimpse of an automatic pistol, snug in a holster built into the bag. He had been denied carrying a weapon into the country, and suddenly felt naked and vulnerable.

Within ten minutes they were settled into her three-year-old white Porsche, which was in need of a wash, and heading out of Bern on route 6, following the river Aare to Thun, the lovely old town which always reminded Bond of the Frankenstein story. If you stand in the small Town Hall Square—the Rathausplatz—in Thun, and look up beyond the Rathaus itself, you can see the great castle looming above you, and the whole view is reminiscent of every Frankenstein movie ever made.

She drove fast, but with experienced skill, her shoes kicked off, stockinged feet dancing on the pedals, and her long, slim arm moving almost lazily over the gearshift. From the moment they left the airport parking area, she made it clear that they would not talk business.

"We're supposed to be an item," she said, glancing at him, a delightful smile glowing from mouth and eyes. "That's what my people have decreed, and who am I to disobey them?"

"Who indeed?" Bond clutched at the corner of his seat as she negotiated a long bend just a fraction too fast for his liking, but hanging into the turn, not allowing the car to drift. "By item, you mean lovers, I presume?"

"Correct. We're to stay where she stayed, and my papers show that I've just flown in from London with you. You're a relative, aren't you?"

"Distant cousin. Was that your people's idea?"

"A joint decision with your Chief. Now, I'll tell you the rest over dinner. Oh, and don't worry, I won't hold you to the entire details of our cover."

"Why a cover at all?"

"Later. Over dinner, I'll tell you."

Silence for half a kilometer, then, "You speak exceptional English." Too late he realized how trite that sounded, and heard her laugh again.

"And we have been getting such good weather this August, yes?" She changed up as they reached a straight stretch of road, piling on a little speed. "I *ought* to speak good English, my mother came from Hastings, where your King Harold was taken by William the Conqueror."

"I know the story. Harold got an arrow in his retina."

"You know what one of the Norman archers said? 'That's one in the eye for Harold.'" Again the laugh. "My father was Swiss, but I got my degree at Cambridge."

"What in, History?"

"Modern Languages. Why would you think . . . ?"

"History? Your exceptional grasp of the Battle of Hastings."

"Oh, I have an exceptional grasp of many things, James."

"I'd bet on it. You weren't up at Cambridge with the deceased by any chance?"

"Later, James. I'll tell you everything later."

In less than an hour they were in Thun. They parked, then walked across to the old Falcon, a hotel in which Bond had spent many happy days years before. Less than fifteen minutes later they were seated in the restaurant, being fussed over and looking forward to dinner.

"So, Flicka. You're ready to tell me a story?"

"Some of it, yes." She rolled a piece of smoked salmon onto her fork, popping it daintily between her lips. "You were right, of course. Part of the reason they've assigned me to this is because I was up at Cambridge with Laura March. I didn't know her well, but we attended the same lectures, had the same supervisor. After Cambridge I saw her occasionally—after all, we were both in the same business—but I really didn't know her well."

"So why the cover? Lovebirds off on a spree. Us, I mean."

"She *was* murdered, James. That's fact. We all know that now, and in our line of work—"

"We can't be too careful."

"Exactly. You have any idea why she was killed?"

"Do you?"

"I wouldn't have asked if I knew. We're completely in the dark, so, as you can imagine, there's a certain amount of panic. Have we got part of some terrorist cell operating on our turf? Did someone choose Switzerland as a killing field? I know it's paranoid, but we need information, and we're not getting it from her colleagues. That's one of the reasons we refused them the okay to come over and work the case."

"You know as much as I do." Bond leaned back in his chair, pushing his plate away, swallowing the last morsel of his salmon. "In fact you probably know more than I do. Her colleagues were about as chatty as a bunch of turtles. I saw her immediate superiors, with my Chief, and we both knew they were holding something back. You knew she worked the Anti-Terrorist beat?"

"Of course, that's why we're nervous. Also, the method was odd and smacked of the old Bulgarian DS." She was speaking of the Durzharna Sigurnost, the former Bulgarian intelligence and security service. The DS had once contained a ruthless death squad, which at one point had access to the highly secret laboratory run by KGB's Operational and Technical Directorate. It was from liaison between the KGB's First Chief Directorate, the DS, and OTD, that plans were made for the secret killing of a number of Bulgarian émigrés, using exotic poisons like the feared ricin, which was almost undetectable.

"Tell me about how she was killed." He leaned forward as a waitress, plump and smiling, cleared their used plates and set down dishes of succulent lamb chops, *rösti*—those delicious potato cakes flavored with onion and cheese—together with tomatoes stuffed with ground lamb's liver, mixed with herbs and spices.

Initially, Flicka had asked Bond to order for both of them. "I never know what I want." She had looked up at him, under flirting eyelids. Now she nodded and smiled as she began to serve him, and the waitress brought the Beaujolais, which Bond sipped, nodding his approval.

Only when they had started to eat did Flicka continue to talk. "The method? I have the entire report with me." Her eyes flicked in the direction of her shoulder bag, which she kept near to her all the time, constantly allowing a hand to drift toward it, touching the leather as though anxious to reassure herself that it was there. "The weapon was undoubtedly a high-powered air rifle or pistol. Maybe one of the type that uses a CO_2 charge. You knew about the capsule in her neck?"

Bond nodded. "What was in it?"

"We've been unusually lucky. Our own people might've gone on looking for weeks. It just so happens that the cops in Bern are hosting three Japanese forensic specialists. They're over here for a year, examining European methods and advising on some of their techniques. It was an off-the-cuff thing. They thought one of these men might be interested. Unpronounceable name, but he spotted a couple of things, pointed them out, suggested the tests. In a word, the capsule contained tetrodotoxin."

"As in blowfish?"

"You've got it. They don't come more exotic than that."

"Remind me."

So, as they ate, Flicka talked, at first almost casually, about tetrodotoxin.

Tetrodotoxin was the poison of choice of the ancient Japanese shadow warriors, the followers of Ninjitsu, the Ninjas. They would use it to anoint the now familiar *shuriken*—throwing stars—and for centuries one of the most secret arts of Ninjitsu was the method for preparing the deadly nerve poison.

During World War II one of the legends of those who fought in the jungle was the story of the silent night-killers who moved, hooded, like cats through dense foliage, reaching out to touch sentries or sleeping soldiers, who would die of "snakebite." Only later did military doctors realize the bite had been delivered from a piece of sharpened bamboo dipped into tetrodotoxin.

The poison comes from the reproductive sac of a species of blowfish called the tetrodontidae. This fish is a native to the coastal waters of Japan and Hawaii, and, as it is a pretty creature, it can often be seen gracing tropical aquariums, in homes as well as zoos. Tetrodotoxin is found in the female fish, and then usually only in the mating season— February.

At this time, the female egg sac is swollen with around two to three liquid grams of tetrodotoxin, which is enough to poison three to four hundred humans. To retrieve the sac from the fish without breaking it necessitates alarming the fish so that it does its best aggressive trick, inflating itself to two or three times its normal size. At that moment you slit the side of the creature with a razor-sharp knife and remove the sac intact.

In recent years many schools of the Japanese culinary art now openly taught the same ancient secret for removing the poison, for removing it is necessary to make a particular delicacy harmless. Skilled chefs would do this trick, for the tetrodontidae is the main ingredient in the gourmet dish *fugu*. Yet, even now, some are not completely adept at removing the sac, and each year there are still a number of deaths in Japan from eating *fugu* which has been improperly prepared.

"It's a horrible way to die." She shuddered, her skin suddenly pale at the thought. "Complete paralysis and respiratory failure in twenty seconds, the Japanese doctor says."

"Fast, though." Bond sipped his wine, holding a little in his mouth before swallowing, savoring the flavor. "Over before you know it. He mention that they still use it for suicide?"

She shook her head: a cross between saying no and driving the specter of death by this kind of poison from her brain.

"I read somewhere that people who want out can buy the stuff from chefs. They get drunk, then prick themselves with a needle soaked in the wretched venom."

"The cops've found the place where the sniper holed up." She was distancing herself from the effect, returning to the first cause. "We can go up there tomorrow. Whoever it was made a comfortable hide for himself, slightly higher up the mountain."

"Must've been pretty sure of his target, unless our Ms. March was chosen at random."

"That's exactly what the cops said. In fact it's what they're afraid of, a killer taking pot shots at people with poison darts or capsules. Not the happiest of thoughts, a random poisoner on the loose."

"Which is easier to deal with? The random killer or some terrorist organization intent on revenge or headlines?"

"One's as bad as the other, really. Scares the hell out of me."

"And you don't look as if you scare easily."

"I don't?"

"You're a professional, so . . ."

"Don't you get scared, James? Don't all of us?"

"Of course I do, but only when the situation warrants it. We're only going through the motions, investigating a murder. We're working like a couple of homicide detectives, there's no danger in that."

She cocked an eyebrow and swallowed another piece of lamb. "That's how you think of it?"

"Naturally."

"Well, I've seen the body, read the evidence. It's like somebody being bitten by a deadly snake, and the snake hasn't yet been caught."

"Yes, but—"

"But nothing, James. Didn't they tell you to move carefully, to watch your back?" Her face was still pale, and there was a new, concerned, haunted look in her eyes.

"My Chief mentioned it, yes, but only in the context of the poor dead Ms. March's employers."

"Well, perhaps he was playing it down. My

boss spelled it out to me. Anyone investigating the death is at risk. If it's a one-off terrorist thing, nobody's claiming responsibility, so they could well have expected a long delay before we worked out the cause of death—if we discovered it at all."

"And if it's some crazy, I suppose he could still be lurking around. That how it goes?"

"Exactly. We've been told to take great care. If it *is* a crazy, we're all still at risk. If it's terrorists, the same applies. So, yes, James, I *am* scared, and I'll be surprised if you don't feel something up on that mountain tomorrow."

"There's something else?" Somehow he felt that she was holding back; delaying facing the truth. "So, what's turned up, Flicka? They've found where the shooter holed up; we know how the girl was killed. Have the cops had any other ideas?"

"She's stayed there before."

"In Interlaken?"

"At the same hotel. At the Victoria-Jungfrau. Three times previously. Each time with the same man. Once a year over the past three years."

"They IDed her friend?"

"No. I've seen stats of the register. Mr. and Mrs. March. His passport showed him as March, we have the number, and her former employers ran a check. The passport was applied for in the usual way, three years ago. You're going to love this, James, and it might make you almost as frightened as I am. It's her brother's passport. His name was David."

Bond scowled, suddenly looking up into her face.

"She was an only child. That's what her service said."

Flicka smiled, and the nervous, haunted look vanished for a second, then returned. "That's what her service thought. I only saw the signal traffic, and got the documents half an hour before you arrived. It appears that she wasn't quite telling the truth. She did have a brother. An elder brother. Black sheep of the family. He died in a hospital for the criminally insane five years ago."

It was Bond's turn to look serious. "Which hospital?"

"Rampton. He'd been there since the age of twenty, and he was five years older than her."

"And . . ." Bond began, but the waitress was beside them again, asking about dessert. Without much enthusiasm, Flicka ordered the cherry tart, and Bond went for the cheese board. "When in Rome," he smiled.

She remained passive, as though the specter of this man, David March, lay across the table between them. "It appears," she said, "that the family moved from the North of England to Hampshire after it happened. It was a pretty big case at the time."

"David March," Bond mused, the name hung on the lip of his memory, but he could not quite get to grips with the man or his crime.

"He killed four girls, in the North of England," she said, her voice calm now. "At the time, the press drew some sort of parallel between March and— Oh, who were they? Monsters? The Moors Murderers?"

"Brady and Hindley, yes. Kidnapped and abused

children, then killed and buried them on the Moors above Manchester. Sure, a *cause célèbre*. Brady's in a secure facility for the criminal insane now, and Hindley's still in jail. That case broke, oh, sometime in the early sixties. An appalling business. Terrible. Yes, monstrous."

"Well, David March made those two look like good fairies. He did his particular thing in the early seventies. I read the file while I was waiting for you to land. He was quiet, unassuming, polite, an undergraduate at Oxford, reading law. The psychiatrists' reports are interesting; the details of the killings are . . . Well, I'd prefer that you read them for yourself, James. I was scared before, but after reading what her brother did . . ."

"So we have a whole series of bogeymen—terrorists, a lone random crazy, and a victim whose brother—" He stopped as the name David March suddenly connected with a jigsaw puzzle in his head. "*That* David March?" He looked at her, knowing his eyes had widened. "The one who kept the heads?"

She gave a fast little nod. "See for yourself." Flicka reached for the leather shoulder bag, but Bond shook his head.

"No. When we get there—I'll read it then. How, in heaven's name? I mean how didn't her people unearth it during her positive vetting?"

"How indeed? I rather gather there're a lot of red faces in London. She didn't even change her name. Nobody in their right mind should have given her a sensitive job with that family skeleton in her closet."

"It *was* her brother, not her."

"Read what the shrinks have to say before you make statements like that. Lord, James, think about it. If you remember only small details of the case, he was a horrific walking, talking, living monster. Yet, two years after his death, sweet little Laura, his sister, lets someone forge a passport with his birth details. What's that make her? To allow someone to use his name, his details. Read it, James. Please just read it." She had reached down and taken a heavy folder from out of the bag just as the waitress came over to ask if they would like to take coffee. They could use the residents' lounge, she said.

So it was, amidst the normal, pleasant chatter of guests enjoying holidays, or passing through on business, that Bond glanced at Flicka, who sat beside him, impassive, as he opened the folder and began to read about Laura March's brother.

He was only two paragraphs into the file when the hair on the back of his neck bristled, and rose in fear.

4

Brother David

He had barely read the first four paragraphs before the whole story came flooding back. At least the facts read in the newspapers at the time returned vividly. Some of it had been lurid, sensationally reported, with the usual sensitivity of ghoulish newspapermen, but he was certain that, even with the gruesome highlights which became public knowledge after the trial, there were still some things that had been left out. He recalled talking some years before to a senior police officer who had assisted in identifying the body of a child buried in dense woodland and found some six months after her murder.

"We don't even bring some things out in court," the detective had said. "I identified that child's fingerprints certainly, but they had to remove the

45

hands and bring them down to London. I never saw the poor kid's body."

The bulk of the file was a detailed and annotated report on the case by the police officer in charge, a Detective Superintendent Richard Seymour, and, even though the lengthy document was couched in official police jargon, the language did nothing to reduce the sense of blind horror.

The events took place in the town of Preston—around thirty-five miles northwest of Manchester—deep in the old cotton mill country. Bond thought of gray granite buildings and the uncompromising, no-nonsense, though cheerful, people of Lancashire who were the actors in this story of terror.

When Christine Wright, of 33 Albert Road, Preston, went missing, just before Christmas 1971, her name was simply added to the missing persons' file. She was twenty-two, blonde, very pretty, and at constant odds with her parents who, she was always telling her friends, still treated her like a child. The file did pass across Superintendent Seymour's desk, but all the indications were that young Christine had run off: she was always talking about getting away, living on her own, or finding Mr. Wright—this last was, naturally, a little running joke with her friends. Later it would smack of grim gallows humor.

She did tell her closest confidante—one Jessie Styles, who worked with her at the National Westminster Bank—that she had met someone truly exciting. The report gave the friend's exact words: "Chrissy said she thought this lad was right for her. She wouldn't talk much about it.

Said he was a bit of a toff, had money. Said it could lead to a new life. They were in love, but then Chrissy was always in love with the latest boyfriend. The difference this time was that she didn't give me any details. Usually she'd have photographs. Tell me everything. She wouldn't even tell me the name of this one."

In the early spring of 1972, a pair of hikers literally stumbled over what was left of the missing girl. Christine Wright was identified by her fingerprints—originally, the police had gone through the motions by taking prints from her room at her parents' house in Albert Road.

What was found by the hikers was simply the torso, in the early stages of decay. The head had literally been hacked off, and the remains buried in a grave less than eight inches deep, near one of the roads leading across the moors above Manchester. It can be very cold in that part of England, and the freezing temperatures that had persisted from early December 1971 to April of '72 had left the body in a well-preserved state, for it was only just beginning to decompose with the first warmth of spring.

Superintendent Seymour began investigating on the day after the remains were identified. He did not get very far. In his notes there was a query regarding the father, and the constant arguments between him and his murdered daughter; but the policeman, after some long question and answer sessions, noted that he thought Christine's father was not even "in the frame" as the English police slang has it.

On Tuesday of Easter week, Bridget Bellamy told her parents she was going to spend the night with her friend Betsy Sagar. She had not returned by Wednesday evening, so it was her mother who eventually telephoned Betsy's home. At first she was angry. Even though Bridget was twenty-one years old, Mrs. Bellamy liked to think that her daughter always told her the truth. Bridget had not stayed with the Sagars, nor had she been at work on this, the following day.

It was only after Betsy Sagar had owned up that Mrs. Bellamy called the police. For the past week, Bridget had been on a high. She had met the man of her dreams, she had told her friend Betsy. They were in love, and he had asked her to marry him. His mother was dead, and the family had a wonderful house which the new boyfriend would inherit, together with a fortune, when his elderly, ailing father died. Bridget Bellamy was a blonde, and the one thing she did not tell Betsy was the name of this wonderful man, though she did mention that he lived in his own house near that of his parents.

Bridget's remains were discovered, again on the moors, in early July. She was more difficult to identify, but there was no doubt, just as there was no doubt that her head had been severed—possibly with an ax and a saw.

There were two more cases during the summer. Both blondes, and in their early twenties; both found headless, soon after telling friends that they would shortly be announcing their engagements.

In those days the name "serial killer" had not yet entered either police or public language, but

Seymour did not have to be told that they had one killer on the loose in his area. Someone who had already murdered four times, who favored blonde females, and whose diabolical work included severing their heads—possibly keeping them as souvenirs.

The Superintendent's notes over the next two weeks gave the impression of someone under great stress. There were no leads; no clues; and he was doing his best to keep the press at bay. At one point he wrote, "If this continues I shall have to let the truth come out. All blonde young women in the area are obviously at risk, but if I release the full details there will be both a panic and a concerted attack on us by the press, who will want to know why we have not arrested anyone. If there is another killing, we will just have to give in and make a full statement. This man is a maniac. I am no forensic specialist, but it is certain that the decapitations are performed in a frenzy, and the two medical examiners who have helped me on this case are both of the opinion that the girls died from the blows to the neck—in other words, died from decapitation. I dread another missing persons' report."

What he feared occurred in the last week of August. Janet Fellowes, aged twenty-one, blonde as they came. However, Janet was different. Her friends spoke of her, not unkindly, as the Pony Girl—"Because she let anyone have a ride," one of them said. Also, Janet talked. On the night she went missing she told Annie Frick who, the Superintendent noted, was probably a member of the same pony club, that she was really having

some fun with a stuck-up young man. "I been
teasing him stupid," she was reported to have
said. "Keeps saying he's in love with me, but I
know what he wants—and he'll get it tonight."

Janet had also said that he would be okay for
a good time, but he would not be around for a
while. The reason, she told Annie, was that he
was a student. "Says he's up at Oxford University.
Has to go back for the new term." Those words
constituted the first and final breakthrough.

There were twenty-four undergraduates in the
Preston area. Only fifteen of them were up at
Oxford. David March was the third young man
to be interviewed by Superintendent Seymour.

Giving evidence at the trial, at which David
March pleaded guilty by reason of insanity—by
then his only true option—Seymour merely said
that after a number of questions, March had
admitted to the offenses. Bond had been right.
Not everything came out in open court. The
Superintendent's official report told the entire
chilling story.

The March family lived in a large 18th-century
house, standing in four acres of garden on the
outskirts of Preston. Behind the main house were
substantial outbuildings, one of which originally
had been a coach house. This, David's father had
completely restored and made into a roomy two-
story cottage so that David, having obtained a
scholarship to Christ Church, Oxford, could have
his own privacy and not be tied to his family
during the vacations.

David was packing, getting ready to return to
university when Seymour arrived, accompanied

by a detective sergeant, and his first impression was that here he had a well-set-up young man: a quiet, good-looking, scholarly type; confident and with a high IQ. He was later to confide that he had immediately scratched March from the list. They sat and talked in a large, book-lined living room, and the detective began a gentle probing, showing him photographs of the girls, taken in life; talking of David's future; and slipping in questions about his activities on the significant dates. At the same time, Seymour had the opportunity to look at the books on the shelves. Most were concerned with law, but one whole section was taken up by books on the occult and comparative religion.

David March behaved perfectly normally for the first thirty minutes or so: eager to answer questions, apologizing for the mess, offering coffee. Then, Seymour noticed a sudden change in him. He seemed to be distancing himself from the two policemen, his head cocked on one side, as though listening for something or someone nearby. In the middle of answering a question regarding his hobbies and other activities at Oxford, David suddenly said—

"They say you've come to look after them." His voice had changed to a dreamy monotone.

"Who?" The Superintendent realized that he could have simply answered in the affirmative.

"The oracles. They're not all gathered yet—but you know that. Isis says there must be at least six. I have only gathered five."

"Does Isis speak with you often, David?" The policeman was interested in Egyptology, so was familiar with the facts. Isis was possibly the most important goddess of the ancient Egyptians, and among March's occult and religious works, he had seen at least four books concerning worship and the ancient Egyptians.

"It's an honor. A very great honor, but you know that, if she sent you." At this point Seymour had written that David appeared to be in some trance-like state. "Isis, mother of all things, lady of the elements, the beginning of all time. Sister-wife of Osiris. Speak . . . Speak through the oracles I have created for you."

Written baldly on the page, Seymour admitted that the words seemed to be the rather dramatic ravings of someone mentally disturbed. In his report, he wrote, "David's voice seemed to change, echo, become distorted. It was the most frightening change I have ever witnessed in a human being. Even his face appeared to alter. I felt cold, while Sergeant Bowles later stated that he experienced the feeling of something terribly evil in the room with us."

"She speaks through the oracles. She says there are enough. That you will take charge of them." David March was utterly wrapped in this bizarre belief. "It is just as she told me. They have started to speak in a chorus."

The Superintendent added, "It seemed very important to him that we believed what he said. A matter of extreme significance, not in any legal or judiciary sense. This was a man proclaiming that he had done what was asked of him."

"Everything," March continued. "I did all that she asked. They were picked with great care. Fair-colored white women. I showed them love, as Isis commanded, and each was sacrificed just as she told me, at the exact time and under the correct conditions. I promise you it was done according to her word, for she is the mother of life. She would speak only through the oracles. Through them she says you will take them from me."

"Good, David." Seymour realized that he was trembling. "Where are they?"

"They're safe. I've kept them safe."

"Then it's time for us to see them."

The heads were in large jars—sealed carboys—floating in formaldehyde, turned pink from the blood which had flowed from the terrible ragged necks. The serrated skin flapped, creating an eerie sense of life. The carboys had been placed in some obvious order in the large refrigerator in David March's kitchen: two were on a top shelf, one in the center middle, and two more on the lowest part.

March even had a pair of great padlocks on the door of the thing, and the heads moved as he opened up, their hair lifting in the liquid, their dead eyes staring with half surprise and half terror, the pinkish stain below the horrible jagged necks rising and adding an almost supernatural glow in the confined light.

"Talk to them," March said in a whisper which had about it a sense of wonder. "Are they not marvelous, the way they speak so softly?"

Sergeant Bowles vomited, and there was a side note from the Superintendent saying that he suffered from nightmares for some time after.

David March's trial, while sensational, did not yield everything to the public. His plea of insanity was so strong, and supported by both the defense and prosecution, that only the bare facts came out. Certainly the press reported hyped-up stories gleaned from the victims' friends, and from bits and pieces they scavenged from the gardener and live-in cook at the March seniors' house—but only after the verdict of guilty but insane was returned, and David had been sentenced to be "Detained at Her Majesty's pleasure," which is the British way of saying life plus 99 years in an institution for the criminally insane.

The trial was almost an anticlimax. It was the brutality of the murders and the discovery of David March that overshadowed everything else. The picture was so strong in Bond's mind that he shivered, looking up, surprised that he sat in this pleasing Swiss hotel, other guests' laughter and talk going on around him. The long report had taken him almost half an hour to read, and, even though it was written baldly, without emotion, the Superintendent had somehow conveyed all the revulsion and shock. Seconds before, Bond had felt he was in that kitchen, with March and the refrigerator, looking at the hideous sight of the five heads floating in their clear, thick, glass carboys.

Now he was staring straight into Flicka's green eyes, which seemed to pull him in, hypnotically, as though they were whirlpools drowning him. Then he shook himself free and saw that she was gazing at him as if his own sense of fear were being transmitted to her. The dread passed between them like static.

"You see what I mean?" She poured coffee for him. "Black?" she asked.

"With a little sugar." His own voice seemed to come from far away. The detective's bland report had the power to stir, like the strength of some long-forgotten force which returned to influence mind and action. "And this is the victim's brother?" he asked, almost of himself.

"Read what the shrinks have to say. That's the clincher, and it's one of the reasons why Laura had to keep the business covered up."

He reached out, took a sip of coffee, then said, "I don't think I need to even look at the conclusions of the shrinks." Bond had always remained dubious of the psychiatrists' powers.

"Let me guess at what they had to say." He smiled, trying to bring humor back into Flicka's eyes. "I imagine that one of the first things they hit on was that David March had nursed an unhealthy interest in things occult since he was very young. Right?"

She nodded. "The Egyptology had begun as a kind of hobby, harmless and instructive. As he grew, he started to believe that the real truths about the universe could be found only in ancient Egypt. His parents became concerned when they found he had built an altar, in the garden, to worship Isis when he was only sixteen."

"I'm not playing Sherlock Holmes." He gave a short, almost humorless laugh. "But my next guess is that the mother had a dominating personality. That her will was law in the March household, and that it was not only David who was affected by her, but also his sister, Laura—

which is why this is important to us."

"Yes. Two of the psychiatrists spent a long
time taking David back through childhood and
his teens. Mrs. March appeared to have been
some kind of martinet. She was also a bit of a
religious fanatic. Laura was only, what?—fifteen?
sixteen?—when her brother was arrested, but the
trauma went quite deep, because by then her
mother had absolute control over her in matters
religious. She, Mrs. March, was a practicing Christian, but took everything to extremes. Sundays in
the March household were like stepping back to
Victorian times. Church in the morning and evening, reading the Bible—or some other worthy
book—in between: no games, nothing frivolous."

"I should imagine that young David told the
same story to each of his victims," Bond mused.

"Which story?"

"That his father was old and ailing, and that
his mother was dead. We know that's what he
told the second one—Bridget Bellamy."

"He admitted that. It seemed he really considered his mother dead."

"Makes sense. Did they help him at all? I mean
at the institution."

"They diagnosed a complex series of symptoms.
He seemed to be a very unhealthy mixture, a
witch's brew of all the worst kind of mental
problems—manic-depressive, psychotic, hysteric,
psychopath. They controlled him with drugs for a
while, but he was highly intelligent. Went through
long periods—I mean months at a time—of appearing perfectly normal, likable, friendly. Then,
out of the blue the terrors would strike."

"There was a need to kill?"

"That's what was said. He tried to murder another inmate, and also attacked a nurse on one occasion. Nearly did her in."

"Mmmm. And, from all this, you think Laura was also affected?"

"Don't see how she could avoid it. One of the shrinks had a very long session with the father, and came to the conclusion that he was seriously unbalanced. The entire mating situation was fraught with dangers. A hyperreligious, superdominant mother and a weak, mentally unstable father. They produced one monster. It makes you wonder if they spawned two of them."

"Let's say Laura March *was* unbalanced. She's the victim here, so, when we begin to examine her murder, we have to take her possible mental state into consideration." He gave another short laugh, heavy with irony. "Her colleagues must be going through all kinds of hell. Courts of enquiry, investigations on those who did her PVs. Couldn't happen to nicer people."

He looked up, and saw the fear still deep in Flicka's eyes. Touching the bulky file on his knee, he said, "This thing's really spooked you, hasn't it?"

"More than I can say. I was concerned up on the mountain, at the crime scene. This story's so horrible that I'm genuinely frightened. Damn it, James, in their wisdom, our respective services want us to go in there and carry out our own clandestine investigation. I'm even nervous of looking through Laura's effects."

"The cops haven't taken them away?"

"As a favor to us, the room she had at the Victoria-Jungfrau in Interlaken has been left as they first found it."

"They've removed nothing?"

"That's what they say. Of course who knows when you're dealing with cops. The room's been sealed. The hotel expects us, but, since reading this stuff, it's the last thing I want to do." She paused, her hand going to her hair, once more raking it with splayed fingers. "James, couldn't we stay here for the night? Put it off until morning?" A weak smile briefly lighting her eyes, and her intentions quite positive. "It's so nice here, no ghosts. We could comfort each other."

The pause lasted for almost thirty seconds.

"We could just as well comfort each other in Interlaken, Flicka, if that's what you have in mind."

"Yes, but—"

"But it's best to face things like this head-on. You say the hotel's expecting us. We should go. Really we should."

She looked away, then back at him with a wan smile, reaching across the low table, allowing the tips of her fingers to touch the back of his hand. Then she nodded gravely and slowly picked up her shoulder bag, ready to leave.

As they pulled out of the car park, Bond caught a glimpse of another car's headlights come on. It was one of those almost subliminal experiences: he was aware of the car starting up, and preparing to pull out, a few slots to their right and behind them. In the sodium lamps illuminating the car park he thought it was a red VW, but would not have put

money on it. When they reached the turnoff back
to route 6, he thought he saw the same car again,
too close for any comfort, though maybe too close
to be a professional. While not dismissing the
possibility of a tail, he put it on the back burner
of his mind. No experienced watcher would use a
red car, nor would he so blatantly call attention
to himself by staying so near.

Less than an hour later they pulled up in front
of the imposing Hotel Victoria-Jungfrau. There
had been no sign of the red car once they had
got fully under way.

Inside, there was the usual gravity over the
formal registration: a neat, unsmiling dark-haired
undermanager, whose little plastic nameplate
revealed her to be Marietta Bruch, watched
them as though intent on taking their fingerprints. She then went through the passport routine before saying that she was so sorry about
what she actually called "the untimely demise of
your relative." Then—

"You have, I believe, papers from the police?"

Flicka smiled, digging into her large shoulder
bag, carefully keeping it below the level of the
reception desk so that nobody could glimpse the
pistol. "Yes, I have them, don't I, darling?" She
beamed, giving Bond a quick, raised eyebrow.

"Well, I gave them to you, but I've known things
go missing from that handbag before now." He
turned away, giving the porter a hint of a wink.
The porter regarded him as though he had just
ordered malt vinegar with Dover Sole.

She pulled out the official documents, passing
them across to the redoubtable Fräulein Bruch,

who inspected them closely, as though looking for possible bacteria. "These seem to be in order," she finally pronounced. "Would you like to see first your cousin's room, before you go to your own? Or do you wish to settle in?"

It was all too obvious that the hotel wanted them to check Laura March's room as soon as possible.

"The police have already given permission for the room to be cleared once you have been through her items." Marietta Bruch gave them a bleak smile, behind which Bond detected the not unnatural desire of the hotel management to get the murdered girl's effects out of the way and have the room free to rent. "We have ample storage space for her cases, if you wish to make use—"

"Yes." Bond sounded decisive. "Yes, we understand, and I think it would be best if we looked through her things now. It will be easier for us also. And we will, of course, ask you to keep her cases until matters have been arranged."

Fräulein Bruch gave a sharp official nod, then asked, "Mrs. March's husband? When she arrived this time, she said he was ill and wouldn't be joining her. I hope it's not serious. She said it wasn't."

"Then she didn't tell you the truth. Mrs. March's husband died several months ago," Bond lied.

"Oh!" Fräulein Bruch looked genuinely shocked for the first time. Then again, "Oh! They were such a devoted couple. Perhaps that's why . . . ?" The thought trailed off as she picked a key from the rack. "Perhaps you would like to come with me?" She came around to their side of the reception desk, back on form, curtly instructing a porter to take Mr. and Mrs. Bond's cases to 614. She put a great deal of stress on the *Mrs.* Bond, as though clearly saying that she did not believe a word of it.

Laura March had opted for an obviously cheap and cheerful room. "It is not one of our luxury accommodations." Unterführer Bruch—as Bond now thought of her—broke the seals and turned the key in the lock. "She made the reservation at short notice, and said one of our cheaper rooms would be convenient."

Inside it was basic hotel: a narrow bed with a side table and telephone; one built-in wardrobe, a chair, a small writing table, and a closet-sized bathroom into which were crammed all the usual conveniences.

The undermanager nodded to them, said that when they were finished, if they came back to reception she would have them escorted to their room, which "is one of our more luxurious suites." The smile clicked on and off, fast as a neon sign, and she backed out.

Bond did the bathroom, noting that there had not really been enough room for Laura to spread out her makeup and toiletries; she had just managed to get most of them into a mirrored cupboard above the handbasin. Her preference seemed to be Lancôme, and he noted a small plastic container of pills, medically prescribed with the address of a chemist in Knightsbridge on the label. The police had probably removed a couple for analysis. He slipped the whole container into his pocket and squeezed out to find Flicka going through the clothes hanging in the wardrobe.

"Nothing remarkable." She flicked through the garments. "One basic black, for evenings, one white, one gray suit—that's nice"—peering at the label—"Ah, Marks & Spencer. That is fairly cheap stuff, but good value, I think. Two pants suits, spare pair of jeans. Shoes. Nothing."

"Go through the pockets." It came out as an order.

"No, James, you go through the pockets. I'll deal with the accessories." There were three small drawers running down the right-hand side of the wardrobe, and as Bond started to feel and fumble through any pockets in the hanging garments, Flicka began opening the drawers, the bottom one first, like any good burglar.

"Nothing in any of the pockets." He completed the jeans as she opened the top drawer.

"Mmmm." Flicka's hands disappeared into lace and silk. "She was a good customer of Victoria's Secret. Look, James. Pretty," lifting several pieces of highly feminine underwear for him to see.

He nodded. "That mean anything to you?"

"That she was sexually active, or had been until she came here."

"Really?"

"Girls buy underwear like this for men to see and remove. I also make purchases from Victoria's Secret, though it hasn't done me any good recently."

"Then Laura could've been in the same boat."

"I think not. This stuff is . . . Well, it's blatant, and it conforms to a pattern. She had a friend who liked certain things. I, on the other hand, just take a good guess. Still hasn't done me much good."

"That could change, Flicka. Who knows what might happen in the good Swiss air." He had moved over to the small writing table and began to look through the hotel folder, which contained brochures, stationery and— "Good grief. I can't believe the cops didn't find this." He pulled out two sheets of hotel writing paper folded in half. A letter, signed by Laura. She had large, bold handwriting. Very large, for she said little and managed to take up one and a half sheets of paper, with great loops and little circles used for dotting the "i."

"What is it?" Flicka was at his shoulder. He could smell her scent and the delicious musk of her hair.

Bond moved a fraction so that she could read the letter. There was no addressee, but Laura had written—

David My Dearest,

Well, as I told you, I have returned to our old favorite place. Nothing changes, the mountains are where they have always been. I also think of you all the time, but know that you are now dead as far as I am concerned. Yet you are everywhere here. Perhaps I should not have come, but I needed to be close to something we both shared.

It has rained all day and I have mooned around the hotel, tried to read, looked out on the mountains which are invisible with the cloud. Tomorrow they say it will be fine, so I shall go to our favorite place.

Oh God, David, my brother, my lover, I do not know what to do.

As ever, my dear dead love—
Your Laura.

"Jesus," Flicka said quietly. "James, let's get out of here."

He nodded, for there was a terrible, creepy feeling, as though the dead woman were in the room with them. If he had any faith in the supernatural, Bond might even have believed that the monster David March, *and* his sister, Laura, were both there, chuckling furtively from the small bed. For the second time that evening he felt the short hairs rise on the back of his neck.

Carefully folding the letter and slipping it into his pocket, Bond turned to face Flicka. She was ashen, trembling, tears starting at her eyes, the marks of shock springing from her, as though she had suffered a wound. He wrapped his arms around her, knowing that he too was trembling.

"Yes, Flicka. Things like this are enough to spook anyone. Let's go."

He locked the door behind them and they rode in silence down in the elevator to the reception desk where the stern Fräulein Bruch looked up without a smile.

"I'm afraid we can't deal with all of my cousin's effects tonight." His voice was back to normal: level and confident. "It's been a long day, so we're going to have to ask you to wait until tomorrow. I'll do it, myself, first thing in the morning."

Marietta Bruch allowed a brief look of irritation to cross her face before saying that she understood perfectly. Snapping her fingers for the porter, she instructed him to show Mr. and Mrs. Bond to their room.

There was one bedroom with a king-sized bed which had a reproduction Victorian head and foot—black metal bars rising as though caging the two ends, and huge ornamental brass bedknobs, polished and gleaming. The spacious sitting room had been remodeled, contrasting oddly with the bedroom. It contained a suite of black leather furniture, a businesslike desk, circular glass table, television, and minibar refrigerator. Bond felt an involuntary chilling shudder as the tiny fridge brought David March's horrible cold storage vault vividly back to mind.

The large French windows, at the far end of the sitting room, led to a long balcony which overlooked the front of the hotel. Flicka had gone straight out onto it as soon as the porter had been tipped and shown out.

Bond followed, standing beside her, looking down on the steady parade of locals and tourists out on their after-dinner stroll in the well-lit streets, part of the ritual of any Swiss tourist resort. By now the air had a chill to it, but they stood close together, in silence for a few moments, until he gently put an arm around her shoulders, leading her back into the room and guiding her to the long black settee.

"There has to be a rational answer to this." He held the letter between the fingers and thumb of his right hand. "We are certain that David March died five years ago?"

"Absolutely. There's no doubt." Color had returned to her cheeks, but her voice still retained a trace of fear. "I've seen the death certificate—a copy anyway—and—"

"What did he die of?"

"A brain tumor. Nothing to do with his mental state, which had really gone downhill by then. David March became a walking, grunting vegetable in spite of the drugs. Three months before he died, the doctors noticed indications of severe headaches, and eye problems. They did all the usual things, X rays, a CAT scan, the lot. The tumor was inoperable. He died in great discomfort, in spite of high-dosage painkillers."

"And do we know if Laura saw him?"

"No. None of his family ever visited him. For them it was as though he had ceased to be."

"Then there are three possibilities." He indicated the letter again. "This is either a plant, which seems quite likely—because the cops didn't remove it—or Laura was writing to someone else, someone she thought of as a brother-lover; or, the last theory, that she was also unbalanced, which could mean it was a piece of mental fabrication on her part. First, I think, we have to make certain it really was written by her."

He crossed the room, picking up his briefcase, thumbing the security locks, and opening it to reveal a laptop computer with a portable fax machine lying next to it. He laughed. "There was a time when my briefcase was a lethal weapon, now the armory is almost totally electronic." He did not add that the case in fact did contain a couple of concealed items that could be lethal if used properly.

After reorganizing the modular telephone plugs and switching on the fax machine, he took a clean sheet of the hotel stationery, placed it on the glass tabletop, and wrote a suitably cryptic message as a fax cover page. This he fed into the machine, dialing the safe fax number in London. The cover sheet went through, followed by the two pages they had removed from Laura March's room.

"By the morning we should have a simple fax back on the hotel's machine. It'll simply say yes or no. If it's yes, then we have to work out what little Laura was up to—fantasy or reality."

"You only asked about the letter?"

"I've asked them to identify the handwriting as Laura's and to recheck the facts regarding David March's death. We'll get some clues in the morning, and first thing I'm going to go through her room again. You stay here, the place has a bad effect on you."

She gave a dry little laugh. "You were completely unaffected by it, yes?"

"No. You know I wasn't. We were both spooked." He went over to the little minibar fridge. "Brandy? Vodka? Whiskey? What d'you fancy?"

"Brandy, I think."

He smiled at her, allowing his fingers to brush her shoulder after he had placed the glasses on the table. She still looked thoroughly shaken.

Bond poured from two miniature Rémy Martins. He rotated his glass, watching the amber liquid as it swirled around. Then he took a sip. "This should help relax both of us. We really should get as much rest as we can. Tomorrow's going to be a long day."

She did not look at him, but nodded as she put the glass to her lips.

"I'll use this couch, here. You take the bed."

Still Flicka did not reply, and after a while Bond said he would shower and leave her in peace. She was sitting, staring into space when he returned, having unpacked his garment bag, showered, and slipped into the robe provided by the hotel.

She left the sitting room, saying only that she would look in and see him before she went to bed. Bond, feeling very restless, poured the last of the wine into his glass and sat back to watch the CNN news. Half an hour later he barely heard the door to the bedroom open, and just caught the whisper of clothing behind him. Looking around, he saw Flicka, framed in the doorway. She wore nothing but a filmy triangle of silk and lace, her hair gleamed, and the green eyes were wide open, so that he again felt she had the ability to drown him with a look.

"Ah, Flicka's secret."

"Your secret, James."

He rose and she came toward him, molding her body to his, one hand reaching up, cradling the back of his head in her palm, fingers outstretched, pulling his lips onto her mouth.

"It's been a long time," she whispered. "But I must have some comfort tonight. Please." The last word was not a plea, but something else which came from deep within her. Then, slowly, she led him into the bedroom.

As he entered her, she let out a little cry of pleasure, rough at the back of her throat: the sound of somebody parched who sees a means to the slaking of thirst. For a second he saw the face of someone else, long lost, instead of Flicka, then it was gone as her own face and body worked a particular magic.

Neither of them heard the door to the sitting room click open, nor the soft tread of the person who crossed in front of their door, for by then, for a short time, the bedroom had become a raft adrift and far from land.

Then, with no warning, Bond softly put his hand over Flicka's mouth.

"Wha—" she began, but he called out loudly, "Who's there?"

From the sitting room a woman's voice, embarrassed, said, "The maid, sir. I'm sorry—I thought you might want me to make up the room."

"No. No, that's all right." He smiled at Flicka, pulling a face. "That could have been very embarrassing," he whispered. "I'd better go through and put out the Do Not Disturb sign."

"If you have to. But be quick about it or I'll start again without you."

He went through into the sitting room, put out the sign, and slipped the night chain onto the door. On his way back he saw his briefcase, and for safety's sake carried it into the bedroom. In the back of his mind something nagged at him. The maid's voice. He thought that he had heard that voice before but could not identify it.

He put the briefcase down at the end of the bed, not knowing that the damage had already been done.

Later, Flicka plowed furrows down his back with long splayed hands, leaving deep scratches, and they moved together, as one. For a long time nobody else existed but the two of them as they blotted out darker dreams and deeper horrors.

5

Little Pink Cells

Bond's eyes snapped open, and he became alert just before the telephone made its soft purring sound, heralding the wake-up call he had ordered for six A.M. He reached out, picked up the telephone and, after two or three seconds of listening, began to chuckle.

He was used to being wakened by recorded voices which, in most hotels, have now replaced the more personal touch of a real human being telling you it is six o'clock in the morning, that the weather is good, bad, or indifferent, and hoping that you will have a nice day. Certainly, the wake-up call at the Victoria-Jungfrau was a recorded message, but with elaborations that could only be Swiss. There was the tinkle of a music box through which girls' voices faded in and out, wishing the listener good morning in German, French, Italian,

Dutch, Spanish, English, Japanese and, as far as he knew, Urdu. This elaborate mixture certainly caught your attention, and he listened to it for a full minute before cradling the receiver and gently shaking Flicka's naked shoulder.

Gradually, with many protests, she woke up, blinked a couple of times, and then gave him a long, pleased smile—a cat-who'd-licked-the-cream look, which Bond realized was probably being reflected in his own face.

She wanted only coffee for breakfast—"Preferably intravenously"—so he dialed room service and ordered a large pot of coffee, with whole wheat toast and a boiled egg.

As soon as he replaced the receiver, the message light began to blink: a fax, they said, had come in from England overnight. He instructed them to send it up immediately. Within minutes a porter was at the door, handing him a sealed envelope.

He read the message, sitting on the edge of the bed, wearing the crested toweling robe. The fax was short and to the point:

Identification positive. Send original immediately by courier. It was signed *Mandarin,* the highest-priority crypto used by M, which meant the Old Man wanted Bond to go through a courier routine involving two telephone calls to Geneva and being physically present when the messenger arrived to pick up the letter.

Still naked, Flicka draped herself over his shoulder.

"Anyone ever tell you it was rude to read other people's mail?" He glanced back at her.

"Sure, but does a fax constitute mail? You can pluck those things straight off the telephone lines; they've all read it downstairs at reception, hoping it would contain something juicy."

"And it doesn't."

"Well, in a way it does. Laura wrote the letter. What's your courier service like?"

Bond playfully slapped her hand away. "Wouldn't you like to know? Come to think of it you probably do, you Swiss being so efficient."

She kissed him lightly on the cheek and gave him a wicked little wink. "Actually you use the same little man as the French—Mr. Hesk in Geneva. We've often thought that could be terribly leaky."

He pushed her back onto the bed, holding her down under his hard body, kissing her eyes, and then her mouth. Before matters could again get completely out of hand, a knock at the outer door signaled the arrival of breakfast.

They sat opposite one another, not speaking, she sipping cup after cup of strong black coffee, he admitting, grudgingly, to himself that the egg was almost, but not quite, done as he liked it. Eventually, Flicka spoke—

"I'm not usually like this."

"Like what?"

"Oh, I suppose, easy."

"I didn't think you were. The chemistry was right, and it was a night to remember. Outstanding. A night to dream about."

"That's true. *You* were outstanding. Can we do it again sometime?"

"I was banking on it. I always try to bank on things in Switzerland." He smiled at her, their eyes meeting. Again, he had that familiar sense of being able to drown and lose himself in the green depths of her eyes. Quickly he shook himself out of the mood, saying he had to organize the courier.

He brought the briefcase through from the bedroom, but when he came to operate the security locks he was surprised to find that they were already set to the correct eight-digit code.

"I could have sworn . . ." he began, knowing that he had automatically set the tumblers after sending last night's fax. It was something he always did without thinking, like breathing, yet, for a moment, he had second thoughts.

Swiftly, he clicked the locks open and raised the case's lid. Everything appeared normal until he opened the small buff folder into which he had put the original letter. It was empty: Laura March's bizarre, unaddressed, and unmailed message to "David" her "lover and brother" was as though it had never been.

"Something wrong, darling?" Flicka sat at the small table, looking at him with an expression of innocence that strangely worried him.

"You tell me?" he asked, unsmiling.

"What is it?"

"I said, you tell me, Flicka. There were only two of us in this suite last night. You saw me lock my briefcase. I slept like a proverbial log."

"So did I, eventually." The ghost of a smile on her lips and a touch of bewilderment in her eyes.

"You sure you didn't go sleepwalking?"

"I don't know what you mean."

"Then I'll tell you. I put the March letter in this case last night. I then locked it, using a sequence that even my masters in London don't know. Now, someone's carefully unlocked it, and the letter is gone."

"But . . ."

"But, apart from me, you're the only person who could have done it, Flicka. Come on, if you're playing games for your bosses, it would be better to tell me now. Save any further accusations and unpleasantness."

"I don't know what you mean! James, I was with you all night. Surely you know that. Why would I want to . . . ?"

"I have no idea as to why, but you're the only possible suspect."

She slowly rose from the table. "Then you're crazy, James. I didn't touch your bloody briefcase, and if you're implying that I invited you into my bed simply to steal something, then . . . Oh, hell, what's the use? I never touched the bloody case." In a second her attitude changed from warm and loving to an ice-cold anger. Red patches appeared on her cheeks as she turned and walked quickly toward the bedroom.

"I suggest you examine other possibilities, James. Also you can find another woman to brighten your nights." The door slammed behind her, leaving Bond kneeling beside the briefcase.

Indeed, he thought, she sounded genuinely angry, but that was often the best defense for the guilty. He cursed quietly. She was a trained security officer and could therefore quite easily

have read the combination code when he had
unlocked the briefcase. Lord knew, he had done
it hundreds of times with people dialing telephone
numbers. Nobody else could have crept in during
the night . . . He stopped, cursed again. Of course,
there was somebody else. The maid who had come
in and almost caught them in the bedroom—or had
she? How long had the maid been in the sitting
room before he heard her? He recalled thinking
that he had known the voice.

Then he remembered the car he thought had
tailed them from Thun. It was just possible that
an unknown other had managed to get in and
steal the letter. After all, he was pretty well
occupied for quite a long time before drifting
into a sweet and dreamless sleep. Whichever
way the theft had been accomplished, *he* was
still to blame, and there was no other option
but to apologize to Flicka, give her the benefit
of the doubt, and watch her like the proverbial
hawk.

He went to the bedroom door and tapped on
it softly, calling her name and then trying the
handle. She had locked it on the inside, and the
next hour was spent apologizing, followed by the
not unpleasant human ritual of "making up."

His message to London was a careful combination of necessary information and excuse.
Like any other intelligence officer, Bond was
adept at covering his back. This time he did
it with greater care than usual, referring to an
unexplained incident, quite out of his control, as
the reason for the original letter going missing.
By the time he saw M in London, he would have

thought out some logical excuse. The message also asked for his service to check on possible Security Service activity in Switzerland. For good measure he mentioned the red Volkswagen. After sending the fax, Bond took a scalding hot shower, followed by a freezing cold one, to open the pores and stimulate the nerve ends. He shaved and dressed, talking to Flicka all the time, as she sat at the dressing table preparing her face for the day ahead.

By this time they were running late for their meeting with the local police in Grindelwald, so on their way out, Bond paused by the reception desk to tell the stern Marietta Bruch that they would go through Ms. March's room on their return. She answered him with a clipped, "Ja?" and her eyes threw invisible stilettos at him. He was certainly not her most popular man of the month.

Though she had more than accepted his apology, in the ultimate way that a woman could, Flicka appeared to have withdrawn again. She was not the ice queen, nor was there obvious anger, but the conversation finally dwindled into one of monosyllabic, sometimes terse, responses, and she drove out to Grindelwald in near silence.

The police presence was obvious. Two cars and a police van blocked the little road to the chair lift, and a large sign, in three languages—German, French, and English—proclaimed that the chair lift up the mountain, to the First area with its great view of the Grindelwald Basin, was closed until further notice. The entrance was also blocked off with yellow crime-scene tape. A uniformed

inspector stood, with a plump, untidy-looking
man in civilian clothes, by the chair lift entrance.
The plainclothesman held a pigskin folder loosely
under one arm, and paid scant attention to their
arrival.

The officer obviously knew Flicka, for he greeted
her by name and, in turn, she introduced Bond to
"Inspector Ponsin." He nodded gravely and turned
to the civilian.

"This is Detective Bodo Lempke, of the Interlaken police department, in charge of the investigation." He waved a hand between them, flapping
it like a fish's fin.

"I already know Herr Lempke," Flicka said
somewhat distantly.

Lempke gave them a smile which reminded
Bond of the kind of greeting he might expect
from a retard, for the man's face had about it
a lumpish, peasant look, his lips splitting into a
wide curving clown's mouth.

"So," he said in uncertain English, the voice
gruff and flat, with little enthusiasm. "You are
what my friends in the Metropolitan Police call
'funnies' yes? Read that once, 'funnies,' in a spy
yarn, and never believed it until my British colleagues said it was true, what they called you."
He laughed, mirthless and without the smile.

All in all, Bond considered, Bodo Lempke was
the most dangerous type of policeman. Like the
best kind of spy, the man was totally gray, lack-
ing any color in his personality.

"Well," Bodo continued, "you wish to view where
the deed was done, yes? Though there's nothing
interesting about it. Few clues; no reasons; except

evidence which gives us the name—or assumed name—of the killer."

"You have a name?"

"Oh, sure. Nobody tell you this?"

"No." This one, Bond thought, was as tricky as a barrelful of anacondas. His type was usually described as one who had difficulty in catching the eye of a waiter. Mr. Lempke would have had problems catching the attention of a pickpocket, even if he had just flashed a wad of money and crammed it into the sucker pocket at his hip.

Flicka rode up the chair lift with Inspector Ponsin, while Bond drew the heavy Bodo Lempke, who certainly carried enough weight to tip the double set of chairs slightly. It was a beautiful short ride up the slope during which Lempke remained silent except to remark on the cause of death.

"You were told of the tetrodotoxin, yes?"

"Yes." Fight innocuousness with blandness.

"Exotic, no?"

"Very."

"Very exotic?"

"Exceptionally."

"So."

At the First viewing point, several policemen, uniformed and plainclothes, were doing what Bond presumed to be yet another careful search of the area, which was marked off with more crime-scene tape. A small group of men and women stood beside the long, log hut which was the restaurant. They looked dejected, as well they might: with the chair lift closed, their usual business would have dried to a trickle of probably discontented policemen looking for they knew not what.

The air was fresh and clear, while the view from this vantage point was almost otherworldly. Bond had his own reasons to feel overawed by mountains. For him, their grandeur—an over-worked word when people described the peaks and rocky graphs of the world's high places—was tempered with respect. His parents had died on a mountain and, since childhood, while he was often moved by the beauty of the crags, bluffs, and jagged outcrops of stone reaching toward the sky, he was also aware of the dangers they represented. To him they were like wanton beautiful women beckoning—sirens waiting to be conquered, yet perilous, requiring defer-ence and care, like so many of God's great wonders.

In spite of the warm sun he shivered slight-ly, turning to see that Flicka had come from the chair lift to stand close beside him. She had said he would feel something strange and frightening in this place, and she had been right. Sites of sudden death, or evil, often gave off signals of fear, just as old places—houses, stone circles, ancient churches—seemed to hold good or evil vibrations trapped in walls like inerasable recordings. Flicka's eyes gave him an "I-told-you-so" look, and Bodo Lempke coughed loudly.

"I show you where the body was found, yes? Where murder happened. Always good for the laugh." He treated them to his mirthless smile and set off, guiding them between the tapes that marked a pathway to a small enclosure. The screens which the police had originally set up around the body were still in place, and signs of sudden death remained—two gashes in the soft springy turf where Laura March's shoes had scarred the ground when her legs had involuntarily shot out and stiffened as the deadly capsule poured the poison into her bloodstream.

"We have snapshots." Lempke reached into the pigskin folder.

"They're not exactly your average holiday snaps, are they?" Bond leafed through the stack of eight-by-ten glossies, all of which showed Laura March in death at this very spot. Apart from an unnatural rigidity, she looked oddly peaceful.

"Sleeping beauty, yes?" Bodo took back the photographs.

"Dead beauty," Bond corrected, for, in life, Laura March had been undoubtedly attractive. He felt irritated by Bodo's seeming callousness, but tamped down his anger. Cops the world over seemed to develop a hard second skin when it came to sudden death.

Lempke turned and pointed up the smooth green slope, toward a small outcrop of rock. "When the forensic folk examined the body first, they drew my attention to the bruise on the back of her neck—I have snapshots also of that. We took some bearings from the position of the body, worked out a possible trajectory. It's up there, sniper's hide."

"But you had no idea that the bruise came from something fired at the victim."

"This also is true. Could have been inflicted from very close, but there were no signs that anyone else had been in this spot. I used brain." He tapped his forehead. "I watch sometimes the television of that detective, Hercule Poirot, by Agatha Crusty—"

"Christie," Bond corrected.

"That's the one. Yes, he calls the brain his little gray cells, no?"

"Yes."

"Then also that's what I use. Little gray cells, only I think mine are possibly pink. I have a liking for red wine. Okay?"

There was really no answer to that, so Flicka and Bond simply followed Bodo up the neatly marked track, rising toward the little outcrop of rock, which was also cordoned off by crime-scene tape.

"This is where the sniper laid his eggs." Bodo made a small gesture to the area immediately behind the rocks.

"Laid his *eggs?*" Bond thought, and knew in that moment his first impression of the man had been correct. Bodo Lempke, with his slept-in appearance and feigned naïveté, coupled with a disarming misuse of the English language, was as sharp as a razor blade. He almost certainly suspected everybody of being guilty of something until he, in person, proved otherwise.

"You see," Bodo continued. "You see how the marksman had a clean shot. Straight down, sixty meters: a good clear shot with plenty of cover."

"How do you know? Did the shooter leave a calling card?"

Bodo gave his blank stare, followed by the imbecilic smile. "Sure. Of course. People like this always leave the visiting cards. Part of their stork-in-trade. They like you to know they've been here, and this one for quite a long time was here. Overnight, in fact."

"Overnight?"

"Came up as one person. Went down as someone completely different. It rained, quite hard, like dogs and cats even, on the day before Miss March died. The shooter got wet and cold, then dried out the next day when the sun came out and when his victim rode up on the chair lift. See, the ground here was softened by rain. He left perfect marks of his body."

Behind the little cluster of rocks there were indentations which undoubtedly showed that someone had lain there for a considerable period.

Lempke gave them his fast humorless smile. "Come," he said with a conspiratorial wink.

He led the way up the rise to a small clump of bushes, also corralled by crime-scene tape. At the base of the bushes was a shallow hole, around two feet square and a foot or so deep. "Maybe he planned to come back for his stuff, but we got here first. I have it in my car."

"You have what in your car?" from Flicka.

"Everything he needed—except for the weapon, of course, and the other personal items he took down on the following day."

"Such as?"

"You don't believe me? You think I'm oaf of detective. Come, I will even buy you lunch at one of my favorite restaurants here. Captain Bond, you accompany the pretty lady, I'll follow. Meet you at the bottom, I have to get these flatfooted policemen out of here. They want to open up the chair lift this afternoon so that the crowds can come up and admire the mountain view."

"You don't like him much, do you?" Flicka asked as they sat, swaying down on the chair lift.

"Cunning as a fox, and he knows far more than is good for him." Bond reached out and took her hand. "Am I forgiven yet?"

"Maybe. Wait and see. I'll tell you tonight."

"Ah."

"What interests me, James, is that this policeman seems to know much more than we were led to believe."

"Bozo Lempke."

"His name is Bodo, I think, James."

"I know; but I like the name Bozo better. Bozo the clown."

Lempke drove like a short-sighted racing driver well past his prime. Rarely had Bond felt so insecure in a car, and Flicka looked both white and shaken when the policeman finally pulled up outside a small mom-and-pop restaurant a few kilometers outside Interlaken.

Being Sunday, when Swiss families tend to eat out, the place was full, but Bodo was known, and they soon found themselves in a private room behind the main restaurant. Lempke waved aside all question of Laura March's death until after they had eaten. "You go into a church to pray," he muttered, "so you go into a restaurant to eat. This is well-known fact, and I enjoy eating."

This became all too clear over the next hour and a half as he efficiently put down two helpings of *Raclette,* that simple yet wonderfully aromatic dish of cheese melted over potato, served with pickled onions and gherkins. He also ate three succulent rainbow trout to Bond's two and Flicka's one. Two extra-large slices of cherry tart, heaped with cream, followed, and he drank the best part of a bottle of red wine with the meal. It was only when coffee was served that Bodo looked satisfied.

He gave an eccentric wink, rubbed his hands together, and announced that they should now get down to business as he really did not have all day to waste.

"My superiors tell me that, as the officer in charge of this case, I am to afford you as much help and information as possible." He looked from Bond to Flicka and back again, as though waiting for questions.

"So what did you find hidden up there, in the hole under the bushes, Bodo?"

"Everything he couldn't take back down the mountain. Particularly as he wanted to go down as a different person."

"What d'you mean by " 'everything'?" Flicka leaned forward to light a cigarette.

"Everything he couldn't carry down. It was all stashed up there."

"Such as?"

"Such as a large canvas holdall. Very dampened by rain and from its contents."

"Which were?"

"Waterproof camouflaged coverall with hood and gloves, battery-warmed, waterproof sleeping bag, the remains of food from what the military call a ratpack, and a thermos flask. Also one spare CO_2 cartridge, so we know what he was using: a high-powered gas-operated rifle. He also left some special attachments for his shoes. Make himself look taller with them."

"And he came up with it? Anybody see him?"

"Sure they saw him. Coming up and going down. One of the men operating the chair lift has identified him, even though he looked quite different both times."

"How?"

"How what?"

"How did he look so different?"

"His tallness, or shortness, depending which day you're talking about. Here, I have artist's impressions." He delved into the pigskin folder, which had obviously been restocked since they were up on the mountain, and placed two photographs of line drawings on the table.

The first was of a middle-aged man, slightly oriental in appearance, with a short drooping mustache and thick-lensed spectacles. As the legend at the side of the drawing told them, he was a little over six feet in height. The raincoat looked very English, probably Burberry, reaching down to lower calf length. This man carried a canvas holdall and a thick walking stick.

Lempke touched the drawing with a stubby index finger. "Came up a tall man, wearing a raincoat." He touched the second drawing. "Went down as a clean-shaved man, around five feet eight inches tall, in black cords and a rollneck, carrying a small rucksack. Too small. If he'd bothered to bring a larger size he could have taken everything back with him."

Certainly the drawing showed someone quite different. Much younger, the face more open. The only thing he had in common with the first drawing was that he also carried the heavy stick.

Lempke smiled, producing a third drawing which he laid between the first two.

"This how he was identified?" Bond's mouth tightened.

"Of course. By his walking stick. Very thick, sturdy, with a brass handle shaped like a duck's head."

"You think that was the weapon?"

"I'm sure of it." Lempke gave another of his mirthless laughs. "I even know the man's name, for it was the real person who went down—or as real as we'll ever get. They identified him at his hotel. An Englishman by the name of David Docking. They had his passport details, as did the local police, which is the law. Arrived on Friday night, dressed as you see him there." He touched the second drawing. "Only luggage was the rucksack— quite small—and left on Saturday morning. The head porter of the Beau-Rivage, where he stayed, saw his air ticket. He was due to fly from Zurich on a British Airways flight on Saturday evening, so it won't surprise you that nobody called David Docking was on that particular flight. Mr. Docking left the Hotel Beau-Rivage at ten o'clock on

Saturday morning and has not been seen or heard of since."

"So Mr. Docking went up the mountain on Thursday morning—"

"Afternoon. Around four in the afternoon."

"Went up on Thursday afternoon, looking like a middle-aged man with a walking stick. Holed up there overnight, and came down, as himself, on Friday, when he booked into the Beau-Rivage."

Lempke nodded slowly. "That's how he did it. One of the men who help people into the chairs noticed the unusual walking stick on Thursday. He was also on duty during Friday afternoon, and his eye caught the stick again. 'Hallo,' he said to himself. " 'A lot of people are going around with thick sticks with brass duck's head handles.' "

Bond grunted, thinking, yes, there was an elderly man with a stick just like that in Washington only two days before Laura March died. Mentally he made a note to check out flights. Could the elderly man with the stick and the funny hat, caught on film near the White House on Wednesday, have been the same man who took the chair lift at Grindelwald on Thursday? The timing would work, and he had little doubt that it could be done easily.

"You see, my little pink cells have worked overtime. The man was already waiting for his victim, and he was quite prepared to suffer minor discomfort—like a night out in the rain on a bare hillside—to get her."

Flicka spoke— "You think she was a definite victim? *The* target? You don't think she could have just got unlucky? That David Docking, or whatever he's called, waited for the first good random target?"

"Even in the rain there were quite a lot of people up there on Thursday, Fräulein von Grüsse. No, this joker—is right in English, joker?—waited for one person. He waited in cold and rain for Laura March."

"Then he must have been pretty certain that she'd turn up," Bond mused.

"One hundred percent certain. My pink cells tell me she was the target, and he waited for her only. He knew she would turn up."

"As you are the police officer in charge of the case, d'you think you're ever going to catch him?"

"Docking, or whatever his real name is? Oh no. No, I won't catch him. Already I think he has long left Switzerland. In any case, I am to hand over my report to your Scotland Yard people, Captain Bond, so that they can take the case forward. As soon as the inquest is over, tomorrow, I act only in an advisory capacity. Had you not been told this?"

"No. There was some anxiety in certain quarters that Scotland Yard should be kept out."

Lempke nodded ponderously. "So, yes. Yes, I understand this, but all is changed as from a very short time ago. The instructions were waiting for me when I came down from First. Really I'm talking to you as a little favor. I pretend I don't get the new orders until I return to my headquarters." Once more the small conspiratorial look. "This, I suppose, means you don't know either."

"Don't know what?"

"Don't know that you also are off the case."

"Off the . . . ?" Bond began. "How in blazes . . . ?"

Lempke touched his nose with his right forefinger. "I consider myself a judge of good character. Just thought you should know what *I* know before you are sent into whatever oblivion is prepared for funnies like you. Now, I think I should drive you both back to Grindelwald so that you can collect your car. Then I can discover they've taken you off the case and show my own contrition and surprise."

"You think they've taken both of us off, for real, James?" They were driving back to Interlaken, with Flicka at the wheel.

"If that's what Bodo says, then it's probably true, though I can't figure him. Why would he want to pass on all that information if he knew we were already being cut out of the loop?"

"Maybe he's concerned that someone's trying a cover-up."

"Who'd want to do that?"

"Your sister service? MI5?"

"They haven't got the clout. My Chief wouldn't go for it. Could be they're furious with me for losing the letter, or maybe there's some kind of danger in our being left in the field."

"I know the dangers, so what's new?"

He said that he would tell her once, and once only, then quickly ran through his suspicions concerning the assassination of the CIA Assistant Director in Washington—especially about the elderly man in the L.L. Bean shirt and the billed cap with the legend *Toto, I don't think we're in Kansas anymore,* and of the walking stick with the brass duck's head handle. "I'm on the restricted file list, and there aren't many of us. The chances of two people using a similar weapon within forty-eight hours of each other must be pretty slim. I just want you to know about this in event we *are* really being taken off the case."

"But I don't want to be taken off it, James. It's the kind of puzzle that I like. I want to solve this business." For a moment she sounded like a spoiled child.

"We might not have any other option."

"Do *you* want to be taken off it?"

"Of course not."

"What're you going to do then?"

"If I'm off the case? I have some leave coming up. I'll demand a month of it now and follow my own private enquiry. But I don't really think that's going to happen."

"Give me your private number in London. Then I can always call you."

The first person Bond saw as they finally walked into the foyer of the Victoria-Jungfrau was M's Chief of Staff, Bill Tanner. He was standing in deep, serious conversation with a gaunt-looking woman, severe-faced, and with iron-gray hair pulled tightly back from a high forehead.

"Hell," Flicka whispered. "That's my immediate superior. Gerda Bloom, known in the business as Iron Gerda."

"Sorry about this, James." Tanner came swiftly toward them as Iron Gerda cut Flicka away from them like a stalking horse. "I'm very sorry about

it, but my orders are to put you on the first flight
out of here. M's furious about the missing letter, and there's been a complaint from the hotel
which, if it's true, means you're up to your neck
in fertilizer. I'm to stand over you as you pack,
and there'll be no further contact with Fräulein
von Grüsse."

6

Smoke and Mirrors

"The Swiss are furious, and so am I!" M barked. He strode up and down behind his desk, brows dark and face an angry crimson. "Why do we always have problems like this when you have to work with any female member of a foreign service, 007? I won't have it. You know that already, so why do you constantly go out there and make fools of us?"

From long experience Bond knew there was no point in trying to argue with his Chief. When the Old Man had the bit between his teeth, and truly believed that his accusations were founded on fact, all you could do was hang on and wait for the storm to pass.

The moment he entered M's office, on his return to London, he immediately knew there was trouble. The Chief was icy and terse as he

made his verbal report, waiting to hear Bond's
side of things before launching into an uncon-
trolled attack, which still continued after fifteen
minutes.

"You appear to have lost a vital piece of evidence,
which is reprehensible. You have also behaved in
a manner prejudicial to both Queen's Regulations
and the discipline of this service. I suspect the loss
of the evidence is partly due to your misconduct,
which was eventually reported to me via Scotland
Yard, who were informed personally by the Swiss
authorities." He stopped in midflow, turning to
glower at Bond. "Well, 007? Well, what have you
to say for yourself?"

"I admit to losing a document, sir. But, in my
defense, that document was secure: locked in my
briefcase, which was inside one of the rooms in
the suite I occupied with a member of the Swiss
Intelligence and Security Service. There was no
reason to think that anything would be stolen
from a room that was locked and safeguarded."

"But it *was* stolen!" M's voice rose on the *was*
and reached a high decibel level on "stolen."

"I don't deny that, sir. I didn't know I'd have to
sleep with the thing chained to my wrist. As far
as we were concerned, Fräulein von Grüsse and
myself were the only people who even knew of the
existence of the letter."

"Oh, yes—Fräulein von Grüsse! The pair of you
are a disgrace. She'll be lucky if she's not actually
dismissed from her service. But for your senior-
ity, Bond, I'd have you permanently out of this
building before nightfall. In these times, when
various parliamentary idiots are calling for the

disbandment of all intelligence services, we cannot afford flagrant moral lapses in the field."

He paused, shaking his head as if in disbelief. "God knows, many people in power, both here and in the USA, seem to delight in telling the world that there is no further need for either security or intelligence operations. I even heard recently of some bestselling novelist doing a Chamberlain and sounding off about peace in our time. We all know that the so-called reformed Russians are still carrying out clandestine operations, and there's been a proliferation of new Active Measures by foreign intelligence services that the politicians—let alone the general public—have never even heard of. So I cannot afford officers like yourself who go out and live the life of Riley on government money."

"What are Fräulein von Grüsse and myself accused of doing, sir?"

"Of rutting like animals, Captain Bond. Of disturbing the peace of the Hotel Victoria-Jungfrau, Interlaken, and of causing grave moral scandal."

"On whose word, sir?"

"On whose word? The hotel management's word, 007. They had no less than six complaints from guests. Heaven knows I have often turned a blind eye to your flagrantly immoral behavior, but this time even I can't disregard it. It appears that you, with Fräulein von Grüsse, made enough noise to waken the dead."

"What kind of noise, sir?"

"The noise of brute beasts of the field. A retired couple called down to reception after midnight to complain of some kind of orgy going on in your suite. Within the hour there were five more complaints from people next door and across the hallway from your suite. One elderly lady, it seems, was concerned lest murder was being done. Screaming, laughter, shouts and—I can hardly bring myself to say it—the noise of furniture being abused. In plain language, the violent creaking of bedsprings."

"Really, sir?" Though he would be the first to admit that Flicka and himself had enjoyed each other's company, it had been a very quiet business. Endearments and whispers, rather than laughter and screams of delight. "And who, sir, reported all this to the police?"

"The hotel reported it."

"Yet they took no steps to pass on these so-called complaints directly to either myself or Fräulein von Grüsse. Wouldn't you say that this is the normal kind of action in a properly run hotel? If there are complaints concerning noise from a guest's room, then isn't it more usual for the hotel to inform the guest and ask him to keep quiet?"

"That's as may be. In this instance, the hotel reported it to the police—you know how the Swiss are. In turn, they checked on your names, realized why you were in Interlaken, and passed the comment back to Scotland Yard, who informed me."

"I'd like to make a bet on which particular member of the hotel staff did this, sir."

"That's not the crux of the matter."

"It is as far as I'm concerned, sir. I would like it on record that, during that particular night, absolutely no noise came from the suite occupied by Fräulein von Grüsse and myself—no screams, no laughter, no shouting, no abusing of furniture. I admit to spending the night in Fräulein von Grüsse's company, but there was no blatant impropriety. Also, I would suggest that the person who made these accusations is a hotel employee, and assistant manager, I think. Her name is Marietta Bruch."

"Really. And can you give me any reason why this Marietta Bruch would lie about something as serious as this?"

"I have absolutely no idea, sir. She was a shade put out when we couldn't complete the search of the late Ms. March's room. Apart from that, she did seem slightly belligerent from the moment we arrived."

"In what way?"

"She made it pretty clear by her manner that she did not believe our cover story. I think if you can get the local Interlaken police to look into *her* story—perhaps even interview the people who are supposed to have complained—you will find it's Fräulein Bruch who's telling fairy tales."

M made a harrumphing sound, half clearing of throat, half dubious grunt.

"In fact, sir, I think I must insist that Fräulein Bruch's accusations are followed up, even if it means chasing former guests halfway around Europe. I repeat, sir, there was *no* noise from our suite."

He looked at his Chief, locking eyes with him, and for an instant could have sworn that deep behind M's glare were the traces of a slight twinkle.

"And what will you be doing while I follow this up—if I follow it up?"

"I am going to apply for a month's leave, sir. I'm going to get out of this building and not return until you, or whoever you appoint, have investigated this business thoroughly, and my name, together with that of Fräulein von Grüsse, has been cleared of any meretricious impropriety."

Again, he saw the small light in M's eyes. "A very good idea, Captain Bond. I would suggest that you go to your office, make your report in writing, and then stay away from this facility until I recall you."

"You're suspending me from duty, sir?"

In the short pause that followed, Bond actually saw his Chief lift an eyebrow. "No, Captain Bond. No, I'm not suspending you. I'm giving you leave to do exactly as you see fit. Go and write your report, then get out of my sight until everything is cleared up."

Bond rose and began to walk toward the door, halting and turning only when M spoke again—

"Oh, Captain Bond, I suggest you also clean out your safe and remove any sensitive papers from your desk. I shall let you know when you may return."

This time there was no mistaking the signals. Though M still maintained his stiff, angry pose, he clearly winked.

"Very good, sir." Bond returned the wink. "I would like your permission regarding one matter."

"Yes?"

"I would like to attend Ms. March's funeral."

"As far as I'm concerned you can do anything you like. Good day to you, Captain Bond." Another wink, this time broad and unconcealed.

It took less than an hour to write the report, which he sealed in an envelope and sent up to M by messenger. There was little of importance in the drawers of his desk, so he opened the small wall safe, provided for all senior officers. When he had left on the previous Saturday, the safe had been empty, but M's instructions, combined with the clandestine wink, had been specific.

Lying inside the safe were four slim buff folders, each flagged "restricted and classified." A quick look inside the first file told him these were the up-to-date reports on the four assassinations that had taken place—in Rome, London, Paris, and Washington—during the previous week. There was no doubt in his mind that M was quietly ordering him to carry on investigating the situation.

Swiftly, he slid the folders into his briefcase, flicked the combination locks, and left his office. At the main entrance he signed out, appending the words *on extended leave,* and adding *Contact at private number.* He then strode out into a pleasantly warm and sunny London afternoon.

Within minutes, as he walked briskly across Regent's Park toward Clarence Gate and Baker Street, he knew there was surveillance on him. Anybody who has spent a lifetime in the world of secrets, leading double existences, prowling those dark and mazelike alleys where truth is so often fiction, and reality becomes illusion, is bound to develop sensitive antennae: a sixth sense.

He could never have given anybody a logical explanation of how *his* antennae worked, but work they did. He *knew* he was being observed and probably followed, though there was no way he could immediately identify those who watched him.

On reaching Baker Street, he decided to sort out the sheep from the goats by giving them a run for their money. Hailing a passing taxi, he told the driver to take him to Austin Reed's in Regent Street. As the driver pulled out into the traffic, Bond glanced back, just catching sight of a young man in jeans and a black shirt desperately trying to flag down another cab.

Austin Reed's store occupies almost an entire block on the west side of Regent Street, a few blocks from Piccadilly Circus. As the cab pulled up, Bond slipped the driver a five-pound note and was onto the pavement almost before the vehicle had come to a stop. He had no intention of going into the store. Instead, he walked quickly toward what Londoners usually refer to as "The Dilly," and disappeared down the steps to the London Transport Underground system.

He took a train to South Kensington, where he intended to change onto the Circle Line, to take a train back to Sloane Square, which would bring him within walking distance of his flat in the pleasant Regency house which stands on a quiet tree-lined street off the King's Road.

As he negotiated the pedestrian tunnels at South Kensington he realized that the young man he had seen in Baker Street was not only still with him but had also maneuvered himself into a position some twenty feet in front of him, anticipating Bond's destination. The young man was a professional, and Bond knew where there is one experienced watcher then two or three others are usually near at hand.

The adrenaline began to pump, and his nerve ends tingled. The very fact of being followed created a tension of its own, and he felt his muscles involuntarily tighten. He had no idea where this team came from. For all he knew, they could be part of some foreign service, or—more likely, he considered—part of the famed Watcher Service of MI5.

The platform was crowded even though the usual rush hour would not get under way for another hour or so. The man in jeans and black shirt lounged against the slick, tiled wall, near a poster proclaiming CATS, NOW AND FOR EVER.

Bond placed himself directly in front of the watcher, giving the young man a good view of his back, waiting for the next train to rumble from the tunnel. It pulled up with a hiss of automatic doors opening, and there was a surge forward as people tried to board the cars while others eased their way out.

He stayed back, as if he had changed his mind about getting on the train. Then he turned, took a pace forward, and asked the young man if he had the time. The watcher lazily raised his left arm to look at his watch and Bond gave him a quick, hard jab to the chin with the heel of his right hand.

The watcher's head snapped back, his eyes taking on a glazed look of surprise.

"There's a man in trouble here," Bond shouted in the general direction of a uniformed BT official before he lunged for the closing doors of the nearest carriage. As the train pulled out, he saw a small knot of people form around the crumpled watcher.

The street off the King's Road where Bond lived was a cul-de-sac, the preferred kind of location for anyone in his profession. "You either live out in the open, with a lot of flat ground between you and the rest of the world, or you choose a street with only one entrance or exit," one of the instructors had told him years ago. "Preferably a short street," the old expert had added.

He knew all his neighbors and their cars by sight, and could spot a strange car or person in a second. Now, as he finally turned the corner and entered the street off the King's Road, Bond realized that, whoever they were, this surveillance team was serious. He saw not only a very strange vehicle—a small closed van—but also a uniformed road sweeper, with his high-wheeled cart, who was making his rounds, working—as Bond's old housekeeper would have said—"as though dead lice were dropping off him." The road sweeper was a total stranger, and not the man Bond was used to seeing.

He showed no sign of having noticed anything out of the ordinary as he put his key in the latch and entered the house through the front door. A pile of mail lay on the mat.

His housekeeper, May, was up in Scotland with her nephew and his wife, so Bond had taken his usual extra precautions—slivers of wood in the doorjamb, invisible thread across windows, just in case anyone had tried to bypass his sophisticated alarm system. Everything was in place, but that did not mean a thing. If he was truly the target of a tight surveillance operation, there could be a tap on his telephone without anyone gaining entrance to the house.

He dumped the mail on his sitting room table, went to the ornate Empire desk, unlocked one of the larger drawers and removed what appeared to be a normal telephone. Unplugging his house phone from its modular jack, he replaced it with the equipment taken from the desk drawer. He did not trust pocket tap detectors, and certainly could not call in the delousing department from headquarters. The telephone now in use was a state-of-the-art piece of equipment, a very distant cousin of what used to be called the Neutralizer phone. With this instrument in place, even the best wiretap was defenseless. The microcircuits within the telephone automatically sent out signals which could not be captured on tape or headphones. Instead, a would-be eavesdropper would be treated to a high-pitched signal known to cause severe cases of deafness for a minimum of forty-eight hours—one of the reasons the service instructions forbade the use of these devices on a permanent basis. The other consideration was cost, for each unit of the Electronic Countermeasures Telephone (ECMT) or Squealerphone, as it was often called, ran to almost £4,000.

Having dealt with communications, he took the briefcase into his small bedroom, felt along the gleaming white painted wainscot until he found a tiny knot of wood which he pulled back to reveal a large, secret fireproof steel safe. Quickly working the combination, he slid the briefcase inside, then locked everything and slid the panel back into place.

Having dealt with the important matter, Bond now turned his attention to the day's mail: ironically enough there was a telephone bill, as well as a red electricity account, meaning that it was time to pay up or lose power; four pieces of junk mail, and a letter in a dark-blue envelope, addressed correctly in a bold hand—female he thought—which he did not recognize.

The envelope contained one sheet of notepaper, in the same shade of blue. The sheet contained neither address nor salutation. In the same round, very feminine hand was a seven-line message:

You should be warned that the Security Service has put permanent round-the-clock surveillance on you, it read. *We have met once, but I should not give you my name in writing. I shall take tea at Brown's Hotel each afternoon this week between four and six. Please throw the watchers and meet me. This is a matter of great urgency and importance, which concerns the late Laura March.*

There was just enough in the short note to rouse his interest. The trick would be throwing the surveillance team. In novels of espionage a hero might disguise himself suitably and hoodwink the sharp-eyed team of watchers. He thought of Buchan's *The Thirty-Nine Steps,* in which Richard Hannay had left the police standing as he exited a building disguised as a milkman. It was almost five in the afternoon; Brown's Hotel lay a good twenty minutes away, by taxi, in Dover Street, close to Piccadilly and Bond Street. If he was going to slip the leash and make contact today, he would have to be very light on his feet.

At least he now knew who he was up against, and that was not the happiest of thoughts, for the Watcher Branch of the Security Service is one of the best-trained surveillance outfits in the world. Softly he quoted Shakespeare to himself: "O, for a Muse of fire . . ."

He stopped, wrinkling his brow, and then smiled to himself. That had done it, the Muse of fire. Smoke and mirrors, he thought as he went rapidly into the kitchen.

May, his housekeeper, was old-fashioned and regarded any utensil made from plastic with the same disdain as a conscientious watchmaker might regard the electronic workings of digital timepieces. Instead of the ubiquitous plastic, foot-operated garbage containers, she insisted on using an old and heavy Victorian all-metal rubbish bin. The plastic variety, she always claimed, were fire hazards—and that was exactly what he needed now, a safe, well-contained fire hazard.

On the previous Saturday, when he had been unexpectedly called into the office, Bond was left with little time to complete any of the household chores usually undertaken by the absent May, so the rubbish bin was still almost a quarter full. It contained damp paper towels, the somewhat pungent remains of the curry he had cooked for himself on Friday night, together with coffee grounds, eggshell, and some discarded toast from his breakfast on Saturday morning. To this now unpleasant stew he added a pile of bundled-up paper towels, tamping them around the garbage and crumpling more, which he threw on top of the moist mess until the bin was around three-quarters full.

Dragging the bin into the small lobby, he placed it in the open doorway between there and the sitting room. Then he went quickly through to his bedroom.

When the old house had been renovated, a skillful architect had made certain that each of its three stories was entirely self-contained. The only entrance to Bond's apartment was through the front door, and to all intents his rooms occupied the entire ground floor. In reality his apartment, like each of the flats above him, lost some eight feet along the right-hand gable end of the house, where a false wall had been put in to accommodate private entrances, each with its own self-contained flight of stairs, for the two higher apartments.

These alterations had in no way affected the original view from Bond's bedroom, where the gold Cole wallpaper contrasted elegantly with deep-red velvet curtains. The bedroom windows looked out onto a tiny garden, with a red brick wall surrounding the lawn and flower beds behind the house. The three sections of the wall formed simple divisions between the gardens of the houses on either side, and, at the end, the garden of the property at the rear. It was this far wall that interested him. The view from his windows included the back of the slightly larger Regency house which stood in another cul-de-sac running roughly parallel to the one in which Bond lived.

There was a drop of some eight feet from the bedroom windows, and the wall that separated the neighboring garden was around twelve feet high, with no barbs, broken glass, or other deterrents to a would-be climber. This house was owned by a merchant banker and his family who, to his certain knowledge, had left for their annual summer holiday in Cyprus on the previous Saturday. Bond liked to keep track of all his neighbors. It was something he did automatically when in London, and, over the years, his personal watch was one of second nature. He also knew that the house had a side entrance giving access from the garden along the gable end to a graveled turning circle and the street.

He opened one of the long sash windows in the bedroom, then went back to the garbage bin. Even a careful team of watchers were unlikely to have any spare people loitering in the parallel street, anywhere near the merchant banker's home, and he considered that, should the ruse in mind work, he could get from his bedroom window, across the wall, and out into the street through the garden door in a maximum of one and a half minutes. It would be a race, for the watchers would certainly react very quickly, but he considered the odds were just in his favor.

Squeezing past the rubbish bin, he opened a drawer in the ornate clothes stand, which stood against one wall of the entrance lobby, and took out a pair of black leather driving gloves. Thirty seconds later, Bond set fire to the paper towels in the bin.

Initially, the metal container blazed alarmingly with flame. Then the fire tried to claw its way into the damp garbage. The flames died, and dense white smoke began to billow from the container. Within thirty seconds the smoke began to fill the lobby, and Bond hesitated, wondering how much the smoke damage would cost him in refurbishing. Then he stepped back, heading for the kitchen to activate the alarm system, which would shriek into action almost immediately because of the open window in his bedroom. A second before the bells went off, the smoke detectors triggered their separate shrill siren, and he made his way to the bedroom with ears humming from the din.

There would not be much time, for the watchers in the van, plus the phony road sweeper, would almost certainly make for the front of the house, intent on breaking down the door. This would be a flushing out with a vengeance, for the team's instinctive reaction would be to assist in what should appear to be a true emergency, and to blazes with their cover. Once they broke down the door, the source of the predicament would be all too apparent, and by then Bond would have to be long gone.

He dropped from the window and hit the ground running, taking a flying leap at the brick wall, his gloved hands rocketing up as he reached the apogee of his jump, scrabbling to get a firm grip on the topmost bricks of the wall. His hands took hold, his body hitting the wall, chest first, knocking the wind out of him so that for a second he almost lost his grasp. Then, with one muscle-wrenching haul, he lifted himself over the wall and dropped into a carefully tended flower bed on the far side.

Not looking back to see what damage he might have caused to the banker's hardy annuals, he plunged across the manicured lawn, running for the large wooden gate that would take him along the side of the house and into the street.

The gate was firmly bolted and locked, and he lost precious seconds in slipping the bolts and smashing the lock with three mighty kicks. Finally, some two minutes after dropping from the bedroom window, he emerged into the street, brushing himself off with one hand and struggling to get control of his breathing.

In the distance he could hear the fire engines, and he thought he could detect the frantic shouts of the watchers. Smiling to himself, Bond reached the King's Road and hailed the first available taxi.

"Looks like a drama somewhere around here, guv'nor," the cabby observed.

"It's quite near my place, I'm afraid." Bond was still flicking brick dust from his navy blue blazer. "I'll know soon enough. Brown's Hotel please, and I'm in a bit of a hurry."

"You'll be lucky this time of day, guv'nor, but I'll do me best."

It was exactly ten minutes to six when they pulled up in front of the hotel's unpretentious entrance. He headed straight for the comfortable paneled lounge to the right of the foyer, where afternoon tea was served in a truly traditional manner. There were only half a dozen people still in the room, and a waiter came up to quietly tell him that they had finished serving tea.

"It's all right, I'm supposed to meet someone . . ." His voice trailed off, for he saw her raise a hand and smile at him. She was sitting in a corner, near the fireplace—decorated with flowers now in summer—where she had a total controlled view of the room, and as he moved closer, he still could not place her.

She wore an elegant black business suit, and the short skirt rode up high, showing an almost erotic amount of thigh. When he had last seen her, she had her black hair pulled severely back from her forehead and fastened in a bun at the nape of her neck. Now the smooth and glossy hair fell down to her shoulders and curled provocatively. The granny glasses had gone and he presumed she was wearing contact lenses, for the deep brown eyes looked up at him, wide and delighted, with just a hint of anxiety.

"Captain Bond, I'm so glad you could make it. I hope you didn't bring anybody with you." The voice was husky and distinctive.

"Please call me James, Ms. Chantry. This is quite a surprise. You look different." The last time he had seen her was in M's office with her superior officer from MI5, the fussy Mr. Grant.

"Then you should call me Carmel—a strange name for a good British girl, I know." She smiled and the entire room seemed to brighten. "You did manage to slip our little phantom friends, I hope."

He smiled and sat next to her, his nostrils noting the subtle trace of a very expensive scent. "They were dealing with a fire in my flat when I left."

"Good. Might I suggest we go somewhere a little

more private. I have a great deal to tell you, and I really don't think I'm going to have all that much time. I fear my immediate boss, the preposterous Gerald Grant, will be out looking for me, and I think his message will be that I've overstepped the mark once too often. Would your service have a job for a former member of the Security Service?"

"It depends what kind of service she's offering."

"Well." She paused, letting a wicked little smile play around her lips. "Well, James, to begin with I have some nasty stories about the way my people fouled up the vetting of Laura March."

"I know about the brother."

"Indeed. Well, for one reason or another, there are secrets deeper than the maniac brother."

"Such as?"

"Such as her last lover—the fiancé and the broken engagement. How would that be for starters?"

"Give me a name, just to humor me, Carmel."

"David?" She smiled, her fingers brushing the back of his hand. "David Dragonpol."

"As in the greatest British actor since Olivier?" He heard the shocked surprise in his voice.

"The same."

"Where can we go and talk?"

"I'm on leave." Again the smile, which was a mixture of wanton invitation and secret amusement. "I've taken a room here for the week, on the premise that little Gerald won't look for me in London."

"You really mean *the* David Dragonpol?"

"The actor, no less. Shall we go?" She rose and

he waited for her to lead the way. As he followed
her out to the elevators, Bond had one of those
strange flashes of intuition which told him that
this way lay monsters.

7

The Man with the Glass Head

The name David Dragonpol slewed around Bond's mind as they rode the elevator up to the third floor. In that short space of time he went through all he could remember concerning the great actor who was, in himself, an enigma.

The world had become aware of Dragonpol in the late 1970s when he had appeared, first, in a television dramatization of the Life of Richard Wagner, then, later in the year, in a National Theatre production of *Hamlet*. It was his first leading role on stage, and he had left the Royal Academy of Dramatic Art only in the spring. What followed was theatrical fairy tale history. Dragonpol had a stunning stage presence, was tall, fine-looking, and with that extraordinary talent of a truly great actor—the ability to change both voice and appearance almost at will. After his huge success as the Prince of Denmark he directed and played in *Richard III* and *The Merchant of Venice*. Both productions had taken, not just London, but the world by storm, and Hollywood came calling with offers he could not refuse.

He did five films before returning to the stage, and by the early 1980s David Dragonpol was hailed as one of the greatest living British actors, second only to Olivier.

During the film period, one reviewer had commented that he was " . . . as impressive in his pauses as he is when speaking the lines of a character. He has that unique gift, known to only a handful of film actors, which allows the audience to see into his head, as though you can view his brain and mind. It is as if he is a man with a glass head."

The jealous few derisively called him the Man with the Glass Head.

Then, as suddenly as he had appeared, Dragonpol—whose ancestry could be traced back to the Doomsday Book—retired from both stage and screen in 1990, for what were described as personal and private reasons.

Rumors spread: he had AIDS; that he had been the victim of a nervous breakdown which had destroyed both his talent and confidence; that some unknown tragedy had struck within his family—he had always kept his private life strictly to himself, and even the most skillful and unprincipled journalists had failed to break into his privacy. They tried to track him down, but David Dragonpol eluded Press and the other media, disappearing as though he had never been.

Bond had seen him on stage and film, then once in the flesh, dining at Fouquet's in Paris with the British director Trevor Nunn, and swore he could feel the creative static right across the busy restaurant.

As they reached Carmel Chantry's door, he felt a strange sense of *déjà vu,* as though the David Dragonpol of that time was very near at hand.

The room was on the small side, though pleasant enough and well furnished. Carmel slipped out of her suit jacket, to reveal a white silk shirt which showed off her slim waist and clung tightly to neat, firm breasts. She dropped onto the bed, propping herself against the padded headboard, indicating that Bond should take the one easy chair.

"Okay, what about Laura March and David Dragonpol?" He tried to look elsewhere as her skirt rode higher up her thighs.

"Oh, James." She gave a little throaty laugh and arched her body. "You mean I have lured you into my web and you still want to talk business?"

He looked up and saw that her lips and eyes were almost mocking him, one eyebrow raised quizzically. "It's all right." She smiled. "I *did* lure you here to talk business, but I get so few opportunities to play the femme fatale that the role carries me away."

"Then why the disguise?"

"Which disguise?"

"I'm not sure. Either the disguise you wore when you came to see my Chief or the one you're wearing now."

She shifted on the bed. "Actually, this is the real me."

"Then why the frumpish outfit, the granny glasses and severe hairdo when you came calling?"

"Gerald." She sighed.

"Grant?"

"Master of the Anti-Terrorist Section, lord of all he surveys. Gerald Grant is the complete paranoid. Because of his paranoia he sees the Red Brigade lurking behind every door, the Provisional IRA in every shadow, the PLO and the Gray Wolves with moles inside the section itself. He demands that his officers practice tradecraft twenty-four hours a day and use disguises when out on the town. To be honest with you, James, I've had fat Gerald up to here." She raised one hand above her head and the silk of her shirt tightened against her breast. "I told you that I was on leave. That's true, but I've also handed in my resignation. Gerald is more dangerous than a busload of terrorists."

"Because of his paranoia?"

"That, plus his incompetence."

"He put the watchers onto me?"

"Of course. He holds executive rank, which gives him more power than he should rightly have."

"Why the watchers?"

"He instructed them from the word go. They were with you in Switzerland, though he had no right to use them. When you came back—in disgrace, I understand—he put an entire team onto you. Said it was an exercise. Bamboozled the head of the Watcher Section. Told him it would be good practice for the lads and lasses." She paused, then shot him a quick and interested smile. "Did you really come back in disgrace? Gerald said you'd been pretty naughty with a lady from Swiss Intelligence."

"Naughty enough to be on leave pending an enquiry."

"Oh, James. You really should control yourself. You can when you try. Look at you now." She moved suggestively and another couple of inches of thigh were revealed.

"Okay, so he put the watchers on me. Why?"

"I think you know why. It's the reason that fat Gerald will get the push. His concern was that you'd find out exactly what you *did* find out."

"Which was?"

"Don't be coy, James. You found out one of Laura's secrets."

"Her brother?"

"Of course."

"Tell me more."

"When Laura March joined the Anti-Terrorist Section, it was Gerald who did the positive vetting. He screwed up—mightily."

"And he realized he had screwed up?"

"About a year ago, yes. Well, in fact, I discovered Laura's secret—the serial-killer brother."

"How?"

"By accident. I was doing some checking on a possible terrorist contact in the North. It meant looking through local newspapers from way back. I stumbled on the David March story. Though it was headlines all over the world, and people have written books about it, the March family somehow managed to distance themselves. They even kept their photographs out of the papers— the national papers, that is. I happened to see a picture of the father with his daughter in a local paper. She was only a schoolgirl, but I had no doubt it was her."

"So you came running to Gerald."

"No. No, I didn't. Laura was super. She was very good at her job, likable, funny, very professional. She was my friend, so I went running to *her*."

"So who broke the bad news to Gerald?"

"She did. You can imagine how she felt. She had buried the past. Done everything to live it down. She had been terrified with the first vetting, let alone the one Gerald did. She knew she'd be out on her ear if anyone linked her to the David March business. One psycho nut in the family puts a terrible blot on the old escutcheon. Nobody in our service would risk employing her—tainted blood and all that kind of thing. The possibility of blackmail was worse than the old days when they wouldn't use gay people. Thank heavens that's changed." Again she shifted on the bed, and for the first time Bond got her message.

"No," she continued. "Laura went straight to Gerald and made her confession. He was appalled, of course, though tried to pass it off. Said he had known all along but felt she was so good that he had buried the evidence."

"She really was *that* good?"

"Laura? Yes, she was stunningly professional. A walking encyclopedia on all known terrorist operations and personalities. To be honest with you, Gerald would have been lost without her, she was so good."

"And now he is lost?"

"Just about. He covered up for her. He even kept quiet about David Dragonpol. You saw that yourself. He refused to discuss her private life with your Chief."

"I still don't see why he put the dogs on me."

She gave a little, mocking laugh. "I think he really imagined that he might still get away with it—I mean hide the little difficulty about her brother and the bloodline, and also keep the Dragonpol thing under wraps. He knew you were good. Has a file on you. Really he wanted someone more inexperienced on the case. He set you up, James, but you must know that."

"No. How did he set me up?"

"He uses someone at that hotel in Interlaken— has been using her for some time."

"Marietta Bruch?"

"The same. Laura spent odd weeks there with David. In fact, he made sure he had someone near her whenever she had any kind of tryst with D.D., as she used to call him. When the engagement was broken off, he seemed very relieved."

He nodded. "So tell me about Laura and the great man. The Man with the Glass Head, as some people used to call him."

"He didn't like that, by the way. There's really nothing much to tell. Gerald was concerned that, should the marriage take place, the press would focus on her, turn up her past, and he'd be given the old heave-ho. Which is probably what would have happened, and what will happen."

"There really was an engagement?"

"Oh, Lord, yes. Laura was nuts about him—and he about her. They met by accident, in 1989. Switzerland, as it happened. Lucerne, I think. Laura didn't even know who he was. David Dragonpol is a great chameleon, you know. Can hide in plain sight, even though his face and name are of the household variety. They met while she was doing a bit of unauthorized snooping for Gerald. The affair began within a couple of days."

"She was like that?"

"Like what?"

"Permissive? Got into affairs quickly?"

"Far from it. Laura was poised, elegant, even beautiful, and very sexy. I tried, but she's not one of the sisterhood." Her hand went to her mouth. "Damn!"

"Don't worry. I had you marked a few minutes ago. Just tell me about Laura and Dragonpol."

"Actually, you might not have me marked. If you want the truth, I'm like the Circle Line. I go both ways. You'd be surprised how many people are bisexual."

"Ah. No, I wouldn't be surprised. Nothing surprises me anymore and, like they say, some of my best friends, and all that." He wanted her to get to the real meat and not spill her own problems or proclivities to him. "Laura and Dragonpol," he said firmly.

"I told you. They met early in 1989, and the whole thing took off. She came back into the office like a Looney Tune. You could almost see the bluebirds flying around her head, tweeting like they do in cartoons. And she put on that goofy, faraway look that people get when they're first smitten."

"And she spilled the beans to you?"

"I forced it out of her, but yes, she talked to me. We had dinner together one night and she told all—as the girls' magazines say. It was better for me to hear it before anyone else."

"But others *did* hear it."

"Of course. In the Security Service you don't keep that kind of thing quiet for very long. Every spare weekend she had, Laura spent with David. When the dogs are out, they soon put two and two together. In a matter of weeks she made no secret about it within the office. I don't think it went further than that. Our people, like yours, are pretty tight-lipped, but I do know that she had girls from the secretariat asking her what he was really like. The usual kind of thing."

"And where did he meet her?"

"They took holidays together, sometimes in Interlaken, which they both thought was safe."

"No, you said she saw him on every spare weekend she had."

"Oh, that. She'd fly out to his place."

"His place?"

"Sure."

"The press and a lot of other people have been trying to find out where *his* place is ever since he went to ground."

"He's never made a genuine secret of it. He has a kind of fairy tale life. Lives in a castle on the Rhine. Very Hans Christian Andersen and the Brothers Grimm."

"Where exactly?"

"Right *on* the Rhine. Not far from Andernach. I've seen photographs of the place—great thick walls, turrets, a huge enclosed garden, moat, the lot. It's even called Schloss Drache—that's German for Dragon. Been in the family for centuries apparently. He lives there with his younger widowed sister. She's quite a handful, I gather. Name of Horton. Maeve Horton, née Dragonpol. You do know his family history, don't you?"

"Only that his publicity used to claim the Dragonpols are mentioned in the Doomsday Book."

"Certainly are. There's a manor house in Cornwall — Dragonpol Manor, would you believe? Yet they really think of themselves as Anglo-Irish. A Dragonpol went to Ireland with the Earl of Essex to put down the rebellion in the late sixteenth century. The Irish problem's plagued every British monarch since Elizabeth I to the present day. Odd, isn't it?"

He nodded her on.

"The Elizabethan Dragonpol set himself up in a huge manor in West Cork. They actually became very respected—the Dragonpols of Drimoleague. Still have a place there. The Irish connection sent Gerald through the roof. He had agents trawling the area—illegally, of course—looking into the family background for weeks after Laura announced the engagement."

"Which was when?"

"Oh, about six weeks after they first met."

"And it was broken off?"

"Yes."

"When?"

"Two weeks ago. She had planned to go out to Schloss Drache for her leave in August. She actually told me they would be getting married in August. Apparently it was all arranged. Then, a couple of weeks ago, she came into my office looking ill—white, unsteady. It was a Friday afternoon and she said D.D. had called her. There was some drama and he was sending his private aircraft for her. On Monday she came in and told me it was all over."

"She was in a state? Emotional?"

"Yes. Very unhappy, but she gave the impression that the reason for the breakup was valid. She actually said to me, 'It's quite out of the question. We can't marry. I just wish he'd told me sooner.'"

"Told her what?"

"I don't know. She said that she'd talk about it when she came back from her leave. Booked the Interlaken hotel at the last minute. Said she didn't know if it was a good idea, because they'd been very happy there, but it would give her some kind of perspective."

"So she was never able to discuss the reason with you?"

She shook her head, biting her lip, plainly upset. When he looked at her again, Bond saw tears hovering in her eyes. "She loved him so much, James. It really was one of those great romances."

"Yet she took the breakup . . . how can I say it? Stoically?"

"She said she understood, and that it was quite

impossible. I mean, when she came into my office on Friday, she looked sick—very sick—with concern. When she came in on Monday, she was together. It was as if she had been able to accept the breakup and knew the marriage would never have worked."

"That's it?"

"That's all I know."

There was a long pause. Somewhere far away, down the corridor, somebody slammed a door.

"So you're going to stay hidden away until your leave is up?"

"Something like that. Gerald won't be too happy. He'll have lost his two most precious assets, and I know where a lot of the bodies are buried. He won't let me go easily."

"You think you're in any kind of danger?"

She shook her head, then laughed. "Gerald's a pompous idiot, but he's not *that* stupid. No, I don't think I'm in any physical danger."

"What about Laura? Did you ever think she was in physical danger?"

"It's something we don't really think about. Anyone in the Anti-Terrorist Section could be in danger."

"But she knew things, knew of people . . ."

"More than most. There was a period when she was working on the hostages business with the Americans. Trying to find out where people like Terry Waite were being kept. She was good, James, so certainly some of the terrorist organizations would know of her, though they might only know her as a cipher—a code name. She was very careful. I told you: a real pro."

"So if you were asked under oath, you would have to say that there was always a possibility?"

"Of course. The same possibility that we all face. No more, no less. There was no particular outfit that she was afraid of. That's all."

Bond grunted and slowly got to his feet.

"Do you *have* to go?" There was a hint of begging in her voice, and her eyes had a pleading look. "I'm very much alone. I mean . . . I could do with some company."

"I'm sorry. I must go. You've given me information that I have to follow up."

"Not even a thank-you cuddle?"

He shook his head, reached out, and gave her shoulder a comforting caress. "Maybe some other time, Carmel."

"That would be really nice."

Outside in the street, the day had turned into evening. Warm, with that wonderful pearly summer sky that you get over London on good August nights.

Back at the Regency house, off the King's Road, he found a police car and a pair of uniformed officers waiting patiently. They told him there had been a fire. "Nothing serious, sir, but it looks like arson, and a break-in."

It was obvious that the cops had not been taken into the confidence of the Security Service. The lock had been mended, and the small entrance lobby was black with soot from the fire. The offending garbage bin had been dusted for prints and removed into the garden. The bedroom window had been broken somehow.

He thanked the police and called a twenty-four-hour glazier who turned up at around eight-thirty. He had just finished with the window when the telephone rang for the first time. It was the red phone, his private and secure line with the office.

"Get anything interesting at Brown's?" M asked quietly.

"Quite a lot, sir. I'm following it up."

"Don't call me." M sounded like a theatrical agent after an audition. "I'll contact you."

"Right, sir. I hope you've taken our sister service apart."

"It's being dealt with. I'll be in touch."

The house phone rang as he was about to go out and get some dinner at a nearby favorite restaurant. He answered warily.

"James, it's me." Flicka's voice was husky.

"Where are you?"

"I've booked into the Inn on the Park. I said my husband would be joining me."

"And is he?"

"I certainly hope you are. I'm registered as Mrs. Van Warren."

"As in rabbit?"

"The same."

"Right. Mr. Van Warren will be with you in half an hour."

"Goodie. I have a tale to tell, James."

"Join the club."

"I can hardly wait."

He cradled the receiver and muttered, "The things I do for England." Ten minutes later he stepped from the house carrying a small overnight case. It was almost ten o'clock, which meant that he missed the television news, and so knew nothing about the young woman found murdered, stabbed to death, in a third-floor room at the exclusive Brown's Hotel. Nor did he hear or see the slightly inaccurate description of himself which had been put out by the police as the last man to be seen with her.

8

This Is How It Must End

"James, it's *you!* Look at it!" Flicka stood in the doorway of the bedroom holding the *London Daily Telegraph* which had been delivered with breakfast. She lifted the front page so that it faced Bond, who was lying back against the pillows. There were banner headlines: BEAUTY STABBED IN LONDON HOTEL! Below, the subheading read, MAN SOUGHT BY POLICE. Side-by-side were two photographs, one of a somewhat elaborate brunette next to a composite picture, produced by a photofit computer program. The composite bore more than a passing resemblance to James Bond.

On the previous night Bond had found himself expected at the Inn on the Park. She had booked a suite which looked out across Hyde Park, not that he wanted to even glance at Hyde Park from the windows, for she met him at the door, a toweling robe loosely knotted at the waist, the knot parting as she stepped back to reveal that she was wearing the bare minimum underneath, with the accent on bare.

They finished saying hello about two hours later, after which he called room service and they sat across a small table eating smoked salmon and a huge chef's salad while he told her how things stood.

"The letter was certainly to David"—he swallowed—"but not to dear departed brother David. I suspect she never intended to send that letter. I believe it was a kind of private therapy. Sometimes people deal with emotions by writing letters to a loved one now out of reach. I'd bet money that's what Laura March was doing."

"And the loved one was?"

He told her. Inevitably her jaw dropped and she asked the familiar question, "Not *the* David Dragonpol?"

"In the flesh."

"Ah." She gave him a sloe-eyed, knowing look. "We know of the famous Mr. Dragonpol."

"Everyone knows of the famous Mr. Dragonpol."

"I mean the royal 'we,' as in my service, know of David Dragonpol."

"Really? Interesting."

"I use the term 'my service' loosely. I honestly don't know if I'm still a member of it. Like you, I'm on leave pending a court of enquiry. But, yes, I've seen the name come across various desks from time to time. He travels a lot."

"My information is that he stays holed up in a castle on the Rhine."

She nodded. "Schloss Drache, sure. He comes
in via Germany, but he's been in and out like a
jackrabbit—you should pardon the simile—over
the last couple of years. A day here, two days
there, a change of planes. Busy man, David
Dragonpol—what a crazy name, Dragonpol." She
ran it over her neat little pink tongue, then tried it
again. "Dragonpol." Then, once more with feeling,
"Draaagooonpool. Weird."

"It means Dragon Head."

"I know what it means, James. It's just a weird
name. He should have changed it to Beastiehead
or something more conventional. Where did you
come by all this information anyway—about
Laura and the demon Dragonpol?"

"First, what do your people think the great
man's up to, traveling around Switzerland?"

"Nobody's sure. He's only been casually questioned, and always has a ready answer: says he
is hunting for pieces to go in his castle, which he
is turning into a huge theatre museum."

"A theatre museum?"

"He plans to open it to the public in due course:
a kind of Disneyland, but dedicated to the history and art of theatre through the ages. That's
what he says he's doing. Mind you, he likes disguises, but then he's an actor, so he would like
disguises."

"Yet your service still knew of his comings and
goings?"

"Usually, yes. He's also very good at slipping
surveillance, but there were some leads—little
things—I recall."

"Such as?"

"Such as a possible meeting with an arms dealer here or a special source there; the odd informer; some people on the fringes of international terrorism. Nothing was ever proved, but there is definitely something sniffy about the actor."

"Iffy," Bond corrected.

"No, sniffy, like in smelly."

"If your people had an eye on him, what about the British Security Service?"

"I wouldn't know about that."

"You share information, though."

"Only when it's absolutely necessary. Dragonpol very rarely went to England. We Swiss like to keep certain secrets."

"Then you Swiss should have known about him and Laura."

She shrugged. "Maybe we did. I don't see everything."

"Well, he was definitely engaged to the fair Laura, and the engagement was broken off a couple of weeks before she went up the mountain and didn't come down again."

She looked at him as though not entirely satisfied; like a woman who has smelled a different scent on his shirt or spotted a lipstick mark on a collar: a shade of lipstick she never uses. "So where did you come by all this information?"

He told her about the skirmish with the Security Service's watchers, and his meeting with the lovely Carmel Chantry.

"And this Chantry person told all?"

"Everything. Including how we were set up by the unlovely Fräulein Bruch."

"Mmmm." She again cocked a quizzical eye at

him. "She tell you this standing, sitting, or flat on her back, James?"

"I was sitting, she was lying on a bed in Brown's Hotel."

"Before she told you, were you also lying on the bed?"

"No, Flicka. It was all very proper."

"What we've been doing is also very proper."

"More than very proper. She also told me that she once made a pass at Laura."

"Doesn't mean a thing—particularly if she's fragile and feminine."

"She volunteered the information."

"Lying on a bed?"

"Yes."

"Huh!" Flicka von Grüsse narrowed her eyes.

"I remained seated throughout."

"Long may it stay that way. You think the wicked witch of the Victoria-Jungfrau will get us off the hook if I alert large muscular members of my service to go and talk with her?"

"Shouldn't be surprised. You might even provoke some kind of international incident."

"Good." She sounded quite ready to start a global incident. "Good. I'll telephone them in the morning. I still have a few favors I can call in. Anyway, someone's going to be in touch with me; give me the inquest verdict and find out when Laura's going to be buried—and where." She took another mouthful of salmon. "What was it the old Inquisition used to call an interrogation? Putting someone on the question."

"To." Bond smiled. "They put people to the question."

"Good again. In a few minutes I shall put you to the question, James. But I shall do it lying down, and the torture will be exquisite."

"You could take a man to an early grave, Flicka."

"No, but I'll soon tell if his stamina has gone down the tubes. Find out if he is telling the truth about this little heart-to-heart earlier this evening with Ms. Chantry."

"I look forward to it . . ."

Now, on the morning after a strenuous night before, she stood in the doorway, one foot tapping and the other pointing to the picture of the elaborate brunette. "Is this the trollop Carmel Chantry?"

"No," Bond said, shifting his body and reaching up as though to take the paper. "No, that's not her, but there is a likeness . . . I wonder . . ." He reached for the telephone and dialed Brown's Hotel, asking for room 349.

A few seconds later the operator came back and asked who he actually wanted to speak with.

"Three forty-nine. Ms. Chantry."

"Ms. Chantry checked out yesterday evening, sir."

"Thank you." He cradled the telephone and looked up at Flicka again. "Does the paper give a name?"

"Of the murder victim? Yes. She was staying in the hotel under the name Barnabus. Heather Barnabus. I read it to you?"

"No, let me see." He all but snatched the *Telegraph* from her, quickly scanning the story. The girl had arrived at the hotel during the previous afternoon, had registered under the name Heather Barnabus, and, it was reported, she had been seen talking to a man in the lounge just after they had stopped serving tea around six o'clock. A chambermaid had found her body at seven-thirty when she went to make up the room for the night. According to the story, she had died from multiple stab wounds. Then came the description that, at a pinch, would pass for Bond. The police, as ever, wished to interview this man in order to eliminate him from their enquiries.

"This girl is definitely not Carmel." He tapped the picture again. "Though there is a passing resemblance. It's possible that someone saw me with Carmel before we went up to her room."

"A passing resemblance? Really? So this Carmel looks a bit of a tart, yes?"

"Not at all. She's been put in a very difficult position . . ."

"Many times, I should imagine . . ."

"By her imbecilic superior who appears to be about as professional as a veterinary surgeon in an abattoir."

"If this one is like the Chantry person, she looks pretty professional to me."

"She's an experienced security officer, Flicka!" He raised his voice, just enough to put paid to the bitchy remarks.

"Don't you think you should do something about it? I mean, somebody's going to connect you with that photofit, and they'll arrest you before you can say cipher."

"I'd feel happier if I knew where Carmel had got to. She has serious problems, as does the

Security Service. The idiot officer who's head of their Anti-Terrorist Section is about as efficient as a wasp in a jar, and I guess he's capable of almost anything, though I doubt if murder comes into it. To be honest, I'm worried in case this other girl, Heather Barnabus, has been snuffed in error."

"You still have to clear yourself with the local law, darling."

He nodded, kissed her lightly on the cheek, and headed for the bathroom.

Some twenty minutes later, shaved, showered, and dressed, he called West End Central Police Station and asked for CID. The line was answered by somebody who called himself Detective Sergeant Tibble.

"The Heather Barnabus murder," Bond began. "I'd like to speak with the officer in charge of the investigation."

"That would be Detective Chief Superintendent Daily, sir. Can I tell him who's calling?"

"Yes. Bond. James Bond."

There was an immediate reaction, as though the detective had been jabbed with a pin. Seconds later a honey-smooth voice came on the line. "DCS Daily, Mr. Bond. We've been looking for you."

"I've just seen the papers. I'd like to get a few things straight."

"So would we, Mr. Bond. Where can I pick you up?"

"You can't. I'm coming to see you."

"You're sure of that?"

"Absolutely. I'll be with you in less than half an hour."

He gave Flicka strict instructions. "Stay here, even when the chambermaids come to make up the room. Don't let anyone else in. If the phone rings, pick it up and say nothing."

"I do know how to handle it, James. I've been in the business for some time."

West End Central Police Station is a utilitarian building, without any personality, which lies off Regent Street. Over the years, an encyclopedia of London's more fashionable criminals have walked up its front steps and through the swinging doors; infamous murderers and insignificant petty villains have sat in its bare unvarnished interrogation rooms. Now, James Bond sat on a chair that was bolted to the floor. Across the table, similarly bolted, sat the smooth-jowled Detective Chief Superintendent George Daily. A second plainclothesman hovered near the door.

Daily's reputation was not unknown to Bond, for he was one of the new generation of policemen, university educated, smart, sharp, and eminently likable. Daily had been with the now-renamed Special Branch when it really was special, so he was well known among members of both the Security and Secret Intelligence Services—which was probably the reason he had been assigned this case in the first place.

"Well, Captain Bond, I've always wanted to meet you. You have quite a reputation, and I recognized you from the photofit."

"Then with due respect, Chief Superintendent, why didn't you blaze my name all over this morning's front pages?"

Daily gave a little half smile. On the table in

front of him were a leather notebook and an expensive gold pen. Bond thought he should mention to the man that it was not always wise to leave something like a pen on a desk when interrogating. He figured his chances and knew he could probably take out Daily by snatching the pen and thrusting it hard into the man's eye. The other cop could be dealt with in a more orthodox manner.

"Why didn't I have you named in the press release, Mr. Bond? Well, I could have been mistaken. We got the photofit from a waiter who says he saw you with the victim. He says you arrived a little before six. He claims to have actually spoken with you, telling you that they had finished serving tea. You replied that you were to meet someone, and he says he saw you join the victim. Eyewitnesses are often wrong. The description could well have been inaccurate: photofits often are, as I suspect you already know."

"So you gave me the benefit of the doubt?"

Again Daily gave his most charming smile. "No. No, not really. I took the precaution of telephoning your Chief when I saw the likeness, and he had a little story for me."

"So you know I *was* there?"

"I do. I also know that you went there to see somebody else, and that's quite important because the someone else looked very much like the victim."

"You know who she was—the person I was meeting?"

"Oh, yes. In fact I've worked with Carmel on a number of occasions, and, while the victim is superficially like her, facially really, she was not at all like her in the flesh so to speak. Yet . . ."

"She could have been mistaken for Ms. Chantry."

"In the dusk with the light behind her, to quote W. S. Gilbert."

"Oh, I do think you educated policemen are wonderful." Bond gave him a crooked smile. "But you think there was a mistake?"

"No doubt in my mind. Once the balloon went up and I'd spoken with your Guv'nor, we removed the other lady from the hotel." His eyes strayed to the plainclothesman by the door. "I think you can leave us now, Meyer." A friendly nod and a wink. The cop shrugged but left, closing the door behind him.

"In fact I have a message from your boss."

"I don't think he'd appreciate being called either Guv'nor or boss."

"No? Well, he's not going to hear me, is he? He says that Ms. C is safe and that your Mr. Grant is also safe, contained, in fact, under house arrest. Strikes me that the ladies and gentlemen of the Security Service are in the midst of a crisis."

"Does it now?" The last thing he wanted to do was to get drawn into any loose talk concerning MI5. You never knew with policemen.

After a pause that went on a shade too long, Daily said that M also wanted him to telephone. "He asked me to tell you that he had removed surveillance on you and would you call him. Been a naughty boy, have we, Mr. Bond?"

"Not so as you'd notice," he said icily.

He telephoned M from a public call box.

"Just wanted you to know that our sisters have got themselves an almost entirely new Anti-Terrorist Section," M growled.

"About time if all I've heard is true."

"Mmm. Well, I fear it is. The former Head of Department has been guilty of much folly, and many a cover-up. The work got done, but he had to watch his back, and he'll now be doing it from an easy chair on half pension—if that."

"You think someone was out to get Ms. C as well as the other late lamented lady, sir?"

"Could be. I've spoken to their Director General, and the lady you saw last night is in very safe hands. Now, I will be in touch. Just make the most of this enforced rest."

"Of course, sir."

He spent almost two hours getting to his final destination, running the back doubles and practicing every antisurveillance trick in the book. M, no doubt, had been keeping an eye on him and he had a healthy respect for that; but, with all that seemed to be going on, he wanted to be certain that nobody else was hard on his heels.

It was almost two-thirty in the afternoon by the time he turned into the pleasant little street off the King's Road, with its plane trees dusty from the August heat.

Inside his apartment, he rapidly did all his personal security checks. Nobody appeared to be watching the house, though he still could not rule out a listening device or telephone bug. With an anti-bug scanner, loaned to him some time ago by Ann Reilly, assistant to the Armourer who provided all hardware for the Service, he scoured

every inch of wall and floor. Only when he was
ninety-nine percent certain that there were no
unauthorized electronics in the house, spiked
through the walls, or hidden manually by some
expert cut-and-run professional, did he telephone
the Inn on the Park.

Flicka picked up without answering.

"It's me."

"Who's me?"

"James."

"How do I know it's James?"

"You have a small mole high on the inside of
your left thigh. That good enough?"

"Yes. Go on."

"Have you heard from your Alpine friend yet?"

"They brought in a verdict of murder by person
or persons unknown—or at least their version of
that verdict."

"And the funeral?"

"Tomorrow. She left instructions apparently.
Two o'clock tomorrow afternoon at a crematorium
in Bournemouth. It appears that she liked that
area. Do we go?"

"Yes, but first I must give you some instructions."

He told her to check out of the hotel and come
over to his flat. "Not the easy way. It would be
best if you ran some interference for yourself. I'm
pretty sure that I'm clean, but anyone could have
been waiting for me where you are now. If so,
they'll pick you up, so give them a run for their
money."

"Will do." She broke the contact. Very professional, he considered. Then he wondered why he

had asked her to come to him. He seldom invited ladies to the apartment. It was one of those things he very rarely did, and even then never had he let them stay overnight.

Flicka arrived just after six-thirty, having come via Heathrow Airport and then the Underground into central London, and again another runaround involving three taxis. For the first time, a woman slept in the apartment, and it proved to be one of those world-champion nights about which most people only fantasize.

The crematorium was about as personal as a public convenience. Bond had the feeling that it ran on the production line principle, with clergy of many denominations doing shifts at the numerous chapels.

Apart from Flicka and Bond, only three other people turned up for the service, which the clergyman read as though he was bored stiff with the entire thing. At last, the coffin slid away and the little velvet curtains closed with only a slight whir of machinery.

Two of the other mourners had MI5 written all over them, if only because they had tried to look completely normal—a man and woman. The woman wept as she left the chapel of rest, and the man did nothing to comfort her. The other person was a man of around forty, dressed in a well-tailored suit. He showed no emotion and walked quickly away from the place as soon as it was all done.

At the door of the chapel, the undertaker told them that there had been a few floral tributes, though the deceased had asked for none. "It was all a bit of a rush, I'm afraid," he said, looking at Bond as though he would know exactly what was meant. He pointed the way to the garden area, where Laura March's flowers were lying in a rather pathetic little row, and they went to take a quick look.

There was a medium-sized wreath with a card that simply said, *From the Director and Members of the Board with tender memories.* Bond thought it reeked of officialdom. There was another from the aunt in Birmingham; a third *To Laura from her many friends at the office. You will always be remembered.*

At the end of this little row, one single flower lay like a boutonnière, the stem wrapped in crisp cellophane and the flower backed by green fronds. The flower itself was enough to cause interest. It was a rose, but a rose that neither Flicka nor Bond had ever seen before: a luminous white, the color intense in its depth, and the most extraordinary thing about the bloom was that each of the petals had a tip, blood red and almost symmetrical. It was as though someone had taken a very beautiful white rose and carefully painted the spots of blood identically at the end of each petal. So odd was the effect that Bond even leaned forward and brushed it with his fingertips to make certain it was real, and not some reproduced piece of plastic. It was real enough, and he bent again to read the card.

The card was plain. No florist's address or little picture: just a plain oblong of white, with a carefully written message. The copperplate writing reminded him of M for a moment, then the words suddenly seemed very familiar. He had read them, and it struck him that he had also seen a description of this same kind of rose at least four times before. The message was very simple—*This is how it must end. Goodbye.*

He stood, looking at the single flower, more eloquent than any wreath or spray, then he turned to Flicka. "I think we should go, my dear. I have something to show you back in London. After that it might be the right time for us to visit Germany."

"The Rhineland?"

Bond nodded, took her arm, and walked briskly back to his car. He knew that he had found in this extraordinary rose a tangible link between the death of Laura March and the four assassinations of that one week of deaths.

9

Richard's Himself Again

The road had been hewn out of the rock, twisting and turning so that one minute they were gazing down an almost sheer drop into the greeny blue waters of the Rhine, and at others they seemed to be pressed against great cuttings, the rough walls of natural stone rising on either side of them. They came upon their first view of the castle suddenly, following a long gentle bend and onto a kilometer of straight road, the Schloss Drache appearing below them like some kind of trick, an illusion, for the castle seemed also to have been cut from the rock itself: a Mount Rushmore in which people lived.

"Bigger than the one at Disneyland," Bond said quietly, and Flicka reached out, putting her hand over his for a second, as the late summer afternoon sun hit one of the turrets, glancing off the windows, flashing light from the castle to the river, as though someone within had directed a prismatic beam directly onto the water.

The legends of the Rhine passed quickly through Bond's mind—the legend of the nymph Lorelei; or the Rhinemaidens and their hoard of gold.

Time seemed to stand still, and it was hard to believe that only forty-eight hours ago they had driven away from Laura March's lonely funeral on England's south coast, as though the hounds of hell were on their heels.

They had made it back to the King's Road in record time, the white Saab 9000 CD Turbo whining through the New Forest and then onto the M3 Motorway, Bond breaking the speed limit whenever it seemed safe, driving hard. The hybrid rose with its strange message ran in circles around his brain, stirring another memory, only half-caught and almost out of reach.

The moment they walked into the apartment he retrieved his briefcase from its hiding place in the compartment behind the wainscot in his bedroom, opened it, and removed the files. He carried the folders through to the sitting room and began to pore over them.

Flicka took her cue and disappeared into the kitchen, making tea, hot and very strong, which Bond sipped as he went through the flimsy pages, searching, making notes here and there. He found what he wanted in the files on Generale Claudio Carrousso's assassination, and then, again, in the papers referring to Archie Shaw. The other two— the Russian, Pavel Gruskochev, and the CIA man, Mark Fish—required further checking.

He called an anonymous number in Paris and waited while his contact went through the more recent information they had on the Gruskochev killing. Bond nodded and smiled, making a note on his file as the data was read quietly to him from an office not far from the Champs-Elysées.

He then called Washington, went through a little game of telephone tag, and finally tracked down the man he wanted, who was dining out, in Arlington, Virginia, with a friend from the Pentagon. The man in Washington asked how quickly he needed the information, and was told yesterday. "If it really is *that* important, I'll go out to Langley and call you back," he said, adding that Bond was about the only person in the world he would do something like this for. An hour later the telephone rang and Bond again smiled to himself as he made notes, the telephone pressed hard against his ear.

"Just what I wanted to hear," he told the caller. "I owe you one."

"And I'll collect." The Washington contact hung up.

Bond then dialed a number in Chalfont St. Giles, greeting an old friend he had not seen for almost two years. After the usual pleasantries, the talk turned to the growing of hybrid roses. The conversation lasted for almost thirty minutes.

Only when he had finished talking on the phone did he call Flicka from where she was reading a paperback in the bedroom.

"So, Sherlock." She dropped gracefully onto the big leather couch. "Have you found the secret of life and death?"

"Enough to tie a few knots together, and enough to put at least one name in the frame. Look." He came over and sat close beside her, the four files on his lap.

"When it comes to murder or assassination, one of the standard procedures—as you must know— is the general surveillance of those who come to the victim's funeral. There were people from both my service and the Security Service there today. You saw the MI5 couple, my guys were not so obvious, but they were around. Again, as you know, the job is to identify everyone who comes to pay their respects, and, when it's all over, someone else usually goes through the so-called floral tributes. Notes are kept regarding the messages, and then the sources are tracked down if necessary. That's straightforward stuff as far as the police and the security and intelligence services are concerned."

"Of course. Yes, it's standard."

"You saw that hybrid rose. Odd. I've never seen anything quite so perfect. The petals all seemed identical, and the blood-red tips could have been painted on, they were so symmetrical. Then there was the message, which would strike the dimmest probationary detective as odd."

"This is the way it must end. Goodbye," she muttered almost under her breath. "Sure, a murderer's message, perhaps? Or a bit of sentiment."

"No, you were right the first time. Those four assassinations which took place last week, just before Laura was killed—"

"Yes?"

"Would it surprise you that the same hybrid

rose, with *the same* message, turned up at each of the funerals? The General in Rome; our MP, here in London; old Pavel in Paris; and the CIA man, Fish, in Washington. In the case of the MP, Shaw, and the Russian, it was made clear that there should be no flowers, yet the rose turned up at each interment."

"And the same message? Exactly the same message?"

"Exactly. Word-for-word, and nobody has been able to trace the source. They simply appeared at the graveside, or the crematoriums, as if by magic. There is one tiny clue—and it doesn't mean much. In Paris, the undertaker saw a young boy—thirteen or fourteen years old—hanging around the graveside before the service. Again, in Washington, there was a schoolgirl, early teens, seen in the funeral home, looking at the flowers."

"Kids paid to drop off the rose?"

"That's what I would go for."

"And the message was *exactly* the same—yes, I asked before."

"Word-for-word. A calling card left by the killer, or killers. It's like a terrorist group claiming responsibility. Someone, or some organization, is telling us that not only did they murder Laura, but also the four high-profile people as well."

"And the rose? I heard you talking to some expert about roses."

He paused, closing the files and piling them neatly on his knees. "That's the most interesting piece of information. The man I spoke to is probably the world's greatest expert on roses. He's responsible for at least twelve new varieties himself, and what he doesn't know about other growers could be written on a pinhead."

"He gave you a name? It's a well-known rose?"

"Not *well* known, but he knows of one person who's been experimenting with a white rose bearing blood-red tips on each petal. As far as he's aware, the person concerned has not actually pulled it off. He told me that one was exhibited at a show last year and it came very near to the perfection the grower is seeking. It was named *Bleeding Heart,* and he actually spoke to the grower, who said she thought the perfect specimen would be ready in a year or two."

"Someone we know?"

"Someone we're going to know. A widow, aged forty-one, by the name of Maeve Horton. Maeve Horton, the younger sister of David Dragonpol. Maeve Horton who lives with her brother in his castle, Schloss Drache, on the banks of the Rhine. Maeve Horton, sister to David Dragonpol who, if we believe that letter we found, was 'brother and dear dead lover' to Laura March."

"So we pay a call on David Dragonpol and his sister?"

"You bet we do."

He worked the phones again for a couple of hours, first checking flights, making bookings and car reservations; then trying his many official contacts, winkling out a telephone number for Dragonpol at the Schloss Drache. By midnight everything was in place.

On Thursday morning they flew to Bonn, took

delivery of the rental BMW, and began the long drive down the Rhine to Andernach, where they spent the night and part of Friday morning at the delightful Villa am Rheine. It was from their suite at this hotel that Bond used the telephone number which he was told would get him in touch with Dragonpol.

The telephone was answered by a woman who spoke fluent German with an atrocious British accent, so he launched straight into English. "Mrs. Horton? Is that Mrs. Horton?"

"Yes. Who's this?" She had a low, very calm voice and sounded as though she was the kind of woman who expected bad news every time the telephone rang.

"You won't know me, Mrs. Horton. My name's Bond. James Bond, and I really need to speak with your brother, Mr. Dragonpol. Is he available?"

She started to speak, then stopped and waited for a moment in silence. Bond had the impression she was not alone. Then—

"What's it about, Mr. Boned?"

"Bond," he corrected. "I'm a representative of a British government agency. I have my opposite number from Switzerland with me, and we really do have to speak with Mr. Dragonpol if it's convenient. If not, we will wait, of course, but I personally feel it would be best to get this over and done with as quickly as possible." He let the words sink in, and felt that she had probably put her hand over the receiver and was talking to someone else.

Then that familiar voice, known throughout the

world, spoke into his ear. "Mr. Bond? This is David Dragonpol." The voice was unmistakable, and the man's face came straight to mind as soon as he spoke: calm, firm, and with an authority you could feel even on the telephone.

"I'm very sorry to trouble you, sir, but this really is quite important."

"You're from a British government agency my sister tells me, so that means you want to talk to me about Laura . . ." He left the end of the sentence unsaid, as though calculating that Bond would fill in the gaps. It was very theatrical.

"Yes, sir. It won't take long, I—"

"I understand, yes. I suppose I've been waiting for someone to arrive on my doorstep. Can you come over today?"

"This afternoon if that's convenient, Mr. Dragonpol."

"Of course. Look, why don't you stay for the night? We can talk. I'd welcome talking to someone else about this whole terrible business. Have dinner with us, then perhaps I can show you around Schloss Drache. If you have the slightest interest in the theatre or any of the performing arts, you're in for a very pleasant surprise."

"It's very kind of you, sir, but—well, there are two of us . . ."

"Yourself and . . . ?"

"Fräulein von Grüsse, from Switzerland. As I said to Mrs. Horton, she's my opposite number so to speak."

They made arrangements. Dragonpol gave him directions to follow what he considered the best route—"The most scenic route anyway, the most dramatic, for you first see Schloss Drache from above."

Now they were looking at it, from a viewing area fenced off at the roadside with room for perhaps a half a dozen cars. Together they leaned on the rails and took in the gorgeous view: the great river, its banks rising in irregular hills of stone and dark-green fir trees.

"Aw, heck." Flicka frowned. "I thought it would be all blue and gold like the one in Orlando."

"Or the one in California."

"Or even the one in Paris, France, now."

"Out of luck, Flick. I don't think Sleeping Beauty lives in this one."

Directly below them the huge rectangle of gray stone seemed to merge with the rock against which it stood. Originally, Bond thought, Schloss Drache was probably built around a large courtyard, but obviously this at some time had been roofed in with reddish-gray slate which rose from the stone walkways behind battlements some ten feet thick. The windows indicated that the massive place was at least four stories high. Huge rooms, Bond figured. In each corner, close to the battlements, a circular turret rose, hugging the wall. Even from this distance it was clear that the turrets could easily accommodate two, if not three, fair-sized rooms.

At the far northwest side of the main structure a chunky square tower rose, like an enlarged version of many of the Norman towers seen on English churches. The top of the tower was lined with battlements, and from there a man would be able to see, literally, for miles, in all directions.

From the viewing area it was also obvious that

the first sight, which made the entire Schloss
look as though it were growing from the rock,
was not correct. Now, you could see clearly that
a thick wall sprouted from the rear, enclosing
what seemed to be a large garden set among the
rocks. They could see stone walkways, and paths,
sudden flashes of color, bushes, even trees and
fountains landscaped into this unlikely setting.

"I wonder if that's where she grows the roses."
Flicka was resting her head against his shoulder
and he turned to kiss her lightly on the forehead,
smelling the fresh scent of her hair. For a second
his mind flashed away to other places, other times,
and the distinctive scents of other women. Twice
he had sworn never to get too involved again,
for it always led to disaster. Yet Flicka seemed
different from the others. She demanded nothing
of him, and gave only affection. Never once had
either of them sworn undying love or demanded
commitment to any sort of lasting relationship.
He gave her a squeeze and slowly they walked
back to the car.

A kilometer or so along the road they came to
a notice in German, Italian, Spanish, French, and
English. It told them: PRIVATE ROAD—TO SCHLOSS
DRACHE ONLY. UNAUTHORIZED PERSONS MUST KEEP
OUT. The access road, a little further on, was also
marked, and, taking it, they found themselves
descending toward the river, down a narrow road
which zigzagged perilously, then plunged into a
dark thicket of pine trees, emerging alongside the
river, then turning until the castle was lowering
down on them. Its mountainous walls appeared
to be leaning in against the sky—that strange

optical illusion made when clouds move as you look up at tall buildings.

"Makes you wonder how many people died when they put this place together." Flicka made no attempt to disguise her awe.

"Certainly puts the building of the pyramids to shame." He eased the car forward. The road narrowed, leading to a small bridge which opened onto a stone turning circle directly in front of a pair of magnificent arched doors reaching up for something like thirty feet. They were old, but their immense brass hinges and fitments gleamed as though they were polished regularly, and the doors themselves were also slick with some kind of wood preserver.

"I wonder how you attract attention. Is there a bell pull? Does Igor come shuffling out?" As Flicka spoke, the doors began to move, swinging back to reveal an open courtyard.

"I think they already know we're here." Bond took the car slowly through the gates and into the courtyard that contained two Range Rovers, a black Merc, and a sleek Lexus. He pulled in beside the Lexus as the gates closed behind them and took a quick look at the surroundings. Three sides of this parking entrance looked like a classic monastic cloister, complete with arches and gargoyles. The wall facing them was cloistered, but split in two where a set of long stone steps ran up to another vast door: this one looking vaguely Victorian, complete with stained glass panels.

As they climbed out, a butler, complete in tailcoat, and two younger men in a green livery appeared from the doorway and descended on the car, opening the trunk and removing luggage with the expertise of a pair of thieves.

"Welcome to Schloss Drache, sir—madam." The butler was essentially English, from the tone of his voice to the way he moved and directed his underlings. The whole thing smacked of a time quite out of joint, like stepping back into a long-dead era.

"If you will come this way, the master is waiting for you in the library." He ushered them into a hallway which smelled of polished wood, and Bond had an immediate impression of trophies in glass cases, stags' heads mounted high on the walls, and some oil paintings which looked suspiciously like genuine Turners.

The butler led them up a small flight of steps and along a corridor lined with pictures, but these were more recognizable. Again there were oil paintings, but their subjects were well known to even the most casual observer, for they were all portraits of great actors and actresses, not from a time long gone by, but from the immediate past, or the present. He spotted Orson Welles, Olivier, Richardson, Gielgud, Jimmy Stewart, John Wayne, Monroe, and a host of others, stage and screen mixed together in stunning colors.

The corridor led directly into a long, airy room lined with tier upon tier of books, all beautifully bound in leather, arranged by color so that there was an extraordinary illusion that you were looking at walls slashed with a rainbow. At the far end of the room, tall, leaded windows caught rays of light which seemed to fall in a prearranged pattern, catching Bond and Flicka in cones of blinding brightness, so that, for a moment, they both blinked, Flicka raising her hand to protect her eyes.

Then, almost as quickly as the light had caught them, it disappeared, leaving only a faint trace of real sunshine shafting in through the huge windows.

"Welcome, Mr. Bond, and you also, Fräulein von Grüsse." The voice was distinctive, with only a trace of David Dragonpol's true voice.

He stood directly behind a large globe which looked like a theatrical prop. One hand touched the globe, while the other rested at his waist. He was quite unrecognizable. Long, full dark hair fell to his shoulders, though in reality everyone knew that the man's hair was light, almost sandy in color. The nose, usually so patrician, was now hooked and beaky, making him look like a predatory bird. Deep-set eyes seemed to glow like burning coals, and his lips were twisted into a deformed curl, like an S lying on its side. He wore a black doublet and hose, the doublet slashed in gold and a huge medallion of a boar's head hung on a golden chain around his neck.

The hand on the globe was more claw than hand, the fingernails long, curling, and obscene, while rings of gold, sparkling with jewels, seemed to weigh down the almost skeletal fingers.

"It's good to see you here." The voice was now completely unrecognizable. "If you have not realized it already, I am Richard of Gloucester. Richard the Third of England."

"Barking mad," Bond whispered, but obviously not softly enough.

"Woof-woof!" said the apparition before it began to laugh, a hideous cackling sound that sent a chill down Bond's back and made Flicka grasp for his hand, digging her nails into his flesh in fear.

"Richard's himself again," screamed the strange creature, and with that he struck the globe, which began to turn rapidly, making a heavy clunking sound with each revolution.

10

Schloss Drache

The cackle turned into a soft laugh. The strange
creature's hands moved, closing together, and the
long-taloned fingers gripped the wrists, one after
the other, seeming to snap off the skin, bone,
and nails. Now, latex gloves dangled from the
fingertips of one hand, while the other moved
upward to rip the long black hair from his head.
The body appeared to change before their eyes,
straightening up, growing.

"Oh, I'm so sorry, but I couldn't resist that. You
should have seen your faces. My name's David
Dragonpol. Fräulein von Grüsse, and Mr. Bond,
welcome to Schloss Drache."

He fiddled with his nose, pulling off the putty
which had shaped the strange crooked beak.
Half revealed before them was Dragonpol himself. Even the voice had returned to normal.

"You see, Hort fancies herself as a painter, and I'm posing for her. She has this idea that oil paintings of me in my best roles will look well in one of the museum rooms. I can't say I agree with her. Hort, come and meet our guests."

They followed his eyes and for the first time saw a woman seated behind an easel set in a kind of niche to one side of the long, book-laden left-hand wall. Putting down her palette, she rose gracefully—a poised hostess, dressed in paint-daubed jeans and a T-shirt, the front of which carried the words GO FOR IT! LIFE IS NOT A DRESS REHEARSAL. She came toward them with a smile and a hand held out to be either kissed or shaken.

"Maeve Horton," she introduced herself. "We spoke on the telephone, Mr. Bond."

Her hand was cucumber cool, and the wide dark eyes seemed to be visibly stripping Bond of his clothes. She was very tall, almost a full six feet, with the slim agile body of a dancer and a face which had the clear skin and regular features of an Irish girl. "I'd have talked for longer if I'd known how good-looking you were."

"Come on, Hort, not so much of the blarney." Apart from the doublet and hose, Dragonpol was fully recognizable now, raking his fingers through the mane of straw-colored hair, revealing the face which had captured the imagination of millions; the actor who could transform himself into any character he chose. "You probably know we have Irish family connections." He gave them both that winning smile, brimming with a near-tangible charisma. "Hort plays the Irish colleen to the hilt. Everyone calls her Hort, by the way, never Maeve."

Maeve Horton made a tutting sound, partway between "whisht" and "ocht." Then she turned to Flicka, as Dragonpol took Bond's elbow and steered him away from the women, speaking softly. "I always try to be delicate in these matters. In this day and age one has to be blunt. I wasn't certain of the sleeping arrangements, Mr. Bond . . ."

"Call me James." He was trying to take in as much as possible, from the obvious charms of Hort to the concealed lighting around the bookshelves and forward of the tall window. He now understood why they had been almost blinded with light as they had come into the library, for there were two rows of baby spots, neatly concealed by a valance, one row pointing down, the others focused toward the library door.

"James, what I need to know is . . . Well, to be blunt, sleeping arrangements . . . Are you and Fräulein von Grüsse merely colleagues or are you an item, as they say?"

"The latter, David—I may call you David, yes?"

"Of course. Glad I asked, because I can now give you the East Turret room. It's a regular bridal suite. Hort spent the bulk of her honeymoon there, poor dear."

"Mrs. Horton is widowed, I believe?"

Dragonpol gave him a wry smile. "It's a sad story, yes. Her husband was—oh, it's difficult. Maybe I'll tell you the whole story later if we have time." He turned to the two women, who seemed to be chatting amicably enough. "Come along, I'll get Lester to show you to your quarters.

Lester used to be my dresser. He really wanted to be an actor and I think he has now taken the butler's role quite well. He enjoys the snobbery of it all."

He strode out down the corridor, shouting for Lester at the top of his voice—an eccentric English country squire: or was that also a piece of role-playing? Over the years Bond had known many actors, and had never met one who was averse to playing parts of his own choice in private. Many of them could not really face normal everyday lives without putting on that second skin of a character, and he had quickly made the assessment that David Dragonpol was one of these. After all, Flicka had pointed out that he sometimes traveled in disguise.

Lester appeared from some servants' quarters with his two flunkies looking like bodyguards.

"Two for the East Turret, Lester. You lads take the luggage up."

Lester gave a majestic bow and indicated in a somewhat superior manner that Bond and Flicka should follow him. He was a tall, dignified man who seemed to think that smiling had become a mortal sin.

"It's good to have you here, James. And you, Fräulein von Grüsse . . . er . . ."

"Oh, call me Flicka, everyone does. It isn't every day that I get to meet a famous actor. It's a real thrill to be here and to see you in the flesh." She almost simpered.

"An *ex*-actor, my dear. A former thespian." Dragonpol even talked like some Edwardian actor-manager. "We'll see you both for dinner, then. Seven-thirty for eight o'clock. Please don't bother to dress, we're very informal here." He began to move away, then stopped, turning back. "I'll send Lester or one of the boys to bring you down. You need an Indian guide to get around this place."

The East Turret turned out to be anything but Edwardian. As they had judged when looking down on the castle from a distance, the turrets were exceptionally roomy, and the East Turret was particularly sumptuous, with its own private elevator and two sets of rooms, one above the other, connected by a cleverly designed staircase which was totally enclosed. The treads were huge oblongs. As Flicka said, "We could dance on these—individually."

The elevator took them directly into the circular sitting room. The decor looked very expensive—blue and white, with large easy chairs, a long settee, and marble tables. The wall above the bar was decorated with theatrical drawings which looked like original charcoal sketches for stage sets.

The unusually wide flight of steps took Bond into the bedroom. Here the design changed. Instead of following the circular line of the walls, the bedroom had been squared off, the windows set very deeply into the walls. The bed itself was the centerpiece—a vast four-poster, like an island in the midst of a green and gold sea.

Bond prowled around, opening doors and taking in the views from the windows. The bathroom, he realized, was slightly above the bedroom and at the very top of the turret. From its main window he could see right across the shallow-sloping roof to the great tower, with clear arched windows set in it at intervals. He returned to the circular sitting room.

" 'It's a real thrill to be here, and to see you in the flesh.' " He imitated Flicka's awed voice.

"Well," she said, "what about you and the Irish flirt—'I'd have talked for longer if I'd known how good-looking you were.' Jesus, this place is creepy, James."

"All huge castles are creepy. What's so different about this one?"

Flicka stood close to the elevator doors. "You do realize that we're virtually prisoners in this place." She demonstrated by pressing the buttons. The small indicator did not light up, nor could they hear the usual whir of machinery. "What do you make of that, James?"

"What do I make of the whole business?" he asked himself. "I'm beginning to wonder if some of those stories about Dragonpol's retirement are true."

"Which ones in particular?"

"That he had a complete breakdown. Was unable to perform: unhinged by his own talent. I mean that whole extraordinary business of the painting—all that dressing up, the makeup, and the lights shone directly on our eyes. That was for our benefit: an act for *us*. He knew we were on our way. Did you get a look at Hort's easel?"

"No, she moved me right away from it."

"Right. You want to know why? It was a daub, a squiggle of lines, paint slashed onto the canvas, no painting of the great man as Richard III. They were both playing with us. I think his first intention was to put the fear of God into us. Maybe he changed his mind at the last minute, but I think we should be prepared for some further bits of fantasy."

"He's living in another world, that's for sure— 'Please don't bother to dress, we're very informal here.' When did you last hear a line like that?"

Bond walked back into the great circular room, his restless eyes looking for possible hiding places for security cameras or listening devices. There were many and there was no way he could possibly sweep the suite without the proper equipment.

"And what about Lester and 'the boys'?" he asked. "They look like ordinary servants to you?"

Flicka was pacing around the room, brow creased and hands moving nervously. "They're more like bodyguards than flunkies."

"Quite. Bodyguards or male nurses. A pair of very tough bantamweights, and I'd put money on them knowing a lot of tricks designed to damage your health. Lester could well have been his dresser, but his own clothes leave much to be desired."

"How?"

"You didn't notice the bulge? The man's carrying. Shoulder holster, and something pretty lethal in it. The other strange thing is that I've seen Dragonpol on stage and screen, admittedly cloaked in the great acting roles, but I don't really recognize him."

"You don't? I'd recognize him anywhere."

"I'm not talking about physical recognition. There's something not quite right with the man. That spark isn't there."

"Oh, come on, James. You know actors, they're like watchers when they're off stage, nude, as it were. Mostly they appear to be terribly ordinary people when they're off. With watchers, it's the other way around. They go invisible when they're working and seem larger than life when *they're* off. Surely it's normal enough?"

Bond frowned. "Maybe. Maybe you're right, but David Dragonpol was not your run-of-the-mill actor, and this man just doesn't feel right. If I didn't *know* it was him, I'd swear he was a ringer."

"Or perhaps you're right about the mental collapse. You've seen people after a breakdown: they look the same, but something vital has gone."

"Could be." He did not sound convinced, nor in fact was he. While Flicka went off to take a bath and, to use her words, "Pretty myself up," he wandered the rooms of the East Turret, poking and prying into every drawer and closet, his mind quietly wrestling with the enigma that was David Dragonpol. The truth, he considered, lay in the man's relationship with Laura March, who had been, according to those who knew and worked with her, a person of high intellect and nobody's fool. If the facts were correct, she had loved this man—unless the breakup was really of her making and because he had become so strange.

He thought again of Carmel Chantry's description of that very breakup. How she had been called here, to Schloss Drache: "She came into my office looking ill—white, unsteady. It was a Friday afternoon and she said D.D. had called her. There was some drama and he was sending his private aircraft for her. On Monday she came in and told me it was all over." That was what Carmel had told him, so it was unlikely that Laura had taken the initiative. Private aircraft? He wondered. Now where would he keep that? Carmel had intimated that there was some kind of landing strip nearby. Well, it could not be within walking distance, the terrain was too rocky for that. He continued to think, going around in circles until Flicka called out that she was finished in the bathroom.

When he reached the bedroom, he saw that she had laid out a long, black, backless evening gown. "So you *are* going to be formal."

"Of course. What about you? Did you by chance bring a dinner jacket?"

"Like certain credit cards, I never leave home without it." He smiled. Then— "Flick, when your people spotted the Dragonfly passing in and out of Switzerland, did he travel by normal commercial airlines?"

"Yes. Usually, that is."

"What do you mean, usually?"

"He does have a private aircraft, but he's pretty sparing in its use. He also has problems with it."

"What kind of problems?"

"He hasn't got any clearance to bring it into Switzerland. I remember we checked that out. He has landing rights in England and France, but none of the other countries. Why?"

"Why, yourself? Why hasn't he got landing rights?"

"Because we nobbled him. Look, James, we've been watching this guy for some time, and my immediate boss was convinced that he had contacts with terrorist groups and dodgy arms dealers. He's been up to no good, so we put the word out in certain quarters. He can use this country—Germany—France, and the UK, but we managed to put a block on him elsewhere. If he wants to go into the Scandinavian countries, or Spain, Portugal, and Italy, he has to fly by the nearest friendly carrier."

"What excuse did you give him?"

"For not getting landing rights? Oh, I guess the various countries used all kinds of excuses—doubts about the safety of his aircraft, or the aircrew. He can huff and puff as much as he likes, but there's no law that says any country has to tell him the reason he's been banned. Sometimes, I guess, they wouldn't tell him at all, they'd just reject his flight plan and refuse any alternates he presented. He'd soon get the message."

"But you have nothing solid against him? No really firm evidence?"

"No, and as far as I know he's never made a fuss about being refused landing rights. I can check if you think the phones are safe."

"Leave it for now."

"I love 'Dragonfly.' I think we should use that as his crypto."

Bond unpacked his garment bag and retreated into the bathroom.

They were both dressed and ready by seven-fifteen, and once more they tried to summon the elevator without success. At exactly seven-thirty they heard the mechanism whir. The cage came up, stopped, and the door opened to reveal the grave Lester, his head tilted as if something unpleasant had been placed directly under his nose. He showed no surprise on seeing the guests dressed formally. Without a word he ushered them into the cage, and he remained silent through the lengthy trek along the many passages and corridors that took them finally into a large oval room: light, airy with a full twenty-five-foot bow window taking up the far end, which looked out onto the large walled garden they had seen from above.

"I said we dined informally." Dragonpol's voice was brimming with surprise, even though he wore a dark-blue silk dinner jacket, and Maeve, by his side, looked coolly exquisite in a white full-length gown into which she might have had to be sewn. At her throat a single diamond drop hung from a heavy gold chain, while around half a million pounds' worth of rings flashed from her fingers.

"Isn't this informal?" Bond feigned surprise. "I naturally thought you meant I didn't have to wear tails."

Dragonpol gave a little shrug, then turned to a nearby drinks table. "It's such a pleasant evening, I thought we might take our drinks into Maeve's garden. What will you have?"

Flicka asked for a screwdriver, while Bond chose his usual vodka martini. Dragonpol then led them through a small door to the right of the

tall window. A few seconds later they emerged
into the garden, which seemed to be enveloped
by the sweetest meld of smells. Bond thought of
England in June, and cloudless early July days
among the most beautiful gardens in Europe. It
was late August, the time when the scent of
flowers fades, and dust settles across borders
and trellises. Here, though, everything appeared
to be in full bloom, and the odors were enhanced
by that freshness which comes from well-watered
lawns and bushes.

"You did all this, Maeve?" She stood quite close
to him.

"Lord, no. Our paternal grandfather did most
of it."

"David called it *your* garden."

"Only because I spend a lot of time out here.
But we have two full-time gardeners. My passion
is roses."

"Really," from Flicka, easing herself between
Maeve and Bond, one hand resting proprietorially
on Bond's sleeve. "I also have a liking for roses."

Dragonpol led the way, along a paved path
flanked with large circular beds and flowering
bushes. "You had better allow me to show you
the way to Maeve's passion. My grandfather had
a sense of humor, and there are many water tricks
in this place. In fact, I will show you one that
you might have seen in America. Stand still for
a moment."

They had just passed a small birdbath set
between bushes to the right. Dragonpol stepped
forward and placed his foot squarely on a tri-
angular piece of stone. With no warning a jet

of water arced from the birdbath, passing over
their heads to land in the middle of a small stone
column forward and to the left of them. The jet
seemed to hit the column and bounce upward
again, leaping forward and to the right where
it struck the head of a piece of statuary. From
the statue the jet leaped back, forming a perfect
arch over their heads, striking another column
on their left, from which it gave the illusion of
jumping again onto the birdbath, from whence it
began its travels again.

"They have a giant version of this water
trick at the Disney Epcot Center in Florida."
Dragonpol laughed like a child, delighted as the
jet of water continued to jump from birdbath
to column, to statue to column, and back to
the birdbath, repeating the sequence again and
again.

"And your grandfather installed that?" Flicka
was also laughing delightedly.

"Oh, yes."

"The castle has been in your family a long time?"
Bond asked, and it was Maeve who replied—

"It looks very old, I know, but it was built in the
1840s on the site of a former castle, the Schloss
Barholtz, which had been destroyed by fire. Our
great-grandfather built it and our grandfather
finished it. Then, when it became David's property, he started to modernize the interior. You
like the East Turret suite?"

"I'd like it more if we were not imprisoned there."
This time Flicka did not laugh.

"Imprisoned?" Dragonpol sounded sharp and a
little angry. "What do you mean, imprisoned?"

"The elevator would not respond. It was as though someone had left it at the bottom level with the doors jammed open."

"That fool Lester. Sometimes he is too much. I apologize. Lester has a habit of doing that to strangers visiting for the first time. The castle is large, as you know; also we have a great deal of renovation going on, particularly on the second and third floors where I'm setting up the museum. He does not like to think of people getting lost. It's quite easy to get lost in Schloss Drache." His voice dropped at the last sentence, giving the impression that this was some kind of threat.

Bond laughed. "Bravo."

"Bravo?"

" 'It's quite easy to get lost in Schloss Drache.' You sounded just as menacing as you did when you played Shylock. The accent was almost the same. I could even see you standing there, sharpening your knife and talking about the pound of flesh you would take."

"Really?" For a second Dragonpol seemed taken by surprise.

"Yes, really. You remember how you did that wonderful bit of business using your belt as a leather strop, and how the knife was shaped like an old-fashioned open razor?"

"Yes. Yes, of course. I'm sorry. In my time I have played many parts. One forgets. Yes, of course, I'm sorry."

They had come to the end of the path now and the garden opened up into a most wonderful trellised rose arbor.

"These are my favorites." Maeve ran forward, tiny steps because of the tightness of her gown.

Flicka's eyes opened wide, and Bond's face froze. She was standing beside a set of four bushes placed symmetrically to one side of an archway thick with more roses, leading into the arbor. The four bushes glowed with a pulse of white-and-scarlet color. Twenty or thirty roses decorated them. Each was the same, identical pure deep white, and each petal looked as though it had been dipped in blood, or that blood had been hand-painted on the petals.

"I have more in my greenhouses," Maeve Horton began.

"Very beautiful." Bond spoke with a cold flatness, for he felt as though ice had entered his veins. "I've never seen a rose like this before," he lied. "Do you sell them? Export them?"

"Oh, no. No, my roses are strictly for family use," she said, and Bond thought to himself that she was lying, just as Dragonpol had been lying when he acknowledged using a dagger shaped like an open razor and his belt as a strop when playing Shylock. Bond had seen Dragonpol's definitive Shylock. He had used an ordinary long stiletto, and had produced a sharpening stone from a leather bag at his waist. It had been an unforgettable moment.

11

The Trail of Blood

They dined in the castle's magnificent great hall which, though David Dragonpol had obviously carried out major renovations, still retained the feel and atmosphere of an almost medieval refectory. Thick wooden beams made it seem as though the hall were built in a post and lintel construction; while a false roof not only gave the impression of height, but also that it was held in place by four massive A-frames: the old wood coarse and stained.

The walls appeared to be made of the original stone, and a huge open fireplace, complete with spit and other ancient iron artifacts, made Bond think of hunting dogs lying on skins before a roaring winter blaze, while men and women in roughly woven clothes made wassail at the long oak table.

To complete the illusion, swords, pikes, shields, and halberds decorated the walls, while the whole was lit by four intricate candelabra on the table. There was electric light, they were told, but it was pleasant, Dragonpol thought, to re-create an ancient setting.

Before dinner they had walked for another few minutes in the garden, and Maeve had insisted that they see her greenhouse—a long and wide affair with its own heating system, run from an Edwardian iron stove. The greenhouse contained literally thousands of blooms—her roses in various stages—and she explained in some detail the work on her hybrid *Bleeding Heart* rose, which had been going on for several years.

"It's a somewhat macabre venture," she had said as they walked back to the house. "But you must admit that it is a very beautiful flower."

Neither Bond nor Flicka had replied or even reacted. The *Bleeding Heart* rose had become a deadly symbol to both of them.

They dined well, Dragonpol explaining that they preferred to eat English food when they were at the castle. "Essentially the Dragonpols are Anglo-Saxon, with a strong Irish underlay." He chuckled. "In my grandfather's time, nobody would dare put German food on the table here, no matter how good."

So they were served a delicious vegetable soup, turbot, very rare roast beef with all the traditional English trimmings, a Yorkshire pudding, correctly placed on the table in a large separate dish, Brussels sprouts, and roast potatoes. The horseradish sauce was not the creamed variety, but real, making the eyes stream.

For dessert, a huge trifle was brought in with much ceremony—"An old recipe of my mother's," Maeve told them, and this was followed by an old-fashioned savory, Angels on Horseback—fat oysters, wrapped in bacon and grilled, set on fingers of toast—before the cheese board and fruit made the rounds. The wines, however, were all German and of exceptional quality, while the entire meal was served by Lester with the assistance of one of the so-called boys whom Dragonpol referred to as Charles.

"You must have a very large staff. Unusual these days." Flicka was fishing.

"No." Dragonpol appeared indifferent. "Apart from Lester and the boys, plus the gardeners, of course, we have a general maid and a very good Irish cook whose mother was married to a German and spent her entire working life in my father's employ. The Nazis left her alone, and she cared for this place during the Second World War. It's an odd old family relationship, but it works well."

On four occasions during dinner, Bond tried to touch on Dragonpol's career and referred to some of his more famous individual performances. Each time, the actor—if indeed he was such—managed to deflect the conversation, turning it back to the one subject which appeared to be close to his heart, that of transforming the Schloss Drache into what he called "the definitive theatrical museum in the world."

It appeared that while the servants lived in a set of rooms in the basement of the castle, both Maeve and himself occupied only this, the first—the ground—floor. "We have all we need here," he said. "There is this dining hall, the library, our drawing room, and two large suites of rooms which we have converted into private quarters. The Turret Suites are there for guests, and this leaves the remaining three levels at my disposal for the museum. Everything I own has been invested in the museum, and I have already amassed an incredible collection. It will draw experts and fans from all over the world."

He went on at some length about how every stage in the development of theatre would be represented, from the ancient Kabuki Theater of Japan and the staging of the early miracle plays in Europe to the theatre of the present day in all its diverse forms.

Dragonpol claimed to have many unique and priceless exhibits upon which he had lavished millions.

"He's always dashing off after some new find," Maeve chipped in, and Dragonpol gave her an evil little smile, then said he would take them through the completed rooms tomorrow.

"That will be most interesting." Bond sounded offhand. "What I *really* want to see is the view from your main tower. Now *that* must be incredible."

There was a small but anxious silence, and he thought he detected a brief signal pass between Dragonpol and his sister.

"Unfortunately . . ." Dragonpol began, and his sister cut in with, "You can't . . ." then closed her mouth like a trap.

"Unfortunately that is not possible," the actor continued as though nothing had happened. "The great tower is, alas, unsafe. We are waiting for a master builder to arrive from Cologne. It's going to need much work, and we are a little concerned. It requires at least scaffolding to be in place before the winter, and I am told the entire business will take some two years. Nobody—not even myself—is allowed into the tower. I'm sorry."

"But you must have been to the top at one time or another?"

"Oh, yes. It was only two years ago that we discovered the cracks, and the architects examined it last year—well, really only eight months ago. It was put out of bounds immediately."

"And the view?"

"Is, as you say, quite spectacular. You have a standing invitation to return when all the work is done. Then you, James, will be able to see for yourself."

"I'm disappointed, of course, but I look forward to it."

When the port was placed on the table, Maeve Horton suggested that she and Flicka retire to the drawing room, and for a few moments there was an embarrassed pause with Flicka on the verge of protest. Several exchanges of eye signals eventually saved the day and at last Dragonpol and Bond were left alone. Lester also retired and there was a long, charged silence between the two men until Dragonpol spoke—

"Obviously you want to talk to me about poor Laura."

"That *is* the reason we're here, David. Do you mind?"

"I'd be only too glad to help if I can." He hesitated, and there was a catch in his voice as he continued—"You see, I feel responsible somehow."

"In what way?"

"If our engagement had not been broken off . . . Well, she would have been here. That was what we planned. It was to be our wedding. If I hadn't—" He stopped and looked up. His eyes were distinctly moist.

"If you hadn't what?"

"If I hadn't broken off the engagement . . . If I hadn't done that, she might still be alive today. Of course I feel responsible."

"But you did break off the engagement, David?"

"In the end we accepted it mutually."

"But you said—"

"I know. I said if *I* hadn't broken off . . . I said *I*. Sure. It was I who first brought up the problem. We spent a weekend sorting it out, and I suggested that it might be the only answer. In the end, Laura agreed. It was a very painful parting, James. Very painful. We still loved each other. Even today, although she's gone, I still love Laura, and I'm sure that on the day she died she still loved me."

"Then why . . . ?"

"Why was the engagement called off?" He gave a little shrug and an odd gesture, his head cocking from side to side. "It is difficult to explain. I don't know how much you know about Laura's background. I don't wish to break family confidences."

"She had no family left, so there are few confidences to break. But I presume we're talking about her parents and her brother. Is that right? Her brother who had the same name as yourself—David?"

"Ah." He raised his hands a few inches from the table, then quietly lowered them again. "Ah, you know about the skeletons in her family closet."

"In some detail."

Dragonpol took a deep breath which turned into a long sigh. "We were deeply in love and we both wanted children. The Dragonpol line, on the male side, runs out with me. There are no other male Dragonpols. I know this will seem old-fashioned, and not a little pretentious, James, but ours is an old family—"

"You go back to the Doomsday Book, yes, I know."

"The Doomsday Book and a lot of other history as well. Dragonpols have served Crown and Country through the ages. We're a proud people."

"Yet you prefer to live here, in the Rhineland, far away from your roots?"

"That must seem strange to you, I know. We have a place in Ireland—"

"Drimoleague?"

"The Dragonpols of Drimoleague as we're known, yes."

"And there's also a manor house in Cornwall."

"Dragonpol Manor. Yes, you're well informed, James, but none of that's a secret. So we have property. We also use it. Hort spends at least half of the year in Ireland. I use Dragonpol

Manor, usually in the autumn, sometimes in the spring. Part of the difficulty is the eternal British problem—death and taxes, or I should say death *duties* and taxes. Also, this is the largest of our properties, and the Museum of Theatre is not a new concept to us. It began with my father. He was a great benefactor of the arts—particularly the theatre. He had the first dream of making this place into a museum. It's the right size. We had to do something with it."

He paused again, his hand and arm moving in a sweeping gesture. "Schloss Drache, as it is—or was—is a great white elephant, my friend. We always knew that we would either have to sell it or make it into some kind of going concern. The world's greatest Museum of Theatre was my father's concept. I'm simply going to see that it becomes a reality."

"And is that why you suddenly retired from a huge and successful career in the theatre?"

He frowned. "Partly. That was only one of many things. People have made wild guesses as to why I so suddenly gave up acting, when it wasn't as sudden as they seem to think. I'd been contemplating it for a while. I'm not going into all the details, but yes, the concept of this International Museum of Theatre was one reason; another concerned things within my family. For the Dragonpols, family comes first and there were certain matters I had to see to."

Bond nodded. "So what has this to do with your engagement to Laura?"

"There has to be someone to carry on the family and its tradition. I wanted sons. Laura also wanted children. We talked of it many times, and we were both agreed. But—"

"But what?"

"About a month before her death, she dropped a bombshell on me."

"She told you about her maniac brother."

"Quite. Yes, she told me about David March. It took a very strong character. She had held back the truth, but finally she told me everything— out there in the garden. It's something I won't forget."

"And that was enough? You broke off the engagement because she happened to have a homicidal maniac as a brother?"

"Oh, come, James. If you've studied the business, you know it was more than that."

"What do you mean?"

"Her father and mother. They were also strange, unbalanced people, far from normal. Laura lived in terror of suddenly finding out that she was also a little crazy."

"And was she?"

"She could become obsessive. She *was* obsessive about her job."

"And you weren't? Being obsessive about one's work doesn't mean—"

"It was slightly more than that. She spoke with doctors—very eminent psychiatrists. Some had evaluated her family when her brother . . . well, after he was arrested. The conclusion was that they were the cause of passing on the seed of madness to her brother, and, if that was the case, she could well carry similar genes. She was told that her children would have a seventy-thirty chance of being born with some kind of mental aberration."

"Isn't that the case with most people? Life's a lottery, David."

He did not look Bond in the eyes. "She was already beginning to see signs of deterioration in herself."

"Such as?"

"When she told me about her past, her family, she admitted that, as well as her obsession with work, she had recently experienced fugues."

"Memory loss?"

"Yes. Often a blanking off of the mind. She had lost the odd hour, but more recently days were missing. During her penultimate visit to this place, she admitted to losing almost an entire day, and she later regained a portion of that lost time. She said it was like a half-remembered dream in which I had become her brother and Hort was her mother. Laura was terrified—convinced that she had begun a descent into abnormality."

"And you could not risk having children with her?"

"James, there is a little madness in all old families. The Dragonpols have experienced their share of it. To have gone on and produced children with Laura would have tempted fate. We decided to end it. That's all there is to it. We were not about to play Russian roulette with the future."

"Okay." He gave the impression of having accepted Dragonpol's explanation. "Forgive me, David, but I have to ask other questions."

"Go ahead."

"Where were you on the day Laura was murdered?"

"Then you really believe she *was* murdered?"

"Take my word for it."

He gave a long shudder. "Where was I? You're not going to like the answer, James. I was in the air. I was flying from Washington to Zurich."

Bond looked up sharply, as if he had been stung. "You were in *Washington?*"

"For one night, yes. Thursday night. I visited a professor of English. We met at the Folger Library and dined at the Willard Hotel. I took a flight direct from Dulles. It was slightly delayed, and I got into Zurich at around ten on Friday night. You can check it if you want."

"You flew from here to Washington? I mean from Germany?"

"No. No, I went in from Paris. There were some papers—letters of the great Sarah Bernhardt—that I had purchased from a dealer. I did not want to risk having them sent by any normal means. So, as I was traveling—"

"How long *had* you been traveling?"

Dragonpol made some calculations, counting on his fingers. "I was away from here for almost a week. It was a quick and short trip. I arrived in Rome on Sunday night, saw a collector of theatrical memorabilia, and bought some beautiful Commedia dell'arte prints from him. On Monday I flew to London."

"What time of day?"

"The afternoon. I got into Heathrow, let me see, around six in the evening. Had dinner with a dealer and arranged for him to bid for me—

certain items of interest were coming up for sale at Sotheby's."

"You're sure it was on Monday night?"

"I'm positive. I have all the necessary information. I keep a very good filing system. Every penny of my expenses is noted for tax purposes because I can offset them against the museum as business. I have tickets, itineraries, everything. Yes, I arrived in London on Monday night—early evening."

"And from London?"

"Paris."

"When?" Already, Bond was doing agitated sums. David Dragonpol, it seemed, had followed the route of the killer, the assassin responsible for the deaths in Rome, London, Paris, and Washington—then, Switzerland.

"Tuesday evening. Just for one night. In Paris I saw one of the directors of the Comédie-Française."

"Then you left for Washington?"

"I arrived very late on Wednesday. On Thursday night I met with my friend at the Folger, and from there we went out to dinner."

"And you were back in Zurich on Friday night?"

"About ten, yes. You wish to see my records?"

"I think, David, the police might just want to see them."

"He was in all four cities, Flick. He made no bones about it. Rome, London, Paris, Washington. All the sites of those four assassinations. He was there."

"But a day late, yes?"

"Mainly only hours late. Hours after the assassinations. If he's telling the truth, he followed those murders as if he was chasing them."

It was past midnight, and he had just been through Dragonpol's schedule with Flicka, sitting close to her on the couch in the East Turret.

"You looked like a ghost when you came out of the dining room," she had said as soon as they were alone, and had—as a precaution—checked that the elevator was now working. He had even joked about it with Dragonpol when the actor had shown the couple back to the elevator to wish them goodnight. Hort had disappeared a little earlier, making the excuse that she had some household duties to which she had to attend.

Once in their suite she had immediately asked what was wrong, and Bond sketched in the entire conversation with Dragonpol.

"It can't be coincidence. The roses are hers. His European jaunt. His presence in every city. He says that he has all the paperwork, but that kind of thing could be fiddled."

"You think it's safe for us to stay here?"

"And risk being the next recipients of the *Bleeding Heart* award?"

"It had crossed my mind."

"He was very open about everything. I didn't really have to jog his memory. He just told me. Even said I wouldn't like it when I heard where he was at the time of Laura's death. Though I fail to see his point, because if he's telling the truth, he got to Zurich after she died—and Interlaken's quite a trek from Zurich. No, if his schedule turns out to be exactly as he's told me, he arrived everywhere just *after* the deaths. But he *did* visit each city, which is quite extraordinary."

"As though he followed a trail of blood?"

"Exactly. Did you get anything more from Hort?"

"She talked roses and the family. Boring to say the least, though there was one thing—"

"Yes?"

"The little tough. What's his name—Charles?"

"What about him?"

"He served the coffee and made a great show of having to speak privately with her. She excused herself and went out of the room with him. They had quite a long conversation."

"Which you listened to."

"Not all. It wasn't safe, though she left the door open a little. They spoke in almost whispers until she seemed to lose her temper. Anyway, she raised her voice. Just for a moment."

"And said?"

"Something to the effect that Charles was a buffoon. That he should know better. I heard bits of that. Then she said, quite clearly, 'They'll be gone by tomorrow night, but for God's sake, don't make that kind of mistake again. The telephone's only there to keep him from fussing. You don't let him use it, and you make sure it's cut off when nobody's with him. You know all this. Pray heaven he hasn't used it.' That's pretty much word-for-word."

"Perhaps they were talking about me—us." He indicated the white, reproduction antique telephone which sat on one of the marble tables. "We haven't tried to use it, but maybe we should." He rose and crossed to the telephone. Picking up the instrument, he put it to his ear, then pulled a face. "Dead. Disconnected. I guess that's what the conversation was about."

Flicka bit her lip.

"Scared?"

"Just a lot, James dear. Just bloody petrified."

"Then maybe you're right. Maybe we should get out while the going's good—or at least in the small hours."

They spent an hour getting themselves ready, dressing warmly in jeans, rollnecks, and light shoes: packing their remaining clothes with care, Bond cursing from time to time that he had not come armed; but neither had Flicka. After all, she was temporarily suspended from duty.

At almost two in the morning, they had everything prepared, their two cases stood beside the elevator, and Bond was just about to press the button to summon the cage, when Flicka touched his arm. "Sorry, James. I have to use the bathroom again."

"Well, for heaven's sake hurry."

She disappeared, and a few seconds later he heard her voice calling, agitated—"James, quickly. Quick, come and look."

He ran up the big stairs, through the bedroom to the bathroom where she stood, in the dark, on tiptoe peering out of the window.

"He said nobody could use the tower. That it was unsafe."

Bond swore under his breath. Looking out across the low roof, they had the same clear picture of the tower they had seen in daylight, only now, in the pitch darkness of a moonless night, the whole structure was illuminated from within, its huge clear windows lit up from top to bottom. Behind the windows figures moved— people ran and gestured.

"Let's get out now, Flick. Something's really screwed up here."

Quickly they went back to the sitting room, and Bond was reaching out for the elevator button when suddenly they heard the clunk and whine of the machinery. The cage was on its way up.

"Stand back, Flick. Get to one side."

The cage stopped and the doors opened.

"Mr. Dragonpol is sorry for this intrusion, but he needs to see you now, quickly, in the library." Lester stepped into the room. In his right hand he carried a Colt .45 automatic. The safety was off, and he held the weapon like someone who was used to handling these things.

"He says *now!* He needs you in a hurry!" The wicked eye of the pistol moved slightly, beckoning them into the cage.

12

The Time Machine

"Do you think we should take our luggage with us?" Bond spoke as though oblivious to the big automatic with which Lester was still gesturing.

"I hardly think that would be appropriate, sir." Even with the pistol, Lester retained the snobbish servility of the complete English butler.

As he asked about the luggage, Bond turned slightly, reaching down as if to pick up his garment bag. Now, frozen, with his hand on the bag, he gave a small shrug, as though acquiescing to Lester's suggestion. Then, in a blur, his fingers curved around the handle, lifting the bag and flinging it, with all his strength, straight at Lester's groin.

He heard the man grunt loudly in pain, beginning to double over, but his right hand came up and Bond saw that the automatic was still very steady, with Lester's finger moving on the trigger.

Then Flicka moved. It was the first time he had seen her do anything violent. She closed on Lester, coming face-to-face, body-to-body, with him, slamming her left arm over his right with great force, crushing it against her raised left knee. Lester's arm snapped audibly and there was a double cry of pain as her knee swiveled, crashing into the unhappy man's groin. The pistol clattered to the ground, followed by its owner, who did not know which part of his body to clutch with his one good arm.

Flicka kicked the pistol back into the room, leaned over, and delivered a fierce chop to Lester's neck. The screaming stopped, he fell sideways and was still.

"You killed him, Flick?" Bond, very impressed, tried to sound calm as he scooped up the Colt.

"I hope not." She prodded the body lightly with her toe, and Lester moved, groaning.

"Better truss him up." Bond was down on one knee, fumbling for the butler's braces. They pulled the tailcoat from his shoulders and the pain made him stir and begin to regain consciousness. Flicka chopped him again on the neck, anesthetizing him once more as they fastened his hands tightly with a handkerchief, then tied his ankles with the braces, stretching the elastic back and securing it around his bound hands. Finally he was gagged with a scarf, which Flicka pulled from her own bag.

"He's going to try and make a lot of noise when he finally comes out of it." She even smiled a shade sadistically, he thought. "That arm's going to give him gyp, as my mother used to say."

"You always as vicious as this, Flick?"

"Only when I don't like someone." She gave him an angelic smile. For the first time he realized how very well trained she was. If, at that moment, he had been allowed to pick a permanent partner from any of the major intelligence services, he knew that she would be his first choice. She was decisive, tough, and uncompromising—all the qualities someone in Bond's job looked for in a partner.

"I think we should go," she said, pulling her own bag into the lift cage.

"Luggage and all?"

"Well, I'm not leaving any of my personal belongings behind. Not in this place."

He dumped his bag beside hers, checked the Colt .45, and pressed the down button. As the lift whined toward the ground floor, they were aware of more light than they had previously seen in the castle, and when the doors opened, the quiet, somewhat creepy calm they had become used to had disappeared. There were shouts and noises coming from the main body of the building, echoing and fading, the thud of footsteps, and, from somewhere, music fading in and out. These noises, and the reverberation of loud voices, had changed Schloss Drache into a Tower of Babel.

"This way, I think." Instead of heading straight down the corridor, Flicka turned right, then right again to where the passage continued toward what they both knew could only be the castle's east side.

Finally they reached a dead end, and a heavy door. She shrugged at Bond, who nodded and turned the doorknob. Light, even more brilliant than before, flooded out at them.

They were in a massive stairwell. The light was unnaturally bright, while the cacophony of sounds became louder, enveloping every corner of the building.

"I always hate it in those movies when people trying to escape go upwards and get cornered on the roof," Flicka whispered.

"There's nowhere else to go but up, except right to the center of things and I don't want to come face-to-face with the Dragonfly and his rose-growing sister. This way we might at least get a look at the forbidden tower."

Eventually they reached a long wide landing which seemed to run across the width of the castle interior, and turned at right angles at each end. Facing them was a pair of oak double doors. The noise seemed to rise and fall: voices, chanting, conversation, mixed with music, as though the castle had suddenly become inhabited by an invading army of ghosts. If he had believed in the supernatural, Bond would have thought they were in the middle of some terrifying haunting.

He was about to put his hand on the doors when they heard Dragonpol's voice, clear and coming from the right and below them, rising above the rest of the clamor. Quietly Flicka put down her case, and Bond leaned his garment bag against it. Softly they moved, clinging to the wall. At the turn they stopped, inching their way out and along the passage.

From this end they could see that, just as the corridor ran for the width of the castle, it also disappeared almost out of sight along what had to be the length of the building. Only in the center did it angle back into the square U shape, with a balustrade. Dragonpol's voice was coming from below a balcony which looked down onto a hallway, or room, at the castle front.

"I can't wait," he was saying loudly. "Where's that fool Lester and the two meddlers?" Then he began to shout. "Hort! Hort! Where the hell's she got to? Surely it can't be taking her all this time? Charles!"

"She's just coming in." It was Charles' voice close and below. "Here!" he shouted.

"Hort? How many this time?"

She was out of breath. "Three . . ." She gasped. "Only three."

"You're certain?"

"Absolutely, and you have the key map. That's still three too many."

"I know it, and I'd better get going. The rest of you—Charles, William—get hold of Lester. Keep our guests safe. I want no stupidness. Just keep them here. Don't hurt them unless it's absolutely necessary."

They heard his footsteps thudding away into the distance.

"I'm glad he doesn't want to hurt us," Flicka whispered.

"Unless it's absolutely necessary. Come on, I'm going through those doors. I want to see what the hell's in that tower."

It was only when they got back to where they

had left their luggage that they realized most of the music and general hubbub was coming from directly behind the big double doors.

Still with the automatic ready in his hand, Bond leaned against the doors, and they entered the strange disorienting world of Dragonpol's embryo Museum of Theatre.

The noise seemed to wrap itself around them in a jumble of sound. As they walked forward into the light, they were both staggered by the sudden change which focused only one sound and one view onto their senses. It was so real that Flicka gasped and clutched at Bond's sleeve. They stood, it appeared, at the very top of a huge Greek amphitheatre. Below them the stone steps were filled with an appreciative audience, which laughed and applauded. He could feel the breeze on his face, and the sun hot above them. He could even smell the crowd, a mixture of spices, bodies, and an amalgam of scents.

Far below, in the stage area, actors proceeded with the play. Long-ago lessons at school slid from his memory and he suddenly recognized the play. It was Aristophanes' *The Frogs*. He knew it because of the chorus which chanted *"Brekekekex Co-ax Co-ax."* The Greek playwright's version of the modern *Ribbit-Ribbit*.

So, as if by magic, they had been brought to a Greek amphitheatre, and to a performance being given some four hundred years B.C. The reality of the thing was extraordinary, and only his logic told him that they were really experiencing a clever use of modern hi-tech and old projection and optical effects, plus the use of advanced robotics. It was quite enthralling and amazing until he spotted something slightly off-key. One of the actors, far below, had lifted a mask to his face. The mask had nothing to do with classical Greek theatre, but was of the kind used in Kabuki performances in the early 18th century.

Just as he spotted this odd chronological error, the whole scene in which they appeared to be standing began to fade into darkness, and to their right a figure rose up from the darkness: a luminous, beckoning figure, so real that Bond turned, gun in hand, ready to shoot if necessary.

The apparition was dressed as an old jester, and it capered and beckoned—another projection, or moving hologram, which bade them follow. Bond took Flicka's elbow and guided her as they followed the strange dancing jester, who suddenly disappeared.

As he vanished, light came up around them and their ears were again assaulted by noise, their sense of smell detecting a mélange of scents, some ripe and unpleasant, others sweet. This time the change of aspect was more realistic than before. They stood in an English marketplace, on the fringe of a crowd. Facing them was a rough platform, an outdoor stage, with beams at each corner, set upon which was a crude upper level on which men and women were working machinery behind cloth cloud shapes.

The players on the stage were acting out some kind of religious story, which Bond realized must be one of the Medieval Mystery Plays, for the actors spoke in an oddly accented English. A clap of thunder came from the people working

the primitive special effects, and it was plain that
the play was the story of Noah, for one of the actors
was bidding his "Wife, come in," as God Himself
leaned down from tattered clouds and declaimed
that the rain would begin at any moment.

Once more, the sense of reality was strong. They
were *there,* present in an English town hundreds
of years ago. People seemed to brush against them,
and one actually spoke to Flicka, asking if she recognized Dickon dressed as a girl. The Dragonpol
set was exceptional. Yet, once more, just as the
scene around them was dissolving, Bond saw one
of the actors consult a relatively modern pocket
watch.

Another figure came out of the darkness, this
time a small man in Elizabethan dress. They could
see right through his body, but, as he beckoned,
he spoke clearly—"Come, there is plenty of room.
Come tonight to The Globe where they perform
Master Shakespeare's comedy and delight, *A Mid-
summer Night's Dream."* They followed as though
mesmerized.

A street rose up around them. There were
cobblestones underfoot, and others pressing in
toward the high curving wooden walls of the
old Globe Theatre. Seconds later they stood, surrounded by an audience, within what Shakespeare
had called a Wooden O.

Again, it was the sense of actually being there
that amazed Bond, and he had to wrestle with his
senses to move himself back out of the light, from
the 16th-century audience enjoying the end of the
Dream—Puck, acted by a young boy, was just finishing the play. Bond literally had to drag Flicka

away, melting through "people" and "walls" into the darkness of what he knew had to be the huge, hangarlike second floor of the Schloss Drache.

"But, James . . ." She began to resist.

"We're losing time, Flick. Things are going on out there."

"But it's like a magic carpet . . . Time travel . . . A true Time Machine."

"I know. But we have to—"

The lights came up suddenly, brilliantly, bringing them up against reality with a terrible jolt. The sounds and pictures had gone, and in their place was—as Bond had presumed—a massive warehouse, with catwalks leading through complicated pieces of equipment, huge cycloramas, automata, and battens of floods, spots, odd-shaped mirrors and projectors.

They stood on a metal catwalk—grilled, and with a chain guard hanging from metal rods set at intervals of around six feet. The catwalk was solid and did not swing or move under them, yet it stood about twenty feet from the ground. This time there was no insubstantial figure, projected by laser or hologrammatic means, facing them.

"I told them you'd got into the display," Charles said in excellent English. "Mr. Lester is really very angry with you. Mrs. Horton is driving him to the nearest hospital. Did you know you'd broken his arm?"

"That was my intention." Flicka's voice gave no sign of surprise or fear. "I also did my best to damage his future romantic prospects."

"If it was up to me, I'd damage more than your romantic prospects." Charles held an automatic pistol very close to his hip. He also stood with legs slightly parted. All the signals were that this man was trained, and it is the training that separates the men from the boys. Lester had not struck Bond as being a trained bodyguard. Charles, on the other hand, knew exactly what he was about. "Just put Mr. Lester's gun down on the catwalk, Mr. Bond. Do it slowly, please. Very slowly."

Bond took a step forward, bent his knees, and placed the Colt .45 carefully on the metal, just to his right and slightly behind him. "Your friend about, is he?" he asked, straightening up.

"William? Yes, sure, William's around somewhere. I wish we could both spend the odd hour in a locked room with you two."

"But you're not going to do that, Charles, because your boss, Mr. Dragonpol, says we have to be kept safe." He took another step forward, speaking softly, trying to get close enough for a move. It was like trying to tempt a wild animal.

"Unless it becomes necessary, Mr. Bond. Far enough." The pistol moved very slightly in Charles' hand. "We don't want any accidents, do we?" He gave a cheeky grin. "Well, I wouldn't mind. We can always *make* it necessary. I wouldn't mind that, and you'd positively hate it."

Flicka brushed against Bond's shoulder as she stepped in front of him. "Oh, Charles," she all but cooed. "You don't think we'd be so stupid as to play games with you. We'll come quietly, won't we, James?" She turned her whole body back toward Bond, and, in doing so, her wide skirt flared up and snagged for a moment on one of the metal stanchions holding the guard chain in place.

For a spectacular few seconds, her upper thighs and lace-decorated hips were revealed, in all their glory to Charles, whose eyes bugged out at the unexpected sight. It was a perfect piece of distraction. Flicka had moved to Bond's right while doing her unveiling pirouette, and he was able to launch himself toward Charles, tackling him low, getting right under the gun hand, his right shoulder connecting with the bodyguard's knees.

Charles gave an uncharacteristic squeal as he pitched over Bond's shoulder. Flicka moved in to grasp the pistol, twisting it and almost wrenching the wretched man's wrist from his arm. There was another scream as Bond dumped him onto the guard chain.

"Let him go, James," she called, and he instinctively did as she instructed, giving the body a little help with his shoulder.

Charles twisted and turned, then fell from the catwalk, landing on the hard stone below with a thud that made Bond wince. The squeal stopped, and was replaced by a groan.

Bond retrieved the Colt, and saw that Flicka already had Charles' pistol in her hand. "Anyone ever tell you how good you are, Flick?" He patted her shoulder, urging her forward.

"Many times, James. My instructors were always generous in their praise—I was head of the school." She winked, then walked quickly, with Bond at her heels. Every sixty feet or so, the catwalk expanded into a viewing platform with machinery, automata, lights, mirrors, and scenery reaching out on each side. Whatever else, Dragonpol obviously possessed a wonderful imagination.

At the far end, they reached a single door. Thick metal with a large heavy lock: it stood half open, and they emerged into the far end of the long passage, which evidently ran right around the enclosed second floor. This time, however, they were facing another metal door that stood open to reveal a narrow stone spiral staircase.

"The tower," Bond whispered, going straight toward the door and up the steps. He almost ran, using the balls of his feet to deaden the sound, and he was aware of Flicka behind him only because of her breathing, light but just audible.

The stone steps twisted upward, finally coming to a bare flagged landing and yet another metal door. This time it was in two sections, a plain steel, hinged slab which contained two very serviceable locks. In turn, this was hinged to an insert of solid bars which had its own lock, the whole forming a secure entrance into a very safe area, in which objects, even a person, could be easily confined.

On the far side of this door a small lobby led to yet another set of bars. These were also equipped with a locking device, and the entire section was designed to slide to one side. It was half open, and they went through into a large chamber with a high, vaulted ceiling. Great cathedral windows were set in two sides of the room, the glass very thick and clearly unbreakable, but it was the décor which stunned them. A large and comfortable bed occupied one corner. There were a couple of leather easy chairs, and a very large rough work table, upon which papers were piled and scattered.

The wall directly opposite the entrance was completely taken up by tall metal filing cabinets, the uppermost part of which could be reached from a ladder, anchored to the top section, and fitted onto a slider. Small wheels at the base of the ladder would allow it to be pushed easily to the required place, and it stood in a central position with one of the higher drawers open, as though the previous occupant had only just retrieved some required file.

Bond went straight to the table, bent, and started to look carefully through the papers. There were charts, drawings, photographs, and even maps.

"Looks like the master plan for the museum." He gestured to Flicka with his hand, calling her over. Indeed, the topmost showed a view of the area they had just traversed. A quick glance showed they had missed seeing a performance at the Moscow Arts Theatre, one at a London theatre in the 1920s, the Royal Shakespeare Theatre in Stratford-upon-Avon in the late 1960s, part of a performance of Wagner's Ring Cycle at Bayreuth, a modern musical in a Broadway theatre, together with about another six exhibits.

"This man's a genius." Bond began to thumb through another pile of papers which seemed to be the working drawings of the large-scale electronics used in the museum.

"A genius, but I think a genius at murder also." Flicka had lifted the larger plans from the table and was rummaging under them. "These look

as though they've been thrown here to hide
something else." She moved several more large
plans until a series of maps, drawings, and notes
emerged.

"Look here . . ." But Bond had already been distracted, walking over to the right of one of the
high windows, where he stood looking in horror
at a bookcase which was anchored to the wall
above a deep glass-fronted cabinet.

"No, you look here."

She went to him, and began to study the spines
of the books, and the lower section of the cabinet,
which contained various items marked with small
cards. The books—beautifully leather bound, with
the symbol DD at the bottom of each spine—were
all works on the same subject—political assassination. Here, there were volumes dealing with prac-
tically every famous public murder, from Caesar
to JFK.

The objects in the cabinet mirrored the same
subject. Flicka caught her breath when she saw
an item neatly labeled *Jacket belonging to Graf
Klaus von Stauffenberg, and worn on the day of
his attempted assassination of Adolf Hitler, July
20, 1944*. Another claimed to be *The pistol used
to kill Mrs. Gandhi*.

"He's into the assassination business with a
vengeance," she said quietly. "Come and look at
what I've found over here."

They returned to the table where, from under
the other papers, Flicka had retrieved several
maps, street plans, and sheets of paper upon
which were scribbled notes. The street plans
were of Milan, Athens, and Paris. There was

also a plan of the interior of Milan's famous Scala Opera House; one of the Acropolis and the Parthenon, in Athens; and several jottings which appeared to depict a certain route leading from the center of Paris to an unknown point near the city.

Among the scrawled notes, the words *Milan, Athens,* and *Paris* were neatly underlined with initials next to each city. Milan equaled KTK, Athens showed the initials YA, while Paris had no less than three separate series of letters—PD. H. W.

"Targets?" Bond looked at her, raising his eyebrows.

"Could be. Most certainly could be. I think we should get out and—" She stopped abruptly, and they both turned toward the door, sensing another presence nearby.

It was only a slight scraping. The sound of leather against the stone outside, but it was enough to send Bond, pistol in hand, to the door.

"No!" he yelled. Then again, "Don't do it or I'll kill you where you stand."

William moved, very fast, twirling backwards out of sight. Bond squeezed the trigger twice, hearing the bullets ricochet off the walls. The outer steel door clanged and the locks clicked shut.

"Damn!" Bond cursed, running forward. The outer door was secure and it would take more than a simple lockpick to get them out.

"I rather think we should see if there's another way out of here." Flicka calmly began to examine the wall of metal filing cabinets. "We've outstayed our welcome and I don't particularly want to be here when they come back for us."

"The windows?" He went over to the high arches and took a closer look at the glass. "We'd need an armor-piercing weapon to break this stuff, otherwise we could have abseiled down—"

"If we had rope, James. Come on, let's be practical, there's some kind of space here around the filing cabinets."

She was right. The entire wall of metal files seemed very solid, but, as Flicka banged on them with her hand, there appeared to be some give, as though they made up a false wall protecting space on the far side.

Bond stood back, his eyes searching for any possible concealed opening.

For ten minutes Flicka moved up and down the wall, while Bond sought a clue from the way the large cabinets were arranged. "It's no good— I can't see any weaknesses," he said at last.

"Change places," Flicka commanded. "Sometimes new eyes—" She stepped back and saw the answer immediately. "Yes. Look. This center area here."

As she pointed he saw what she meant. In the middle of the wall one section of the cabinets appeared to be surrounded by a darker line, the size and oblong shape of a door.

"The ladder." He went across and drew the sliding ladder over until it was level with the right-hand section of the darker outline.

"No. No, that's not it." Flicka stepped to the files on the left of the now obvious door and began to move the sliding metal drawers in and out. "I'm sure there's a simple way." As she spoke they both heard a click from the file she was pulling out. "That's it." She pushed and pulled and the drawer seemed to click into some hidden position, but nothing else happened. She tried the drawers above and below. They also clicked and stuck in place. "I'm sure—" she began, then Bond leaned against the oblong of cabinets and they moved, swinging inward.

"Open Sesame," he whispered as they walked through into a cold and clinically white chamber, one side of which was given over to a long console with an array of inlaid computer monitors, controls, a switchboard, and two large TV monitors. The wall facing this large control panel contained row upon row of large mainframe computer tape machines, while in the wall in front of them was a door marked GANTRY: DANGER HIGH VOLTAGE.

Conversation was superfluous. It was obvious that they stood in the main control room for Dragonpol's Theatre Museum. In the center of the long console a glass panel covered a detailed electronic map of the exhibits, with winking lights to show exactly where the various sections lay in relation to the entire display. It was now clear that each of the many spectacles was activated by heat-and-movement sensors, so that the approach of visitors immediately turned on the various projections, holograms, sound, smell, and the lifelike automata. At the moment the master switch was in the off position, and the two large TV monitors gave a panoramic view of what seemed like a jumble of small theatres, cycloramas, and lighting battens, all joined together by the walkway over which the unhappy Charles had been pushed.

"Look." A flicker of movement caught Bond's eye. His hand hesitated over the controls until he found a small joystick that operated one of the many closed-circuit TV cameras. He gently moved the stick, focusing and then zooming in on the movement. There on the walkway, William was climbing down to help Charles to his feet. The latter looked shaky and a little stunned, while the pair of them were obviously talking and trying to decide what should be done.

The walkway itself broadened and sloped onto firm ground at each exhibit, so that visitors were able to move directly from this main path around the museum into each presentation, which would come to life at their approach and, cunningly, direct them back onto the higher metal path when the show was over. Groups of people would be automatically led from one exhibit to the next, probably in a state of disorientation which would lead to a greater sense of wonder.

Bond's hand worked the joystick again, tilting the hidden camera up to view the walls of the museum. High above the exhibits was a second catwalk—obviously the gantry—which would be used for maintenance and possibly security. At intervals, metal ladders led straight down from the gantry, giving access to the main walkway and the complex set pieces.

"The man's got a gold mine here once it's completed." Flicka moved behind him, her voice almost a whisper of awe, adding, "If it's ever completed."

"I vote we use the master switch, turn on all

the fun of the fair, and go down to hunt that pair of heavies on their own ground." Bond bent over the controls, memorizing the layout and making sure he could lead them through the maze of exhibits.

"It says DANGER HIGH VOLTAGE." Flicka inclined her head toward the door to the gantry.

"So, have you got some other magic way out of here?"

"No, but I'm not really partial to getting a few thousand volts of electricity run through me."

"Then don't touch anything. Keep away from the wall. Look."

He began to carefully outline his plan, moving the closed-circuit TV camera around with the joystick to show her exactly which way they should go.

"I always wanted to be in a big Broadway musical," she said, for the plan was to surface from the rear of the display which took visitors onto the stage of a musical—one of the exhibits they had not seen on their short tour, which had been interrupted by Charles.

Once more Bond moved the camera to focus onto the area in which he had last seen the two supposed male nurses. They were still there, with Charles rubbing a bruised shoulder and testing the strength of an injured leg.

"William's on the ball." Flicka nodded at the screen as William handed a spare automatic pistol to his colleague. "Thinks of everything. I imagine you want to get this show on the road before they both come dashing up here and do unspeakable things to us."

"I think it would be the wisest move. Ready?"

She nodded, and Bond's hand once more hovered over the console, finally stopping just above the lever that bore the legend MASTER SWITCH. He hesitated again. "Just for the hell of it, Flick, could you make sure that door to the gantry is open?"

She opened the door and found herself looking down into an elevator shaft.

"There's a call button." She nodded back toward Bond. "How very thoughtful. If we had rushed in, we would've been clawing air." She pressed the button and they heard the whine of machinery.

Bond kept one eye on the TV monitor to check on Charles and William, who seemed undecided about the next course of action and appeared to be arguing. William, he considered, was probably all in favor of doing away with them, while Charles probably wanted to at least wait until Maeve was back before taking any drastic action.

The cage rose and Flicka pulled back its sliding door.

"Okay, let's go."

He pulled the master switch, saw the museum plunged into darkness on the monitor, and walked quickly into the cage, which smoothly descended at a touch of the down button. The elevator stopped and they found that they were in a narrow sloping passage which would clearly lead down into the main part of the castle, and the gantry high above the museum.

They went forward at a jog trot. "Remember we have no spare ammunition. If they start shooting, make every round count." Bond checked the Colt, and saw Flicka glance down at the handgun she had taken from Charles.

On reaching the door leading onto the gantry they paused, Bond telling her to move as quietly as possible. Then they crossed through into darkness, standing for a few seconds to allow their eyes to adjust.

Below them, far off to the left, there was noise and action from the Globe Theatre exhibit near which they had been stopped by Charles. Slowly they traversed the catwalk, very much aware that they were suspended, dangerously high, above the vast cavern that was the museum.

Bond's eyes were quickly conditioned to the darkness, and he led the way, feeling the safety bar to his left, trying to judge the distance to the metal ladder that would take them down, close by the Broadway Musical exhibit. He counted four chained-off ladder sections, stopping when he came to the fifth, turning and whispering to Flicka, making downward motions with his hands.

He saw her nod, then he swung out onto the ladder, slipping the Colt into his waistband, momentarily wondering how she would cope with her weapon. The narrow rungs were cool and firm to the touch and he gradually increased his speed, descending rapidly into the blackness below, waiting at the bottom for Flicka to join him, gesturing with his arm toward where he considered the exhibit to be.

They were behind a high curving stone wall, the cyclorama at the back of the display. Silently they moved forward, crabbing their way to the

end of the wall. Bond nodded to her, took a deep
breath, and they plunged forward.

Neither of them was prepared for the effects
which suddenly assaulted all their senses. As they
stepped into the dark area, it became alive. For
a few seconds they were almost blinded by the
light and deafened by the noise: it was as though
they had walked through some magic looking glass
onto a stage full of prancing, dancing figures, lit by
floods and full battens of theatrical lighting, and
singing their hearts out: "There's no business like
show business. . . ."

The figures moved with precision, following a
set pattern of dance steps, the men in white tie
and tails, the girls in silver tailcoats, top hats,
and abbreviated spangled briefs. The noise was
deafening, and Bond could just see an orchestra
conductor through the glaring light.

Close-up, the dancing automata had a bizarre
appearance, with sparkling staring eyes, rouged
cheeks, set smiling faces, their mouths opening
and closing like ventriloquists' dummies, the
dance steps prescribed by the patterns set in
their computerized, robotic brains.

The impact of the scene slowed both Bond and
Flicka, who lost precious moments as they stood,
almost confused by the spectacle.

Then the shooting began.

A male automaton was lifted off its feet, almost
at Bond's side, as two bullets ripped in from somewhere beyond in the darkness. He had been aware
of the muzzle flashes from the darkness, and fired
twice in the general direction from which the shots
had come as he blundered forward, nudging one of

the female dancers so that the robot was pushed out of alignment and continued to go through her dance steps moving away from the other females.

He saw and heard Flicka fire into the black hole behind the lights and thought he heard a screech of pain above the din of music and singing. Another bullet cracked past his head, and the face of the second male robot disintegrated into wires and microchips as Bond leaped forward through the lights and into the cavern of darkness beyond.

The music and singing did not stop, but he was aware of the robotic confusion now reigning on the stage. From the corner of his eye he saw Flicka jump across what was supposed to be the orchestra pit, firing as she went. Then he was also on the far side of the lights looking at Charles, spread-eagled on the ground, his shirtfront a bloody gushing mess where one of their bullets had struck him.

"There!" Flicka shouted, swiveling to the right and getting off two rounds, aimed at the fleeing figure of William, who ran clattering along the walkway.

Bond followed and, on reaching the metal path with Flicka close on his heels, the din of the Broadway show cut off, the music suddenly silenced, and the lights going off as they crossed the invisible electronic eyes which operated the display. Now the only sound was of William's feet on the metal as he ran from the fight.

They followed, Flicka slightly behind Bond, who fired once at the retreating man just as he

momentarily activated another of the displays—
a modern play, set on a proscenium arched stage.
Dialogue and movement began and was then
stopped as William reached the far side of the
display.

The scene came alive again as Flicka and Bond
went past, then, ahead, they saw the stocky little
William run into the next exhibit as though he
were trying to make it to the area behind the
displays.

Again there was noise, a huge overpowering burst of music recognizable immediately as
Wagner's *Siegfried*. William was attempting to
get across the stage, which was a full-sized mod-
el of the famous opera house—Richard Wagner's
great dream theatre at Bayreuth, built especially
for the performance of the composer's gargantuan
operas.

Bond stopped, legs parted, the Colt an extension
of his arm, sighting in on the figure of William
as he blundered forward toward the automaton
of Siegfried singing his microchip heart out and
raising the legendary magic sword which is such
an integral part of the massive Ring Cycle of
operas.

He fired once and saw William lifted off his feet
as the bullet struck him, sending him curving
toward the half-rising sword, then, in a flurry
of arms and legs, William crashed down on the
operatic automaton. Sparks flew from under his
body, and a small burst of smoke immersed both
man and robot for a few seconds. When the smoke
lifted, William lay impaled on the sword, while the
opera continued, the tapes playing on even though

the reproduction of Wagner's stage remained still, with the macabre bundle of corpse and electronics at its center, the very real sword reaching bloodily up through William's back.

13

A Ride in the Country

"Don't you think we should wait for Maeve? Sweat her?" Flicka stood in the great hall. They had seen this part of the castle on their arrival, therefore getting only an impression of a heavily decorated Victorian-like entrance. Now, for the first time, they noticed the long Minstrels' Gallery, high above.

"That's how we heard the Dragonfly talking to his sister." Bond pointed to the balustraded U-shape above them.

"Yes, but don't you think we should wait?"

"No. For one thing I don't particularly want to do any explaining concerning two dead bodies. Also, if we're to catch up with Dragonpol, we should head for Milan. That's his first stop, isn't it?"

"According to the notes, yes. But, James, how do we set about finding him?"

"We might have to get a little help, Flick. What I do know is that the longer we hang around here, the more time it gives Dragonpol."

He went up to the place where they had left their luggage, carrying it down to the hall and then out to the BMW, which he checked meticulously. He had read the full report of how Archie and Angela Shaw had died in London, and one thing was certain: Dragonpol knew about explosives, just as he knew about other kinds of weapons and more exotic ways to death.

The car was clean so they just drove away, leaving Schloss Drache lit up as though for some festival.

They speeded toward Bonn, stopping only for Flicka to make one international call to Switzerland from a public telephone.

"I won't be long, but I have an idea, and it might just make all the difference when we get into Italy," she told him, refusing to say more.

In all, Flicka spent over half an hour in the phone booth.

"Getting back into your service's good books?" Bond asked when they were on the road again.

"Not likely, my dear. I called our old chum Bodo."

"Lempke? The Swiss cop with the turnip head?"

"The same. He's a damned good policeman, and he also owes me a favor."

"Will he pay up?"

"We'll see when we get to Bonn."

When they reached the airport and turned in the BMW, she made another call, while Bond got them onto a flight to Milan.

"All set," Flicka told him. "We have a booking at the Palace."

"Oh, you couldn't get us in at the Principe di Savoia?"

"I didn't even try the Principe," she snapped. "If you want kitsch, overdecorated five-star places, you can go and stay there on your own. Anyway, Bodo is expecting to find us at the Palace."

"He's repaying your favor?"

"More. He's coming to see us, with information, I hope."

He did not press for explanations. Already he had learned that Fredericka von Grüsse liked to do things her way, and she would tell him only when she was good and ready. Bond respected that, for he knew it mirrored his own attitude in arcane matters.

They arrived in Milan at a little after six in the evening, and by seven were settled into the Palace, amidst chrome and furnishings which were serviceable, though far from the luxury Bond would have preferred. However, the minibar was well stocked, and it was Flicka who suggested that they break out the champagne.

"We have something to celebrate?"

"Getting away from Schloss Drache in one piece is enough for me. But this might be a case of " 'we who are about to die.' "

"What a charming idea. Why are *we* about to die, Flick?"

"Work it out for yourself, James. It's quite simple really. We're both marked men—well, you are. I, on the other hand, am a marked woman."

"But shouldn't we begin to try and find the Dragonfly?"

"You like looking for needles in haystacks?"

He thought for a minute. She was right, of course. Without some official assistance they would be unlikely to track down Dragonpol. He had even suggested that they make contact with some kind of authority. Yet something else was nagging away in the back of his mind, there just out of reach. Something they had overheard during that last conversation between Dragonpol and his sister.

"I suspect he might well come looking for us. The Dragonfly, I mean."

"With a little homicide on his mind? Hence, " 'we who are about to die'?"

"Possibly, but Bodo doesn't think he's out to kill *anybody* at this point." She paused, gave him her most beautiful smile, and added, "With the exception of the meddlers—that was what he called us, wasn't it? The meddlers?"

"He also said we should be kept unharmed." Again the overheard conversation swirled around his mind, with something significant hovering off stage.

"Unharmed until he returned, presumably. We have to face the fact, James, that friend Dragonpol, actor extraordinary with a great eye for detail, does not really like us. So, unless he gets lucky and sees *us,* he's unlikely to start killing anybody."

"No? What about the bloody list? Milan equals KTK and so forth."

"If Bodo's correct, KTK is not even in Milan.

Think of La Scala, James. Then think about who KTK could be."

"I already have. Milan equals one of the greatest opera houses in the world—La Scala—and there's only one KTK connected with opera. The beautiful Dame Kiri Te Kanawa."

"Quite. And she's nowhere near Milan at the moment, though she will be in December. You worked out who YA is, in Athens?"

"Arafat?"

"Give the man a cigar. Yes, Yasser Arafat, the Old Man, the PLO leader with a thousand lives, or so it seems."

"And?"

"And he is nowhere near Athens, and not likely to be until December, when he has agreed to take part in a joint meeting with other Arab leaders, together with representatives from the British and United States governments. Dame Kiri's going to be in Milan for the second week in December doing three performances of *Tosca,* and making one charity appearance in the Cathedral, on the night of the thirteenth. Arafat is due to arrive in Athens on December fourteenth. All that's a long time off, but if Dragonpol's up to his usual form, he's planning to do those two in a row. Of course, there's always Paris."

"I have one idea about Paris, but it really doesn't bear thinking about, and there's no way that Dragonpol could have any advance warning."

"Then keep it to yourself until we've talked to Bodo."

As if on cue, the telephone rang and within seconds Flicka was having an animated conversation with the Swiss detective.

Finally she put the telephone down and turned to face him. "He will have all the information we need by tomorrow, and we are to meet him for lunch."

"So?"

"So we're on holiday unless David Dragonpol comes calling. Why don't I go and change into something loose and stimulating while you call down for room service?"

As Fräulein von Grüsse said the next morning, it was a night during which they both deserved to be awarded gold medals. "World champions," Bond agreed with a sly smile.

They were seated at a small restaurant in Milan's famous Galleria—possibly the world's first shopping mall, Flicka said—lunching in style and watching all the girls go by. Bond had said that he thought the smartest women in the world were to be found in Milan, and Flicka, after only a few minutes, said she felt positively dowdy.

Lempke arrived on the dot of twelve noon.

"You've got everything?" Flicka asked.

"Funnies." Bodo made his clown's face, then looked from side to side furtively. "Funnies, both of you. Don't know why I put my entire career on the lamb for you."

"I think you mean on a limb, Bodo, but I know you do it for me because you love me to distraction." Flicka took a long sip of her wine, looking up at the fat cop from under batting eyelids.

Bodo followed her lead with his glass of red. "Adds more to my little pink cells, eh?"

He refused to say anything worth hearing until he had eaten. "If I am playing hockey from my job, then at least someone should buy me a good meal," he announced.

It took Bodo a good ninety minutes to dispatch antipasto, minestrone, spaghetti alla Milanese, and a huge piece of disgustingly rich chocolate cake. With thick cream. When the coffee was served he wiped his mouth with a napkin and settled back.

"I think I told you everything already, but your friend with the strange name, the David Dragonpol, isn't about to start killing anyone here in Milan or Athens. Mind you, it would not surprise me if he tried to knock the pair of you into oblivion."

"Contacts," Flicka prodded. "I asked you to fix up some discreet contacts for us here in Milan."

"Sure. I done it. Just like you asked. But, as I said, I'm not going to lose my pension for a couple of busybody funnies."

"So who is he?"

"Who is who?"

"The contact you've arranged."

"Ah—I have to take you to him. Cloak and dagger." He laid a pudgy finger against the side of his nose. "The pair of you should know all about cloaks and daggers."

"One question." Bond rightly felt that somewhere along the way he had been left out. "Just one small question to put me into the picture."

"Sure." Bodo gave him another of his clown's faces.

"You seem to have done some snooping and

also arranged things for us. How do we know Dragonpol's still here in Milan?"

"Trust us, James." Flicka laid a hand on his sleeve. "If Bodo's here, then Dragonpol is almost certainly still in town. Someone had to get in touch with authority, and that's just what I've done, through Bodo. We can't do this alone." She turned to Lempke, who was looking at the bill with a face which spoke of heart attacks.

"You bought lunch for the entire restaurant." He passed the slip of paper over to Bond, who paid with a credit card.

"Okay." Bodo appeared much relieved. "Okay, I take you to my man now. Come."

None of them even noticed the dapper Englishman dressed in navy blazer and slacks, one hand smoothing a mane of gray hair, the other clutching a stout walking stick with a brass duck's head handle. The Englishman had been sitting only a few tables from them. Now, as they left the restaurant, he too paid his bill and followed them, at a distance, as they walked out onto the street.

The traffic was snarled in a way unique to Milan, the air heavy with the smell of diesel and gasoline. Bodo sniffed. "The end of summer," he said. "Soon you won't be able to get a flight in or out. Always the same in Milan. Come autumn and the place gets socked in. Soon it will be time for the smog again." He lifted a hand, and a sleek Ferrari seemed to materialize out of the banked-up traffic, snaking over and pulling up by the curb.

"Have to be quick or we'll get a ticket." Bodo hustled them in, and the driver, a short young man with the eyes of a pickpocket, smiled and nodded. "Just going for a little ride, like the old gangster movies say. A ride in the country."

On the pavement outside the Galleria the very obvious Englishman, with his military blazer and the stick with the duck's head handle, watched them drive away. He saw other cars weaving behind them in the traffic and he frowned. There was no way he would be able to follow them now. He made a small, petulant gesture with his head, then turned back to find a telephone. The meddling Swiss woman and her English boyfriend would have to return to their hotel, and he had plenty of time. Everyone would wait, but one person had to know what was going on if the whole business was to be pulled off with a minimum of fuss. Somebody had to be lured, and he knew just the woman to do the luring.

"There are a couple of cars on our tail," Bond said as they pulled away. "A black Fiat and a dark-green Lamborghini. Possibly a taxi as well."

"Good." Bodo turned to him and smiled. "We don't want unauthorized vehicles on our tail, do we?"

Within minutes they were taking the road out of Milan, heading toward Lake Como and Cernobbio.

"We wouldn't be going to the Villa d'Este by any chance?" Bond asked.

"You know Milan well?" Bodo gave him another smile.

"I know the Villa d'Este. It's pretty high-profile for a secret meeting with your contact. Also, your man must be a very well-connected Italian police-man if we're meeting him there."

"Who said he was a policeman? Anyway, you'd be surprised who stays at the Villa d'Este these days." With that, Bodo made himself comfortable and appeared to go to sleep.

The Villa d'Este is, arguably, one of Italy's greatest hotels. For almost five centuries it was a private estate on the shores of Lake Como, some thirty miles from Milan. For over a hundred years it has been a summer oasis for the rich and noble: a refreshing gem set in parkland, with tennis courts, swimming pool, horses, an eighteen-hole golf course, and amazing Lombardian food. Its famous park and terrace have been the meeting place for deposed, and reigning, royalty, politicians, and people whose names are legends, while the service approaches the grandeur of a lost age.

They were expected. Bond spotted two security men watching in the parkland and a small black van placed strategically near the main entrance. Ten miles from the hotel, a pair of nondescript bikers had pulled in front of their car, while the other vehicles he had spotted as they left Milan now closed up in convoy. They swept up to the main entrance like a visiting presidential party, and an overtly plainclothes policeman opened the door.

"Straight through to the elevators. Suite 120 on the first floor." He spoke in almost unaccented English and escorted them through the grand foyer and up to 120, where he tapped softly at the door and ushered them in.

"James, how nice to see you. And this must be the lovely Fräulein von Grüsse." M sat, looking

incongruous, behind a delicate Louis XV desk.
Bill Tanner stood beside one of the windows, and
a short Armani and Gucci clad Italian hovered in
the background. Bond quickly introduced Flicka
to his Chief, and M took her hand, holding it for
considerably longer than necessary.

14

At the Villa d'Este

"Do sit down, the pair of you." M waved them toward chairs and they realized that Bodo Lempke had somehow disappeared along the way.

"I did say that I'd be in touch, James." He was in a suspiciously good humor, and Bond must have shown surprise. "Incidentally, your nice Swiss policeman's returned to his duty. Good man, Lempke. As soon as he was able to answer Fräulein von Grüsse's questions, he did the right thing and got straight on to us. Filled us in with all the details we did not know, and arranged the little clandestine runaround so that we would be able to have a talk without any interruptions." He smiled as though this were all a game. "You didn't think we'd let you get into difficulties in that odd German castle, did you?"

"I didn't notice any surveillance, sir."

"Good. You failed to spot anyone at Brown's, I recall, which means my people are much better than M15's Watcher Section. Rest assured, though, we have been tracking you all the way. And now we've reached the really dangerous part, James, bearing in mind that we now know what we're up against."

"We do?"

"Tell them, Chief of Staff." M moved his head slightly in the direction of Bill Tanner.

"Friend Dragonpol needs to be corralled." Tanner spoke in a low voice, as though he were about to let them into some terrible and highly confidential secret. "Unhappily we have no solid evidence. Nothing on which to pull him in. What we're dealing with here is a man with a deadly aberration, only we can't prove it, which means we have to catch him in the act."

"What kind of aberration?" from Bond.

"In some ways the man is almost certainly a serial killer, but one with a particularly nasty quirk." He took a deep breath. "We've run everything through records, the computers, and the Americans at Quantico who deal with serial-killer profiles. What we've finally come up with is a real ticking bomb." He paused again as though waiting for some signal. M nodded.

"Dragonpol announced his retirement at the end of '89, and it took effect in 1990." Tanner spoke as though he had learned a lesson by heart. "Here are the statistics. February 1990, in the space of three days, a known terrorist was shot dead on the street in Madrid; a Scandinavian politician died in a bomb blast in Helsinki; and an elderly, revered musician was killed when the brakes of his car failed a few miles outside Lisbon. Later, it was proved beyond doubt that the brakes had been bled—purposely. The Portuguese police are still investigating that one as murder, the other two have been presumed acts of terrorism, but no group has claimed responsibility."

"And . . . ?" Bond began, but M held up a hand. "Let him finish!" he commanded sharply.

"November 1990," Tanner continued. "In the space of two days there were terrorist acts in Berlin and Brussels. Two known members of the Abu Nidal organization were killed by some kind of silenced weapon as they sat in the lounge of the Steigenberger Hotel. Nobody saw it happen, nobody heard it, nobody claimed responsibility. On the following morning a senior American officer died when a bomb totaled his car during the rush hour in Brussels. Again, nobody claimed responsibility."

"But do we—"

"Please, James, there's more."

Bond shrugged, resigned to waiting out the list of deaths and disasters.

"April '91." Tanner consulted a clipboard. "London, New York, and Dublin. Three days this time. A close friend of the British Royal Family run down by a Mercedes-Benz which was never identified. Happened in the Strand at ten in the morning. The car was found two miles away. There is no doubt that this was not a normal hit-and-run. The man was murdered. Again, no responsibility. On the following afternoon, outside the Waldorf-Astoria, in New York, an American

diplomat was—wait for it—shot dead with a bolt
from a high-powered hunting bow. On the side-
walk and in front of at least thirty people. No
leads and no claims. On the next afternoon, a
woman entered a bar just off Stephen's Green in
Dublin, pulled a pistol out of her handbag, and
shot an Irish politician dead. Everyone thought
it was the Provos because the fellow was outspo-
ken against the Provisional IRA. But they denied
having anything to do with it. Neither was it some
extramarital scandal.

"December '91. A double-header: Paris and
Monaco. A diplomat in his Paris office and an
internationally famous lawyer leaving his hotel
after lunch in Monaco. Both shot in the head at
close range. No witnesses. No responsibility.

"Lastly we have this year's little series of trag-
edies. The General in Rome, Archie Shaw in
London, Pavel Gruskochev in Paris, and the CIA
man in Washington. Followed, of course, by the
tragic death of Laura March in Switzerland."

Bond could not hold back any longer. "This is
all very well, but can we tie them to—"

"To David Dragonpol, James? Yes. Or, I should
say that we know he was not in his Schloss
Drache, or the place in Ireland, or in Cornwall
at the relevant times. The rest is hazy. We have
documented proof that he was in the countries
concerned either on the days of all these killings
or within a few hours of the killings. The man
used two passports—blatantly his own in the
name of David Dragonpol and the one he used
when taking little weekend trips with the late
Ms. March, under the name of her brother, David

March. It's as though he wanted us to know he was around at the times of the killings."

Bond nodded. "When I questioned him, he admitted to being in Rome, London, Paris, and Washington, but not at the actual time of those murders. He also said he was in the air, flying from Washington to Zurich, when Laura March was killed. Do we know any more about that, and the presumed attempt on Ms. Chantry at Brown's?"

"We do actually." Bill Tanner seemed to brighten up. "The stabbing at Brown's had no connection. The police have the man and he's confessed. It was *not* a murder of mistaken identity, but a rather nasty love affair that went very sour. We've also talked at great length with Ms. Chantry. It would seem that, on reflection, her impression is that Laura March called off her engagement to Dragonpol. She was upset, of course, but that would give him a motive."

"Doesn't tie in with what Dragonpol told me."

"Would he want you to know the truth?"

"Maybe not. Is Carmel Chantry still being kept safe?"

"She's out of a job. They've got rid of everyone who worked closely with Grant. The man really wasn't up to it, so it's spring cleaning time. Chantry's been given a handsome golden handshake and sent on her way. After all, she's in no danger now."

Bond frowned. "I'm still concerned about the March killing. It really doesn't tie in. I think we should run some kind of check on Dragonpol's movements. Go through the travel records."

M stirred. "We've come to the conclusion, James, that he does have some kind of accomplice—witting or unwitting—who travels quite close to him, within hours as a rule. It's the only thing that makes sense."

"Why?" Bond thumped his knee with one hand.

"Why an accomplice or why is he executing people?" M cocked his head toward Bill Tanner again.

"It would seem that he was always a kind of obsessive." Tanner flicked through the papers on his clipboard. "In his career he was so meticulous that he got carried away. In fact, that's an oddity, a quirk. He would make errors—usually rather stupid historical errors. When they were discovered, he'd fly into towering rages and blame everyone but himself. Why does he kill in this fashion? The psychiatrists all agree that it is part of his obsession with detail, combined with his need to express himself by some devastating act. The serial-profile people at Quantico maintain that he really gets his kicks in the planning stages. The actual killings are like curtain calls. They doubt if he realizes the importance of killing."

Bond asked if that made sense.

"They say it does." Tanner began to quote written reports by psychiatrists and a long paper by the head of the psychological-profile people. "We have absolutely no doubt that he's a dangerous crazy. He is also a very clever crazy, and I don't think we could put him away with what we've got."

"But how in the hell does he get his information? I mean just take the death of Generale Carrousso.

Nobody but those really close to the Holy Father had the slightest hint that Carrousso would be in the Vatican at that time. And the Russian— what about the Russian? His press conference was called only hours before it took place."

"Quite." M stirred again. "You should know that, earlier this year, in the spring, Dragonpol visited Rome, London, Paris, and Washington. It is as though he were doing a dry run—as we believe he is now for Milan and Athens. As to how he gets his information, I think you must understand that, during his peak years as an actor, David Dragonpol made many friends in high places. The German police have already begun to check back on the telephone logs in and out of Schloss Drache. He gets calls from the most unlikely places. Also he makes calls in the same way."

"And how do we know he's here, in Milan, at this moment?" Bond's mind had slipped far away, to the conversation about telephones which Flicka had heard at Schloss Drache.

"Be assured that he is, Signor Bond." The beautifully dressed Italian spoke for the first time.

"Oh, James." M actually half-rose from his chair. "I'd like you to meet Gianne-Franco Orsini. Gianne-Franco is, for want of a better word, my opposite number in Italy, and he's been very cooperative. We owe him a lot, and, by the time we're finished, *you* might even owe him your life."

Gianne-Franco Orsini made a polite little bow. "Believe me, Mr. Bond—and you, my dear Fräulein von Grüsse—this man, this Dragonpol, flew into Milan only a few hours before yourselves, and I have very good reason to believe he is still here."

"Casing the joint in order to kill Dame Kiri in December?"

M winced. "James, please try not to use criminal slang. It can offend people terribly. But, yes, it appears that he has approached one person in an attempt to get a private guided tour of La Scala. We, or I should say Gianne-Franco, happens to control that particular person. So the tour is on hold for a couple of days, though he could easily go with the normal daily tours. We suspect that he's seeing the sights. We also believe that should he catch sight of you or Fräulein von Grüsse, he will switch his plans and dispose of you—either here or in Athens."

"So you think he'll definitely go to Athens?"

"If his December timetable is going to work, he *has* to go to Athens. But of course it could all have changed by now."

"Because of Paris?"

"Maybe. We sincerely hope not, but maybe. No, he really has nowhere else to go."

"Not even back to Schloss Drache?"

"Most certainly not back to Schloss Drache. The German police have that tied up, and his sister, the rose-growing Maeve Horton, is being questioned."

"Has she talked?"

It was Tanner who replied. "Unfortunately she won't say a thing. I understand that she's screaming bloody murder and asking for lawyers. She just will not say a word about her brother."

"And the dead bodyguards?"

"That's all being taken care of. Incidentally, there's one thing about those bodyguards you should know . . ."

"That they were both well-trained?"

"That they were both trained nurses as well as minders. They'd seen action in some of the best high-class mental institutions in the world. Obviously, Charles and William were employed to keep tabs on Dragonpol. We'll break the Horton woman eventually. In the meantime . . ."

Nobody spoke. The silence twisted around the room. Bond glanced at Flicka, and she raised her eyebrows at him. Finally he opened his mouth—

"Basically, what you're saying is that you'd like us to do a trick that I've had to perform several times before?"

"And what trick would that be, James?" Coolly, from M.

"The one where I go out and play at being a tethered goat. A target for the crazy Dragonpol."

M nodded like a Buddha. "That was the general idea. You won't, of course, be in any danger—"

"Of course not."

"Gianne-Franco's ladies and gentlemen will always be near at hand." He smiled his foxy smile. "There's no danger at all."

"If you'll forgive the expression, sir, balls."

M grunted. "Ideally," he continued as though Bond had never spoken. "Ideally it would be nice for you and Fräulein von Grüsse to take in a bit of sightseeing together, here in Milan, and then, when Gianne-Franco tips you the wink, in Athens. But I cannot order you to do that. I can ask you, James, but I really can't even *ask* Fräulein von

Grüsse, for she is a completely free agent."

"With respect again, sir, there's no such thing as a free agent."

"Oh, there is in Fräulein von Grüsse's case, but she probably doesn't even know about it yet." He turned to Flicka with the look of a saint. "Has your former service been in touch, Fräulein?"

"No, sir."

"They will be. As of yesterday you ceased to work for them. Discharged for acts prejudicial to good order and discipline, etcetera."

Flicka gave a little "Oh" and looked as though she might burst into tears.

"However, *I* can offer you a job."

"A job? With your service?"

"Naturally. My Chief of Staff brought along the necessary forms just in case you fancied coming aboard."

"And if I took the job, I would remain on the current assignment with Captain Bond?"

"Officially, Captain Bond is on leave awaiting the result of a board of enquiry, but—as he well knows—that's a bit of a bluff."

It was Bond's turn to grunt.

"Well, my dear, what do you say? You and Captain Bond seem to make a nice team. When this business is over, we have plans for reorganization. You could be a great asset to us."

"I would still work with Jam— Captain Bond?"

"A consummation devoutly to be wished, to quote the Bard."

"Then I'll take the job, sir."

"Good. Then you'll both go and do some sight-seeing, yes?"

"Give us the guidebook, sir." Bond knew it was no good arguing. "But what happens if we haven't got him after his stay in Athens?"

"Do not even think about that, James." M had gone deathly serious, all good humor dropping away like a snake shedding its skin. "If you have to go on to Paris, then we're all in trouble. The target there is unmistakable and refuses to alter plans. We have four days before Mr. Dragonpol's one possible kill on this particular outing."

"Don't you mean three possible kills?" Bill Tanner asked.

"One or three, it's all the same. If it came to that, we would face a terrible decision, and the target for Paris just will not budge."

"Then Fli— Fräulein von Grüsse and I will have to drag him out either here or in Athens, sir."

"Your head's in a noose if you don't, 007."

M, Bond thought, was all heart.

15

My Brother's Keeper

Before they left, Bill Tanner produced an expensive-looking briefcase. "With the Armourer's compliments, James. He says there's nothing new or special. But he claimed you'd know what to do with it." Bond nodded and treated the case as though it contained gold bullion.

M, looking very serious, delivered the final instructions. "We'll stay here until it's all over, but you must not attempt to contact anyone, unless there is another death, of course. This man is very dangerous and, if it weren't for the Security Service's involvement, we'd have left it all to the police. Give it three days here," he said. "Three, and three only. In fact, I think you should reserve seats on a flight to Athens, and do it as openly as possible. Go about your business, loiter, behave as tourists, but do not look for our own people or Gianne-Franco's ladies and gentlemen. They'll be there. Just try to be unaware of them. Your focus must be on Dragonpol. When and if you spot him, your job is to lead him to a place of your choosing. Somewhere public, where Gianne-Franco's people can take him. I want him alive, James, you understand?"

He understood, all right. He also understood that Dragonpol would probably be harder to spot than Gianne-Franco Orsini's watchers.

Now Bond sat close to Flicka in the back of a cab with the unopened briefcase between his knees. It was very late.

"I feel naked." She leaned toward him, half whispering. The taxi was an ordinary saloon and had no partition, so the driver had already tried to make light conversation, first in Italian and later in fractured English. They had pretended to know neither.

The Italian driver with the pickpocket's eyes had taken them along the lake, dropping them off in Como where, for a few hours, they forgot the dangers lurking in the shadowy world in which they now found themselves. Hand in hand they wandered around like young lovers, even buying the kind of souvenirs they would normally not touch with a barge pole: little pots and ashtrays with *Lake Como* printed on them, and a pen and ink drawing of Como.

At one point Flicka slipped away, returning with a small box containing a pair of exquisite cuff links: narrow strips of what looked like woven gold with a large clasp at each end. Bond opened his gift as they sat outside a small bar.

She sipped a Campari and he nursed his usual
vodka martini. His pleasure in the gift was like
that of a small child on Christmas morning.
"People don't often actually give me presents,"
he said, then told her to stay where she was as
he strolled off up the street. He returned with
a gold ring containing a magnificent sapphire,
in a claw setting, surrounded by a circlet of
diamonds.

"Oh, James, you darling man." She leaned
over and kissed him on the cheek. "Please,
you put it on my finger." She stretched out
her left hand and indicated the third finger.
For a moment he hesitated, then took her right
hand, whispering, "Not until this is all over."
Tenderly, he slipped it onto the third finger
of her right hand. "I don't want to tempt fate.
Women with whom I get deeply involved have
a tendency to meet what bad novelists call an
untimely end." He kissed her gently, and they
walked down to the lakeside where they found
a small restaurant.

The sky was like velvet, speckled with stars.
Out on the lake there seemed to be a thousand
lights from the small, coracle-like fishing boats
which trawl the waters of Lake Como and the
neighboring Maggiore.

It was a night of magic, and during dinner they
spoke to each other more with their eyes than
voices.

Then, suddenly it was over, and they were hag-
gling with a cabdriver over the price of a ride back
to Milan.

"I still feel naked," she said.

"Soon you will be."

"No. No, I didn't mean that. I feel we're going back into a war zone and I'm not armed."

"We can probably change that." He indicated the briefcase, which he lifted onto his lap, taking care their driver could not see them through his mirror.

Inside the case were documents, a couple of files, and a diary, but that was mere window dressing. He touched the hidden pressure points and lifted out the false bottom to reveal a pair of weapons, ammunition, and two holsters: a shoulder rig for himself and a thigh strap for Flicka.

The guns were Browning 10mm automatic pistols. Both were loaded, and the false bottom of the briefcase contained a shielded partition which meant it could be safely carried through any security checks.

Keeping the pistols below the driver's sightlines, Flicka transferred one to her shoulder bag while Bond stuck his into his waistband, behind his right hip.

"Like carrying a cannon," she whispered.

"They're not peashooters. These things're real stoppers. The FBI are using them now instead of the old 9mm."

They pulled up in front of the Palace at a little after midnight.

As he paid off the driver, Bond spotted at least two of the Italian team. He did not notice the smart Englishman who was out for a late stroll, still wearing slacks and a navy blue blazer, striding out with the aid of his walking stick, which sported a brass duck's head as its handle.

At reception, the duty manager smiled at them and spoke in his near flawless English. "Mr. and Mrs. Bond. A nice surprise for you. Your sister, Mr. Bond. She has arrived earlier this evening. Naturally I allowed her to wait in your room. She's there now, and said you'd be delighted to see her."

"Your sister?" Flicka asked once they were in the elevator cage.

He shook his head. "I'm an only child. Could even be friend Dragonpol in drag. He's done it before—the Russian in Paris."

At the door to their room, he cautioned her to wait, flat against the wall to one side. Then, slipping the lock, he went in, crouching low, the pistol ready at his side.

"I'm sorry to arrive like this." Carmel Chantry sat in the one easy chair facing the door. She was dressed in a white silk suit and looked as though she had just stepped from the pages of *Vogue*.

The introductions were embarrassingly stilted, with Flicka watching Carmel's every move, speaking only when necessary.

"Your Chief asked me to come," Carmel began. "I went through everything with him, and his people in London."

"Yes, he told me." Bond was also suspicious and wary of this sudden intrusion. "He gave me a rundown on what you had said."

Carmel shook her head. "I have to tell you, face-to-face, James. You see, I did not tell your people everything. This afternoon, my conscience . . . Well, I felt bad about it, so I got in touch with your office. They put me through to your Chief and I gave him the gist of what I had left out. He told me to contact you, tell you everything. You see, I might possibly be able to lead you to David. To Dragonpol."

"Really?" Flicka remained cool and distant. "How could you do that, Ms.—er—Chancy?"

"Chantry," Carmel said with a sweetness that could have withered flowers.

They raided the bulging minibar again and opened a couple of half bottles of wine, drinking while Carmel Chantry told her story.

"When they debriefed me—after the business at Brown's Hotel—I was quite frightened," she began. "I knew far more than I even told you, so I let them have a little of it."

"According to my Chief, you said that it was Laura who broke off the engagement."

"Yes, that was part of it. What I didn't tell him was that I really became quite close to Laura, and to David. I visited the castle with her several times. Got to know David and Maeve quite well. Yes, it was Laura who broke it off."

"You were with her that weekend?"

"No. No, I didn't go, though she asked me to come along as moral support. The point was that David finally told her there was a history of mental instability in his family. He even confessed the full reason for giving up acting. David Dragonpol had a complete nervous breakdown. During the year before he announced his retirement he had twice gone through memory losses, and on occasions he would completely lose control of his temper."

"And?"

"He was afraid. Very frightened of what might happen, but he did hope that Laura would help him. He felt that with her as his wife he could return to normality. He really needed care and treatment."

"He wasn't getting treatment?"

"Only a self-imposed treatment. He had a pair of male nurses—"

"We met them," Flicka muttered.

"A pair of male nurses who were with him, or near him, at all times. Also he had a secure room built into the Great Tower at Schloss Drache—"

"We saw that as well."

"When he began to get hyperactive, or there were signs that he was about to go into what he called one of his lost phases, they would take him up to the secure room in the tower and make sure he was looked after and kept safe. But Laura couldn't take the strain. They really did care for each other, and they wanted children, though when she found out the extent of his condition, she knew the engagement had to be broken off as soon as possible. David was fine for ninety percent of the time, but the other ten percent was truly frightening. And it was dangerous. There's no doubt about that, it was *very* dangerous."

"So the only new things you're telling us are that you knew him quite well and that it was Laura who broke off the engagement? You've told nobody else about your side of the relationship?"

She gave a little nod. "I knew him *very* well. Too well, in fact, and he knew me, in all senses. He also knew about my . . . Well, my preferences. Laura never had any idea that there was a kind of relationship between David and myself, but I went out to see him the weekend after she broke it off. He was becoming very hyperactive. Charles—that was one of the nurses—said he was concerned. David had begun saying that if he couldn't have Laura, nobody else would. James, I knew he had killed Laura as soon as I heard the news of her death. I then got worried that he might just come after me."

"So why are you really here, Carmel? You haven't flown all the way to Milan just to unburden your soul and make your confession to me."

"No. I think this all has to end. I talked to Maeve on the telephone before I spoke to your Chief. I have a pretty good idea where David will be."

"Then tell us, and we can do something about it."

She shook her head again. "No. I don't want him hurt or hunted down."

"He won't be hurt. The orders are to get him alive."

"He won't know that, nor will he believe it. But I can probably lead you to him. If anyone can talk him down, I can. Maeve never could. Laura was good with him, but I can really do the trick."

"So what do you propose?"

"I'm going to try and contact him. Then I'll bring him to you. I'll arrange things so that he'll suspect nothing, and I'll bring him to somewhere open—a public place."

"You really think you can do this?"

"I'm a hundred percent certain I can."

"Where do you plan to spend the night?" Flicka asked, making it perfectly clear that she wanted the girl out of their room.

"I have somewhere. It's okay, I'm going now. I'll be in touch tomorrow: probably sometime in the afternoon. If I'm lucky I'll have got hold of him and talked him into a meeting with you."

There was silence for a full minute, then Bond asked—

"Carmel, what's your true relationship with him?"

"With David? I suppose I'm now like a sister—different from Maeve, because she could never control him. I can calm David when the going gets rough for him. It really works. I can influence him in a way that neither Maeve nor the nurses ever could—nor Laura really." She gave a bitter little laugh. "I suppose he looks on me as a sister, and, as such, I am my brother's keeper."

"Do we trust her?" Flicka asked after Carmel Chantry had left.

"We have no other option."

"I don't buy her whole story."

"Neither do I. But we can't check her out, and we're on our own. I suggest that in the morning we do what we've been told to do. We go out and behave as though nothing has happened. We buy ourselves tickets on the first flight out to Athens on Thursday—which will give us the full three days. Maybe we can take one of the Scala tours as well. Then we come back here and wait. If Carmel doesn't get in touch by, say, three tomorrow afternoon, then we go out again. Show ourselves and hope that we spot him before anything desperate happens."

Below them, Carmel Chantry walked slowly across the foyer of the Palace Hotel. She wore a stylish white, belted, thin trenchcoat that had cost her a fortune in Paris.

Outside, the doorman asked if she wanted a cab.

"No." She nodded to him, looking left and right up and down the street. Even at this time in the morning there was still a fair drizzle of traffic. "No, I'm waiting for someone."

"I'll stay out here until your friend arrives, Signorina." The doorman thought she might possibly be a high-class whore, and he was really letting her know that she should move on.

Five minutes later she saw the car flash its headlights as it approached. When it came to a stop, the doorman ran across to open the passenger-side door for her. She tipped him with a smile.

"It worked?" the driver asked as she settled next to him.

"I did just as you told me. They bought most of it, I think."

He nodded, put the car in gear, and smoothly pulled out into the traffic.

"Then we only have to draw all the threads together."

"You think it's going to work?"

"I hope so. It's a last chance. Possibly the only chance we're going to get. Thank you for coming at such short notice."

She looked at him in the dim light. Nobody would recognize him now, dressed and disguised as he was. He had become an expert in disguise, and had learned a great deal, she thought.

Glancing toward the rear of the car, she saw the long walking stick with the brass duck's head handle.

"You brought it then," she said.

"As a last resort, yes. For proof, if necessary."

"And you'd use it?"

"Only if I have to. If there's no other way."

"We'll have to be very careful."

"I think we've been careful for too long. My fault really. This should have been done months ago. With luck it'll all be over by tomorrow night."

The morning came, bright and cheerful, another lovely day. It was hard to believe that the summer was almost over. There were still plenty of tourists around, savoring the last days of the holiday season, bracing themselves for the journey home and the return of autumn and winter.

As they had planned, Bond and Flicka strolled through the streets. They did not take taxis, or any other form of public transport, but walked everywhere, considering that, should Dragonpol be looking out for them, he would be more likely to spot them on the streets.

First they went to one of the larger travel agencies, where they booked seats on an Alitalia flight direct to Athens for Thursday morning. They even lingered, bombarding a harassed girl with questions about the best places to stay and gathering up as many brochures as they could.

Flicka carried a little pile of leaflets with the name *Athens* in full view, and they walked into the Piazzale San Giornate and toward the wonderful façade of the opera house, the Teatro alla Scala. Inside, they joined a tour and admired the building; had the wonderful acoustics demonstrated to them; looked at the statues of Rossini, Bellini, Donizetti, and Verdi in the foyer.

Neither saw anyone who could be remotely identified with Dragonpol, though Bond was aware of Orsini's watchers everywhere. They arrived back at the Palace after a light lunch, just before two-thirty.

By a quarter past three, Bond was saying that Carmel would not call, that it was some kind of runaround, when the phone began to ring.

"You know who this is?" Carmel asked at the distant end.

"Yes. Anything for us?"

"He'll come to meet you, with me, at four-thirty."

"Where?"

"The Duomo. On the roof."

"We'll be there." Bond hung up.

"She says he'll be on the roof of the Cathedral at four-thirty," he told Flicka.

"You believe her?"

"I have no reason not to believe her. You want to stay behind? Wait for me here?"

"You must be joking. If you're going to be face-to-face with Dragonpol high up above Milan, then I want to be with you."

"Then we'd better try to make it ahead of time. I'd rather be waiting for him than find he is waiting for us."

They reached the Duomo at twelve minutes past four, when the light had begun to take on a wonderful filtered reddish glow. It was, they heard a passing guide remark, the best time to visit the Cathedral.

The Duomo, Milan's great Cathedral, is one of the wonders of Europe. It dominates the city, colossal in size, yet somehow almost ethereal, with its statues, belfries, pinnacles, and gables; a monster cake built in white marble to the glory of God, standing at the far end of an imposing esplanade.

Flicka went up by the elevator, while Bond took the stairs. Both were conscious that Dragonpol, with ease, could be waiting for them, or even lurking on that hard spiral climb.

When Bond reached the top, he saw Flicka viewing the exit points from the far side of the roof. Above them towered the famous Tiburio, the central tower, dominated by the statue of the Blessed Virgin.

It was almost four twenty-five and, following a quick conference, they spread out to right and left so that they both had clear views of the stairs and elevator cage: relatively safe in the knowledge that even Dragonpol could not look in two directions at once.

On the dot of four-thirty, Carmel Chantry, still wearing the white silk suit of the previous night, emerged from the cage. She stood blinking in the sunlight for a moment, then she reached back and took the arm of a distinguished, gray-haired, tall man wearing the uniform of the retired English officer—the double-breasted navy blue blazer and gray slacks.

Bond peered at the man, who also looked around him suspiciously. Then Carmel saw him and waved, her voice just carrying across the space—"James—we're here, James."

They began to walk toward him, and he now saw that her companion could well be Dragonpol, but in baffling disguise. Then he saw the thick walking stick with the brass duck's head handle. Carmel's companion faltered slightly. His expression changed, looking first toward Bond and then, sharply it seemed, at Carmel.

Bond moved on the balls of his feet, one hand reaching for his hip and the big automatic pistol. His hand had just touched the gun when the shooting and screaming began.

16

Rise of a Deaf-Mute

Bond heard Carmel cry out, "No! James, no! He's—" Then the front of the white silk shirt and jacket blossomed crimson, her head went back, and she flew forward, arms outstretched as though taking a plunge into a swimming pool. For a split second he thought of Maeve Horton's *Bleeding Heart* rose, then he was dragging the pistol from his waistband, hearing the crash of shots echoing across the roof, aware of people throwing themselves to the ground, and the distinguished gray head of hair levitating under a fine mist of blood, while the deadly walking stick went flying through the air. The man who had been with Carmel went down, pitching forward, hitting the stone with a crash, leaving blood smearing the ground.

Gianne-Franco's men and women were suddenly very visible. At least six of them—two women and four men—had weapons out: one of them carried an Uzi, and they were closing in on a tall man who stood just outside the stair entrance.

Bond could not believe his eyes at first. The man had an automatic pistol held in the two-handed grip. The shots had hardly crashed out when he simply opened his hands, dropped the pistol, then straightened up, placing his hands on his head.

Later Bond had difficulty in reconstructing the entire incident, for everything happened within seconds, and it was not until the man placed his hands above his head that he saw it was David Dragonpol.

"I didn't mean to hurt the girl!" Dragonpol was shouting almost hysterically. There were tears running down his face, and he moved toward the two bodies, in spite of the Italians threatening and ordering him to stand still.

Nobody was stupid enough to fire on Dragonpol as he bent over the male corpse. He was now openly weeping, and by the time Bond reached him, he had started to mutter, "Oh, David. David. I'm sorry but it had to end like this. There was no other way. No other way. You'd have just gone on killing and killing. It was already too much. Enough."

Other words, from some recent time, flashed through Bond's mind. There for a moment then gone. "Three's still three too many," the voice in his head called out.

Now, close to the sprawled body, Bond took in two things. First, in spite of the wound to the top of the head, the face was identical to that of

Dragonpol, who now bent over him. An obscene-looking bloody mass of what had once been a gray wig lay a few feet from the body.

"David?" He put out a hand and rested it on Dragonpol's shoulder, though his mind had yet to take in the strange mirror-image that seemed to pass between living and dead.

Dragonpol looked up and shook his head. "James," he said. "I'm so sorry about the girl. I had to take out David. He would have killed you with that damned thing." His foot kicked at the walking stick. "Then he would have gone on and killed more people."

"I wasn't expecting—" Bond began, then peered at Dragonpol's face. "David?" he asked again, and Dragonpol slowly shook his head once more. "That's David." His hand caressed the shoulder of the corpse. "That's my brother, David. I should've told you when you were at Schloss Drache, but I didn't have the guts. In the end, Laura knew about him, but she thought like you. She believed I was David. I was the one who was to marry Laura. Give me a minute and I'll tell you everything."

The police had joined the Italian security men by now, and people were being shepherded from the roof. Someone snapped handcuffs on the living Dragonpol and led him away. He went very quietly, dignified, and without protest.

"What in the name of—" Flicka began, standing very close to Bond. "James, what's—"

He cut her off with a sharp, "I don't know."

As the activity on the roof began to take shape and settle into a crime-scene pattern, Gianne-

Franco suggested they all go to a safe house which would be used for the debriefing. "You're both expected there," he told them, and neither Bond nor Flicka had the will to argue.

The house was large and set in its own grounds, somewhere on the outskirts of Milan. There was ample security. A plain van blocked the gates leading to a drive, and had to be backed out in order for them to get through. Other cars were already drawn up in front of the building—a pink-and-white two-story villa. Men prowled the grounds, and two police cars and another van were parked almost out of sight behind a clump of trees.

Inside, the furnishings were bare and without frills, the walls painted in an institutional green. Telephones purred and low conversations drifted from half-open doors. Unsmiling, silent men and women moved between offices, carrying files.

They were escorted into a large room which had a rough table as a centerpiece. M sat near what had once been an ornate fireplace, while Bill Tanner stood looking out the window.

"I wanted him alive, James." M's eyes were full of reproach.

"I know, sir. I'm sorry. There was nothing I could do. Why didn't anybody know there was a brother?"

"That's what we're waiting to find out." Tanner spoke quietly, as though distracted. "The Italians are getting a statement from him now, then we're going to be allowed to interrogate him."

"Somewhere along the line everybody slipped up." M gazed into the empty fireplace. "It appears there were identical twins. David and Daniel, but even the theatre press didn't get onto Daniel, so I fail to understand it. Someone as famous as David Dragonpol must have been investigated by the press. The media are pretty hot about these things. Usually they can quote every relative, living and dead." He made an angry little noise through his teeth. "But that doesn't really excuse any of us. Nobody, not even myself, bothered to check out the family. We all simply believed what was printed by the press and what appeared in the biographies. The Dragonpols of Drimoleague. Two children, the last of the line. Maeve and David."

An orderly came in with coffee and sandwiches—slices of baguettes stuffed with cheese and ham—but none of them seemed to have an appetite. Then Gianne-Franco Orsini arrived, looking as neat and clean as though he had just dressed for a party.

"Well, he saved your life, Captain Bond. This is for certain. I have forensics people—ballistics and weapons experts—who will bring the weapon up in a moment. Diabolical. This brother, the Daniel Dragonpol, has told us much. David made the weapon with his own hands. Diabolical."

They saw just how diabolical it was a few minutes later, when a pair of white-coated ballistics and firearms experts brought the thick walking stick into the room, placed it on the table, and, with a nod from Gianne-Franco, demonstrated exactly how deadly it was.

"There was a second handle tucked into a specially made holster, on the deceased man's body." One of them, speaking good English, placed another brass duck's head on the table next to the complete stick.

Close up, they could see that the handles were much larger than any ordinary walking stick with such a decoration. The stick was also much thicker than normal, and made of a hard, highly polished smooth wood.

It was in reality made up of three sections, each hollowed out to a 9mm bore. One of the men unscrewed a length of some eighteen inches from the bottom of the stick, revealing that this was plainly a noise-reduction unit. The next long section also unscrewed. This was undoubtedly the barrel of the gun, while the last six inches, together with the heavy brass carving, made up the real works of the weapon.

The six inches of metal, encased in wood, was larger than the barrel and contained a chamber and a side opening for the ejection of used cartridge cases, while the duck's head could be stripped down, showing a cunning magazine and breech mechanism. There was room for three Equalloy rounds—one in the chamber and two in the duck's head. The breech was operated in a standard manner, and the workmanship was precise and hand-turned.

The duck's bill moved, forming the trigger, and there was even a safety catch built into one of the brass eyes. When the bill was squeezed, a firing pin made contact with the chambered round, and the gases threw the entire mechanism back, ejecting the used casing, automatically reloading with the second round, and so on for the third.

"We assume the noise-reduction system would

have to be replaced after three rounds have been fired," the ballistics man told them. "We have yet to test the thing, but my guess is that it would be accurate up to around a hundred and thirty meters—in yards, about one hundred forty."

"And it was loaded, just like this?" Bond asked.

"Loaded with the safety off, sir," the other expert said gravely. "As I understand it, he was bringing the thing up to his hip and aiming directly at you. If he hadn't been taken out, *you* would have been."

Flicka's fingers dug into Bond's arm.

"You always had the devil's own luck, James." M did not sound impressed. "What of the second mechanism?" pointing to the other duck's head.

"Even more cunning." The expert began to dismantle the brass and wood. There was no doubt what this had been used for. The head again contained a breech block, but this time of a much smaller bore, while the mechanism contained a CO_2 cartridge. In the chamber they could just see a tiny gelatin capsule.

The two firearms men both agreed that there had to be another, smaller-bore, barrel somewhere, and that the capsule would have to be examined by forensics. "But with the information we have been given, I think it's obvious what this one does, gentlemen, and what the capsule contains. We're handling it with great care."

"Diabolical!" Gianne-Franco used his favorite word again.

When the firearms people had left, Bond decided it was time to eat. He bit into one of the large ham-filled baguettes and M winced at the crunching noise.

Eventually they all ate, as it was obviously going to be a long night. They had almost cleared the large plate of sandwiches when several security men and two senior police officers came in with the man they now knew as Daniel Dragonpol. He looked tired and haggard, but it was quite clear that, as far as build and features were concerned, he was identical to his brother, David. He looked around the room, and gave Bond a bleak smile of recognition.

Nobody tried to restrict his movements, and one of the police officers passed a small stack of typewritten pages over to Gianne-Franco Orsini.

"I have told these gentlemen everything," Dragonpol said, sitting down at the table as though holding a press conference. The voice had the same timbre known to theatre and movie aficionados all over the world as that of the great actor. "I'm quite willing to answer any questions, and I realize that I might well have to stand trial for the murder of my brother and the, admitted, manslaughter of Carmel Chantry. I don't know what happened. I was aiming at my brother and she shouted something. It must have been a reflex." He hesitated. "I was very fond of Ms. Chantry who—like you, James—thought I was my brother, David."

"And I must thank you for saving my life, Dav—Daniel. Is that correct? Daniel?"

Daniel Dragonpol nodded. "Quite correct, James. I'm very sorry to have misled you and a lot of other people. Our family is close and proud. Wrongly, we tried to keep David's condition hidden." Something stirred in Bond's

mind. Daniel, he thought, sounded as though
he was on autopilot. Perhaps it was some kind
of shock. He remembered Dragonpol at Schloss
Drache talking about his family's pride.

"That's what I want to know about." M had
moved to the table, shoulders hunched, and his
chin in his hands. "Why did nobody know that the
famous David Dragonpol had an identical twin?"

"Many people *did* know. It was a fact to everybody in Drimoleague, where we were born, and
older folk in Cornwall knew. But they were also
very loyal, and after a couple of years the family put it about that one of the twins had died.
Anybody who cared to take a good look through
the Public Records—births, deaths, that sort of
thing—could have found out."

He paused, looking around the table, as though
seeking support. "It amazed me that the fact of us
being identical twins never once appeared in the
press. Later, of course, it became very useful. You
see, David was born without the power of speech,
and was unable to hear. He was born a deaf-
mute. While I, on the other hand, was a normal
little boy. The family, being what they always
were, found that facing the fact of David's huge
handicap was more than they could bear. Doctors at that time were convinced—and my family
believed it—that David would spend a short life
within a world of his own. They regarded him as
a vegetable, utterly lost to all of us. So they did
what so many old aristocratic families used to do.
They covered their embarrassment by hiding it;
refusing to accept it."

"So they put him away? Institutionalized him?"

Dragonpol slowly shook his head. "No," he said in almost a whisper. "Telling the story makes it sound like one of those old Victorian melodramas. David became the little boy shut away in an attic: the Grace Poole of *Jane Eyre* or the boy Colin in *The Secret Garden*. He was an embarrassment, cared for by three nurses—until the accident."

"Accident?"

"As children, Maeve and myself were educated by a series of governesses. We moved between Ireland and Cornwall. Wherever the family went, David was brought along. Nobody dared leave him behind. If we were in Cornwall, so was he. In Ireland, he was also there. The accident happened in Ireland when we were three years old— David and I, that is. Three years old," he repeated, as though momentarily lost.

"You would see your brother regularly?" M asked.

"Yes. Yes, I saw him, though I don't remember a great deal about it. I have a vague recollection of this other little boy who was kept apart, but most of our childhood was spent together. After the accident."

"You want to tell us about that?" M used his best interrogator's voice, as if it did not matter to him one way or the other.

Dragonpol asked if he could have a cup of coffee. More coffee was ordered, and until it arrived he simply sat there, looking sad. Bond recalled his Hamlet, and almost saw him sitting with the same melancholy look on his face. Then he realized that it had not been this man, but his brother.

When he had taken a few sips of coffee, Dragonpol started again. "Most of what I can tell you is from family talk—the family tradition, if you like. Though I do recall the sense of drama and of wonder. My life also changed after the accident."

Once more he sipped the coffee, and it was as though he were playing for time, building tension.

"We were in Ireland. At the house in Drimoleague, and a cold, stone, dreary place that was. David was kept, literally, at the top of the house. There were two attics, one on either side of a large landing, and two sets of stairs. One went right down to the front of the house, but there was a little trapdoor with a kind of ladder that dropped to a tiny landing with a narrow flight of stairs that went right down to the servants' quarters.

"The three nurses looked after him very well, but—I can't remember this, it's what I was told later—one of them had to leave. Someone sick in her family or something. David needed constant attention because he was a danger to himself. Two people were not enough to manage him. It was tiring, trying work.

"Odd, I do remember a woman's name—Bella. You don't often hear the name Bella nowadays. Well, Bella was supposed to be on duty and she fell asleep, it appears. David somehow got to the trapdoor and the ladder contraption—it's not there now: we had it taken out years ago. He fell. What? Twelve? Fifteen feet? Fell right onto his head. I do remember the fuss. The local doctor coming out, and I recall being told to be very quiet. Told that David was probably dying."

"But he didn't die." M sounded as though he were accusing Daniel of some gross and terrible act. "Instead of dying, he got better, didn't he? Got completely better?"

"Yes. By some miracle he came out of the coma. He was unconscious for almost a week, I was told. Yes, when he came out, he could hear, and he made noises. Within a year he could speak. Within two years he was like all other little boys. He could read, play, get into scrapes."

"Is there any supporting evidence of this?"

"Yes. Plenty. At Schloss Drache we have letters, and our parents' diaries. I've only briefly looked at them. I like to live with what I can remember, but Maeve's read them."

"So, suddenly all was changed. You had a playmate. Your brother."

"We had a wonderful childhood together. Except—"

"Except what?" This time it was Bond's turn to sound doubtful.

"He was a little obsessive. And he was cruel. Very cruel."

"In what way?"

"Obsessive?"

"If you like, that first."

"Well, the family did not make any fuss about David and his newfound normality. They didn't even deny the stories that he was dead. In a way, I think my parents had some idea that he was not truly normal, even though they didn't say anything to suggest abnormality. You see, David liked to work to a routine. He set himself tasks, goals, and if he did not—or could not—meet the goal, then he would fly into terrible rages. Later, of course, he became obsessive about being an actor. As with everything else he had to be the best actor ever. He could not settle for second best. If something he did was not quite right, he would become uncontrollable with rage. He learned to check it in time, but in private it could be very frightening."

"So you rather played second fiddle to him?" M again.

"Very much so. He was a brilliant man. In the end I suppose I was the only one who really knew him. He learned to control himself in public, and even among his peers, but never in front of me. I suppose I became his real keeper."

Bond remembered Carmel Chantry on the previous night—"I suppose he looks on me as a sister, and, as such, I am my brother's keeper."

"And the streak of cruelty?"

Daniel Dragonpol let out a long sigh. "Animals to start with. He would invent the most terrible traps and snares for animals, and revel in it when he caught one—birds, squirrels, sometimes a dog or cat. They were like old-fashioned man-traps. Awful things which caused distress and pain but usually did not kill the creatures." Another pause. "He would do that. He would kill them."

"And eventually the animals became human beings?"

"Yes, something like that. With the traps, he became elated while he was designing them. The actual catch was something he looked forward to. But the killing? Well, that seemed to be nothing."

"But eventually the animals became people?" M repeated.

"I've told you. Yes." Sharp, on the brink of anger. "Yes. He killed people. But that only happened recently." He closed his eyes, shook his head. Then, softly—"I think it was only recently. There might have been something during the height of his success. I know of one actor and a theatre technician who died by accident while working with him. Those accidents could have been planned traps. But I really believe all the rages, the obsessions, and the cruelty were mainly contained by the brilliance of his career, because he *was* bloody brilliant." He stared about him, as though challenging them.

"Oh, he was bloody, all right. Yes, *bloody* brilliant," M snapped. "Your problem, Daniel, is that you knew. You knew what he was up to and you said nothing. You reported nothing."

"I know. I take full responsibility for it. They'll probably lock me up—"

"And throw away the key, I hope." M had become very angry. "Now tell us about his retirement from the theatre. This time the truth. What happened. How it happened. Who did what."

Dragonpol nodded meekly. "I believe that my brother was, in some ways, insane from birth. Or maybe it was simply a case of what happened when he had that fall at three years old. It brought back his hearing, loosened his vocal cords, but left him . . . Oh, I don't know . . . Left him some kind of emotional cripple. A very dangerous emotional cripple."

"The retirement," M prodded.

"In that final year I spent a lot of time with him—come to that I've spent most of my life with him. But in that last year he began to crack. The strain of performing, even of rehearsing and learning, became too much. By then of course he was channeling a lot into his dream of the Theatre Museum at Schloss Drache. In the end he did have a breakdown. Completely. Maeve and I nursed him. Lester—his dresser—came with him, and we brought in the two nurses: Charles and William. Eventually I persuaded him to stay at Schloss Drache and just work on the museum. I don't think he even realized that he had retired from the theatre."

"But he'd gone into a new line of business as well, hadn't he? The assassination business."

This time the pause was even longer than before. "You want to tell us about your brother's penchant for organizing public executions, Daniel? You want to tell us why you didn't even try to stop him?"

"There are two sides to everything." Daniel seemed to have gathered strength and was prepared to fight back. "Yes. Sure. I'll tell you what happened, and I'll tell you how I tried to stop it. I did everything I could. I—"

"You did everything short of actually bringing it to the attention of the police, I think."

"Well, you know it all, I suppose." Now he suddenly changed. It was the third or fourth time that Bond had sensed a sudden mood swing.

They didn't break for another four hours. M went meticulously through every suspected killing: from the February 1990 shooting of the terrorist in Madrid; the bomb blast that had killed the Scandinavian politician in Helsinki, followed by the musician whose brakes had failed outside Lisbon, right through to the series of recent deaths, ending in the murder of Laura March.

"She was your fiancée, after all," M thundered. "You must have known that he killed her—and you still didn't do anything about it."

"That was his revenge," Daniel said quietly. He looked ready to drop with fatigue. "I was shattered because Laura had called off the engagement—and quite rightly, once I'd told her the truth about David."

"But she thought you were David, right?" from Bond.

"Yes. Yes, I played the part of David for most people. Especially Laura. He knew. There was no doubt about that. It was his revenge and, yes, it was the last straw. I knew it couldn't go on after that. I'd already made up my mind that David would have to disappear. To tell you the truth, I was going to do away with him. But your Captain Bond and Fräulein von Grüsse suddenly turned up. We knew he was planning something else, and—"

"You knew *what* he was planning?"

"A December spree. He came here to make his arrangements and do a dry run. I was sure of that."

"Tell us about it."

"You know already."

"All the same, we'd like to hear it again."

"I'm pretty certain he was planning to kill Dame Kiri Te Kanawa on the stage of La Scala, then go on and do away with Arafat in Athens. He came here to set it up. Another day and he would have gone on to Athens."

"How do you think he chose his victims?"

"Publicity. Most were famous—politicians, terrorists. Now he was out for one of the great sopranos of our time, and the leader of the PLO. I think he chose at random, or when a good idea for a target presented itself. As simple as that."

"Then what? Then what was he going to do after the dry run in Athens?"

Daniel stalled. You could see it. He was so like his brother, but this was real life, not acting. You could see almost into his brain, as if he were asking himself if they really knew or if they were guessing.

"After Athens," M prompted.

"There wouldn't have been an after Athens. I had him pinned down this time."

"He didn't know that. Tell us about what was to happen this coming Sunday, outside Paris."

Again, a sigh of capitulation, followed by a deep breath. Then he jibbed again and remained silent.

"His notes," Bond said. "His notes indicate Paris with the initials PD. W and H. Does that jog your memory?"

Daniel Dragonpol gave a tight-lipped nod. "Okay. Right. Yes, I think it was probably his idea of a big coup. What do the terrorists call it? A spectacular? A royal princess, together with her two children, who are direct heirs to the British throne, are to be entertained at the EuroDisney complex outside Paris on Sunday. I think he planned to kill them as a kind of public spectacle. In his mind it would be the ultimate irony for a princess and two little princes to die at Disneyland."

"And I wonder how you know all that," M questioned almost to himself. "I wonder how you both knew that she was taking her children to EuroDisney on Sunday. It hasn't exactly been advertised."

17

The Dragons Are Loose

It went on until after five in the morning, with everybody but M getting more and more exhausted. The Old Man seemed to thrive on the long and hard, question-and-answer routine. His interrogation techniques were a copybook lesson to everyone present, and he dragged every last piece of information, and then more, from the cowed Daniel Dragonpol.

Brother David, it seemed, had carefully kept up all his old contacts, in government as well as the arts. According to Daniel he had informers everywhere—in financial areas, big business, and highly regarded social groups, as well as among his old colleagues in the theatre. He knew many friends of friends, and even had the ear of insiders within royal circles. So information regarding the schedule of the princess and the two young princes would be no problem.

"David set great store by the telephone," Daniel told them. "We tried all kinds of tricks, but in the end there was no way we could keep him from a phone." He made a gesture of hopelessness. "Nor could we keep him under lock and key. We knew when he was brewing up for some kind of expedition, just as we knew when he became deflected from his preoccupation with the museum."

"Did he make those silly little errors when his mind moved to other things?" Bond asked.

"What little errors?"

"Well, he's got a Greek actor, four hundred years B.C., putting on a Kabuki mask. Then there's the watch on—"

"I haven't noticed anything like that!" A shade sharp.

"Well, the mistakes are there."

"Then they'll have to be put right before the museum is opened to the public." Daniel seemed to stop, as though realizing his predicament for the first time. "If it is ever opened," he added.

"But you found it impossible to keep him confined or away from telephones? That what you're telling us?" M sounded alert and relaxed, his mind razor sharp.

"That's exactly what I'm saying."

Bond recalled the conversation about telephones which Flicka had overheard between Maeve and the nurse Charles—who was more than a nurse, though Daniel never mentioned that side of things.

"Let's go over it again," M prodded. "You tried to catch up with him during the terrible killing spree which included the death of your former fiancée?"

"I've told you. Yes. I tracked him down, but on each occasion I was too late."

"How do you think he knew where to find Laura March?"

"He listened at doors a lot. In the castle. I mean, it was creepy. He moved around the place like a ghost when we didn't have him locked in the Tower Room. When Laura was there for the last time, she told me she'd try and get to Interlaken to rest and—well, put herself straight. We were both in a very emotional state. David knew we had spent time in Interlaken. I have photographs, and I talked to him about it. He knew we liked going up to First and sit looking at the view."

"So you followed him on that last occasion and tried to catch up with him. What of his other little trips?"

"I didn't really find out what was happening until '91. I found some notes which indicated what he'd been up to during the previous year. I did try and catch him in April '91, when he did the London, New York, and Dublin ones. In fact I almost got him in Dublin. He was staying at The Gresham and I really thought I had him, but that was the occasion he disguised himself as a woman. He walked right past me in the foyer of the hotel, and it wasn't until he came back that I realized what had happened."

Around four-thirty they came to the question of the flowers and the notes left at each funeral.

Daniel seemed bewildered at first. When he started to talk, it was about Maeve's attempts to create her perfect hybrid rose. Bond stopped him—

"Daniel, we know what Maeve was doing with her roses, and we're all aware that she has only recently managed to produce the perfect *Bleeding Heart*. What we're asking is, did David do the business with flowers from the start?"

"Yes."

"Then what did he use before the last outing, when he was able to get his hands on Maeve's *Bleeding Heart?*"

"She had come quite close. He used what was available—at least he did on the April '91 sortie."

"And how did he manage *that* trick? First, how did he keep the roses fresh; second, how did he set up delivery?"

"He had a small cooler, like a miniature version of the ones you take on picnics. He always took buds with him—roses that were a few days from being ready. You know, Maeve—" He was off again, telling them how Maeve had roses in varied conditions; how she had her greenhouse set up with the flowers in different stages of development, rambling on until they stopped him.

"Yes, but how did he get them to the funerals? He was always long gone by the time his victims were buried."

"I think he anticipated the funerals. I'm not sure, but I'm pretty certain he left a rosebud, with a suitable message, in the hands of someone else. Someone he paid to deliver them when the time came. Children, I suspect. To be honest, I'm not absolutely certain."

"But you knew he took Maeve's roses?"

"Of course."

"And she knew as well?"

"Naturally."

Bond stepped in again. "On this, the final trip, did you know what he had taken? I mean when he left Schloss Drache while we were there."

"Sure. Maeve went out to the greenhouse, I think. Worked out what was missing."

"Three," Bond half murmured, remembering the overheard conversation between Dragonpol and his sister.

"Three?"

"This time he took three."

"Six."

"I was there, Daniel. I heard you talking to your sister before you went after David. She told you he had taken three."

"You have to be mistaken. He took six . . ." He trailed off, then brightened. "Oh, yes. I remember now. On the previous jaunt we discovered for the first time that he always backed up on the roses. You heard Maeve tell me three?"

"Clearly."

"Then she meant there were three targets. He always took double the amount. She would have said three, meaning three targets, which in turn meant six buds."

A picture of Maeve Horton came into Bond's mind. Tall, agile, with the slim dancer's body and the predatory dark eyes, her skin smooth and clear. Everyone called her Hort, he recalled, yet all through the interrogation Daniel had spoken of her as Maeve.

"Daniel?" he asked. "When I first met you, at Schloss Drache, you indicated to me that there was something funny about Hort's husband. Actually, you said that you'd tell me about it if you had time. Would you care to share that with us now?"

"Hort," he repeated, as though savoring the word. "Yes, poor old Hort. I only call her that when I'm around her. Yes, there was a problem regarding her husband."

"Killed in an accident, as I understand it," M broke in. He shuffled through some papers that Bill Tanner had placed in front of him. "Yes. Killed in a riding accident, near the Dragonpol House in Drimoleague, West Cork, Republic of Ireland. January 6th, 1990. So what was the problem, Daniel?"

"Please, I'm very tired. I need to rest."

"What was the problem?"

"Only a suspicion."

"What kind of suspicion?"

"David was there when it happened. Maeve's husband . . . They were having difficulties. He was talking about a divorce. My sister used to be a little headstrong as far as men were concerned."

"Meaning that she put it. about?" Bond remembered Maeve's X ray eyes, wide and dark, looking at him as though she was undressing him.

"That's a crude way of putting it."

"How else should I put it?"

"She liked men. Yes. Okay."

"And her husband was talking about a divorce?"

"Yes."

"And she didn't want one?"

"No. No, she didn't."

"Why?"

"Look, I'm exhausted. I—"

"Just a little longer. Please answer Mr. Bond." M leaned forward over the table.

"He had money. Was very wealthy. She would've been the guilty party. Wouldn't have got a cent."

"And you think your brother David had something to do with his death? You were going to tell me about it during my visit?" He sounded almost shocked.

"I've already told you. I was on the verge of putting an end to my brother when you and Fräulein von Grüsse arrived at Schloss Drache. I was off-balance. It was in my mind to say something to you . . . But . . . Well . . . Yes, okay. David was there, and when I went dashing over for the funeral, there was some whispering and giggling between him and Maeve. It didn't feel right, that's all. Maeve hinted later, but they were only hints, so I don't know for certain. Anyway, it's all over now."

"I hardly think it's all over, Mr. Dragonpol. You knew what David was doing, though you did little to stop him."

"Please. I'm—"

"Tired, yes. Yes, we're all tired. One more question." M had become peevish. "A question regarding your sister, Maeve. What did she think of David?"

"She'd have done anything for him. She adored him."

"Even though she also had more than an inkling about his killing trips?"

"Yes. Naturally she wanted that to stop. She wanted him treated. But she really would have done anything to help him."

"Like yourself?"

"No. I saw only one way. To have him permanently removed. Maeve—Hort—would never have condoned that. She loved him very much."

"And she did know he was a killer? That he went out, planned assassinations, and then came back to get on with building the museum?"

"Yes, she knew. I think she would have killed *for* him: to keep him safe."

"Really." M looked at his watch and seemed surprised by the time. "Enough for now. We'll convene again at midday. You can take him away." Crisp, as though on the bridge of a Royal Navy ship.

Daniel Dragonpol sagged with fatigue and allowed himself to be led from the room.

"This is all very interesting." M scanned the papers Tanner had put in front of him. Then he looked up at Bond. "You know that we had an address from Daniel Dragonpol? I mean an address for David?"

"No, sir." Bond felt waves of fatigue rolling in over him. He thought his old Chief's stamina was quite extraordinary for a man of his age.

"When the Italians first brought him in, they asked if he knew where his brother had been staying. It was some hole-in-the-wall hotel tucked away behind La Scala. They searched it. Found odd clothes, bits of disguise, but no flowers either in or out of a cooler."

"Really?" He could not summon up a great deal of enthusiasm.

"Really, James, yes. Not even a petal, let alone a bud, or six buds. By the way, I'm truly sorry about the Chantry girl. Decent member of our sister service, I think. Really pretty terrible."

"I haven't completely bought the accidental shooting, sir."

"No. Neither have I, to tell the truth."

"Why did you send her directly to us last night, sir?"

"Send her . . . ?"

"She was at the hotel when we got back from Como. Said you'd sent her."

M looked grimly concerned. "Said I'd sent her? No. I didn't even know she was here in Milan. That's rum."

"Very." Bond passed a hand over his brow, and M looked at him closely, like a doctor examining a patient.

"You look all in, James." He peered closer. "Look, why don't you and that nice von Grüsse girl take some time off. You've been working quite hard, after all."

Through the fog of his weariness, Bond felt surprised. It was unlike M to even suggest something like this, for he strongly disapproved of his agent's way of life. It struck him as being particularly odd now that Flicka had been welcomed into the service over which M held total authority. The Old Man rarely condoned anything even hinting at a liaison between two members of the Service unless he had some ulterior motive.

"Are you sure, sir?"

"Course I'm sure, James. Wouldn't give you time off if I wasn't sure. Take the rest of the week. It's only, what? Tuesday morning? Report back to me in London on Monday. Leave your whereabouts with the Duty Officer, though, just in case. Right?"

"Thank you, sir. Yes." He turned and nodded Flicka toward the door.

"Oh, James?"

"Sir?"

"Maeve Horton?"

"What about her, sir?"

"She strike you as being odd?"

"Not really. Gave me a bit of a come-on. Attractive enough in a gypsyish kind of way. Why?"

"I'm unhappy about what Dragonpol said. Just a hunch. A thought." He sniffed the air, as an old seaman will sniff for signs of a change in the weather. "I'm going to have her pulled in by our German friends. Maybe get them to take her to London. We'll be moving Daniel back as well if the Italians are cooperative."

"Right, sir." He thought it was not for him to reason why. The words "but to do or die" came into his head and he went deathly cold. Tiredness, he thought.

One of the Italian uniformed men drove them back to the hotel, and on the way, Bond suggested to Flicka that they should leave Italy. "We have seats booked on that flight to Athens on Thursday. Why don't we see if we can change them? Get out now? I don't know about you, Flick, but I'm fed up with Milan. Fed up with the Dragonpol business as well."

"Oh, yes, please. Please let's do that."

"Then can we do it before we pass out? Just get our stuff, check out, and head for the airport."

"Gladly. I've never been to Athens."

By eleven-thirty that morning they were driving into Athens in a hired white Porsche. From the airport they had tried to get bookings at the Grande Bretagne and Le King George. Eventually they settled for the Hilton, which he assured Flicka was the most beautiful of all that chain's hotels.

She believed him only when they arrived and walked through the brown-and-white marble entrance into the lavish interior with its never-ending halls, restaurants, arcades, and the two beautiful atria.

She was even more ecstatic about the suite, which had everything, it appeared, in triplicate. "Oh, darling, I'm going to have a lovely time here."

"Yes, Flick. We can do the Acropolis and the Parthenon."

"Yes, I suppose we could fit those in as well." She gave him a dazzling smile and said she was going to freshen up. Why, he thought, did she seem to be fit and wide-awake when he felt absolutely shattered?

He picked up the telephone and dialed the international number for the screened line which would put him in touch, in complete privacy, with the Duty Officer at the headquarters building in London.

"Predator," he announced when the other end picked up.

"Yes, Predator?"

"The boss wanted me to leave an address. I'm at the Hilton in Athens."

"Lucky somebody." The Duty Officer was a woman. She was also, he considered, not politically correct.

There were two bathrooms, so he took a shower, then briskly rubbed himself down with a towel, slipped into a bathrobe, and went out into the bedroom.

Flicka was lying on the bed, wearing next to nothing.

"I've put the Do Not Disturb sign on the door, darling. Come and disturb *me.*"

It was almost two hours later before they both fell into a deep and contented sleep.

He was wakened by the telephone and for a moment did not know where he was. Forcing himself up from the ocean bed of sleep, he reached out for the phone, while Flicka grumbled as she came awake.

"Predator?" the voice at the distant end asked.

"Who wants to know?"

"Levon."

"What's your occupation?"

"I make cartoon balloons."

"Then you're a good man."

"Predator?"

"Yes."

"Flash urgent from M. Return London soonest. The dragons are loose. You want me to repeat that?"

"The last sentence."

"The dragons are loose."

"Is that dragons plural?"

"Yes, sir. You copy?"

"Tell him I'll be back soonest." He replaced the instrument and cursed. Twice.

"What is it?" Flicka, naked, leaning up on one arm.

"Get yourself dressed. We have to get to London." Already he was dialing the airport to see if they could get a flight out that night. It was already eight-thirty.

Seconds later he was pulling on clothes, and throwing things into the garment bag, checking the shielded section of the briefcase, and calling for Flicka to hurry. "We've got just over an hour and a half to get a plane to Heathrow via Paris."

"Why this?"

He told her and she queried dragons just as he had done.

They had the bill ready for him at reception. "If you miss the flight, there'll be a room for you here tonight, Mr. Bond," the girl at the desk told him.

Outside, one of the car valets asked for the number and Bond gave him the little brass ticket. The boy retrieved the keys and walked the fifty yards or so to where they could see the little white Porsche was parked.

Bond tapped his foot, willing the boy to get the thing going. The streets out of Athens are nearly always a racetrack no matter what time of day or night. The boy was sliding behind the wheel. Then the whole area lit up. A great crimson flame shot from within the car before anyone's eardrums were assaulted by the explosion.

Bond pushed Flicka to the ground, covering his head and flattening himself across her as pieces of metal clattered around them.

Then came the silence followed by the screams and the terrible scent—a mixture of gasoline and the sweet sickly odor of incinerated flesh.

Flicka was just behind him as he raced to what was left of the car. "Dear God," she said, with a curious little sob. "Oh, dear God," pointing.

His eyes followed her finger. Something had been thrown out, landing intact just to the right of the shattered and burning wreck that had been their car.

"Jesus," he said.

There, on the ground, almost at his feet, was a pure white rose, its petals tipped in blood red.

18

The White Knight

In spite of urgent appeals by M, the Greek police did not let Bond and Flicka leave for London. Instead, they were subjected to lengthy interrogations, and it was almost thirty-six hours before they were allowed to sign statements and go. As with anything else in Greece, time appeared to have no meaning. So it was not until late afternoon on Thursday that they attended what amounted to a council of war in M's office.

Bill Tanner drove them in from Heathrow, talking the whole way, briefing them on the situation.

The villa, on the outskirts of Milan, in which they had interrogated Daniel Dragonpol, belonged to the local police, who shared it with the Italian equivalent of the Security Service. For several years they had used this house as offices and a special briefing center for police and troops preparing for VIP visitors. Because of the limitations of its use, the facility had no truly secure area in which to keep anyone under detention.

During Dragonpol's long debriefing, the Italians had argued about the relative merits of preparing some makeshift accommodation on the spot or driving Daniel five miles or so to a police precinct with cells. In the end it was decided to secure an area on the spot, so new locks and some bars were fitted to one of the outbuildings. They reasoned that if they left a pair of police officers with the subject, he could be kept safe until midday, when M had asked for the next session to begin. There was no cause for alarm. After all, this was not a high-risk suspect.

Unfortunately the bulk of those who had been working the case had done almost twenty-four hours on duty by the time M stopped the interrogation. The result was some very tired people who wanted sleep, and only sleep.

The two police officers detailed to act as guards for Daniel Dragonpol were as tired as anybody else. They locked themselves into the specially prepared outbuilding, which had been equipped with two bunks and a chair. Their instructions were to see that Daniel got as much rest as possible, and they planned to watch over him in shifts—one man sleeping on the spare bunk while the other remained awake. They had taken two flasks of coffee in with them, and nobody seriously considered Daniel Dragonpol to be dangerous. As one of the senior police officers later said, "He seemed relieved that his brother was dead, and untroubled about the future. He appeared to have grasped the fact that he would probably serve some kind of a prison sentence for manslaughter, but that didn't seem to worry him."

At just before nine-thirty in the morning, several well-rested police officers were bused out to the facility from the center of Milan. Two of these fresh men were immediately instructed to relieve the Dragonpol guards.

When they reached the outbuilding, they found the door open and the two police guards dead. One had burns on his face and had been garroted with his own tie. The other had died from gunshot wounds, killed at close range with his own pistol. In all probability this man was already unconscious when his killer had placed a pillow over his head and fired through it twice, thereby reducing the noise but in no way impeding the deadly progress of the bullets.

The strangled policeman had been stripped of his uniform. There was no trace of Dragonpol and few clues as to where he had gone.

Neither was there any way to determine the sequence of events. A spilled flask of coffee indicated that Dragonpol most likely had been allowed to pour his own beverage, which he had flung into the face of one cop, turning and felling the second man with a blow to the head.

One thing had been proved definitely. When the strangled cop went down, his watch had struck the floor and smashed, giving investigators a time frame. The deaths, and following escape, had taken place at six-thirty, a little more than an hour after the interrogation finished. The only other certainty was that Daniel Dragonpol was loose and dangerous.

"Looks like our Daniel was really David," Bond mused.

"We consider that an absolute certainty," Tanner agreed. They had just come off the M4 Motorway and were heading into the center of London.

"So who did Carmel think she was bringing to us?" Flicka asked.

"Yes, what *did* Carmel think she was doing?" The scene on the rooftops of the Duomo replayed in Bond's mind. Carmel waving and calling. Then the lethal walking stick coming up. Carmel shouting, "No! James, no! He's—"

He saw the stick again. Heard the shout in his head for a second time. Now, in retrospect, he wondered if the man lifting the stick was really only raising it in greeting, just before the shots crashed out.

"Maybe—" he began. Then, "Maybe we all made some terrible mistake." The more he thought the scene through, the more he became convinced that Carmel, and the man they thought was David, came in peace. Presently he asked—"And Maeve?"

The Chief of Staff gave a long sigh. "The German police did not do as we asked. They did not even have one man watching Schloss Drache. When the orders went out to pull Maeve, they found she had flown—probably two days ago."

"And one or the other of them took a shot at us by filling the Porsche with explosives." Bond did not seem to be talking to anyone in particular.

"Did he have time to catch up with us?" Flicka was now more animated.

Tanner sashayed the car between a bus and a taxi. The cabby did not like being cut off and made it clear. "And you, mate," Tanner said quietly, then carried on as if nothing had happened. "If Daniel was really David, then we can't rely on anything he's told us. The place behind La Scala, where David was supposed to be hiding out, for instance. That's almost certainly a red herring. Yes, David probably could have caught up with you. It's even possible that he has another bolt hole, complete with the means for a disguise, and a cache of weapons and explosives. He might even have spotted you out at the airport and decided to have a go—a spur-of-the-moment kind of thing."

"That's not his usual MO." Bond still sounded distant.

"Who knows? He went for high-profile targets of opportunity and usually made long-term preparations. But in your case he would certainly have made an exception. Time is on his side. After all, he's got until Sunday morning before he pulls off the royal assassination."

"You still think he's going for that?"

"It's the reason some of the best people in the business are sitting waiting for you in M's office at this very moment. And you, James, are the designated slayer of dragons."

Indeed, the group sitting and standing around the glass and chrome desk in M's office did consist of the best. He recognized a senior Special Air Service officer and a Commander from the Metropolitan Police. The latter, whose name he thought was Robb, controlled the Diplomatic Bodyguard Section, which included the so-called Royal Detectives. There was also a roly-poly little man with a constant smile—introduced simply as Ben—who turned out to be Head of Security for the EuroDisney complex, some twenty miles east of Paris. Yet another member of the group had sharp, chiseled features and looked distinctly French. He also did not seem at ease in civilian clothes.

"This is Colonel Fontaine, of GIGN." M introduced them and the Frenchman gave a little nod of recognition. "Captain Bond, you've worked with GIGN before, I think. Colonel Veron speaks highly of you."

There was a slight release of tension in the room which Bond put down to the stiff attitude Fontaine had obviously been taking. The French Special Forces Unit—GIGN—is not known for willing cooperation, even with its allies, and particularly on its home ground.

"The French authorities have kindly agreed to members of the SAS and, of course, detectives from the royal bodyguard to assist in this operation." In spite of this, M did not appear to be a happy man. There had probably been a battle of wills before Bill Tanner had brought them into the office.

"Then Her Royal Highness is definitely taking the princes to France on Sunday?" Bond tried to make it sound matter-of-fact, but the news was worrying. "Doesn't she realize—"

"No, Captain Bond." It was the policeman, Commander Robb, who answered. "We've put it to Princess Diana. Her answer was completely uncompromising. She says that they're always possible targets for terrorists and—to quote her—'nut cases,' so why should this be any different? She also said she had complete faith in her detectives, the GIGN, and the SAS."

"The point is." M sounded as though he were about to become highly sarcastic. "The point is, we have yet to ask her if she has faith in you, James."

"Me, sir?"

"Mmmm. You see we've come to a kind of decision in your absence. You ever play that game 'tag' when you were at school?"

"Yes, sir, only we called it 'he.' There was a dangerous variation known as " 'chain he.' "

"Well, be that as it may, to quote from our various childhoods, you, James, are 'he' or 'it,' or whatever other designation. You're the one who's going to get us out of this."

"I don't suppose I have any right of appeal?"

"None at all. You're going to be the White Knight who saves the beautiful princess. After all, you know the man Dragonpol better than we do. You've been close; sniffed his lair and all that. So you get the plum job."

"And what am I to do, sir? Specifically, I mean."

"Catch the blighter. Kill him if you have to."

"There are no alternatives?"

"Tell me what else we can do if we're not going to see an assassination on Sunday morning?"

"There is one other way, sir. We could remove the target."

"No. We try to remove the assassin."

"Everybody really believes this man Dragonpol will attempt an assassination?" Commander Robb sounded dubious. "I mean he must know that Their Royal Highnesses'll be protected in an unprecedented—"

"With all due respect." Bond's eyes hardened. "You could put every member of the NATO Forces, plus the SAS and GIGN into the theme park. You could even dress Her Royal Highness, and the princes, in bulletproof underwear, and Dragonpol would still probably hit them.

"With him it's a vocation. It's what he does best. I've simply got to look at the thing logically. We know what he's done before. We had him— though we didn't realize it at the time—and we've let him go. He's a specialist, and he does this for the fun of it. It's his job, and he takes pride in it. The killing is a by-product. The main thrill for him is setting things up. For David Dragonpol this is better than any drug high, better than sex, better than anything. He's going to kill the princess and the two young princes—"

"Unless we stop him. Or I should say, James, unless *you* stop him, and beat him at his own game. Now, do you think that can be done?"

Bond heard himself, as though from a long way off, saying, "Possibly."

"Then we have some kind of a chance. As I said before, we came to an understanding before you arrived, James. If you cannot, or do not, take Dragonpol before the royal party actually arrives at EuroDisney, then we *will* force a change of schedule. The GIGN, SAS, and her own detectives will head her off at the pass, so to speak—

it's our only fail-safe. They'll manufacture a problem with the aircraft, or the helicopter: something which makes it impossible."

"If *that* has to be done, sir, then I shall not be alive to see it. You should know that, in all probability, if she does not put in an appearance, he'll only get her somewhere else. Now let me look at the arrangements for Sunday."

Once more, within the room, there was a sense of tension released, and Bond knew what many of them were thinking—"Thank God it's not me."

"What do you need, James? Ask for anything."

"A few hours alone with Ben, here." He indicated the roly-poly Head of Disney Security. "Then, when we've talked, I want a couple of hours on my own to work it out. After that can we talk again, sir?"

They were given a large empty office on the third floor where Ben spread out a chart of the entire Disney area and began to recite the arrangements which had been coordinated between the Disney organization and those who advised the princess.

He talked for a long time, showing exactly where the royal party would arrive and what exhibits and rides had been selected. He added that the bulk had been chosen by young Prince William and Prince Harry.

"Our own people and the French police will be there for crowd control."

"You mean the park is going to be open to the public as usual?" Bond looked up sharply.

"Oh, yes. It's one of Princess Diana's stipulations. She wants her party to mingle with the public for as long as possible. We, of course, are arranging that one car of each ride is specially set aside and decorated for her and the children, but the rides will run normally and there will be other people on them at the same time as the royal party. Naturally they get to jump the line." He gave a nervous little laugh, which Bond did not return.

"The Disney Board of Directors is very worried about all this." Ben did not lose his smile. "It would be terrible publicity for the entire company."

"It wouldn't actually make the royal family's day either." He gave Ben a sharp, unsmiling look, but the security chief maintained his cheerful expression. Probably the happy face came with the territory.

"You know, the first time I went to the Magic Kingdom, in Orlando, I didn't think I was going to like it." Bond thought he might put the man at ease by telling him the truth. "Funny, I went with a girlfriend and we only booked for two days. I thought the whole thing would be tasteless, tawdry, and a bit phony. In the end we stayed for a week. The great thing about Disneyland is that it works. The moment they walk through those gates and find themselves in the Town Square and Main Street, the visitors know that they're going to have one hell of a good time. The rides are a knockout, and it *does* become wonderful.

"I'm pretty case-hardened, Ben, but there's a child in all of us, and that place brings out all the wonder of childhood. I noticed then that there were as many adult couples having a good time

as there were children. I tend to get a little angry
when people knock your outfit."

"You don't work there unless you feel like that."
Ben's smile broadened.

"Is the Euro complex the same as the others—
Orlando, Anaheim, Tokyo?"

"If you know the layout of those, then you'll
recognize EuroDisney. We have the same dis-
tinct areas—Main Street USA, Adventureland,
Frontierland, Fantasyland, Discoveryland, with
the Sleeping Beauty's Castle dominating the
whole thing—though it's called Le Château de
la Belle au Bois Dormant, like we've also got
Blanche-Neige et les Sept Nains, and La Cabine
des Robinsons. But you'll recognize it all, even
with the few additions—Star Tours, which is a
terrific ride through the *Star Wars* experience,
with a novice robot at the controls of your space
vehicle."

"So which areas will the royal party be seeing?"

Ben went through his list. They were to arrive
at eight-thirty on Sunday morning, an hour before
the park opened. The tour was to include Main
Street USA; the EuroDisneyland Railroad, which
circles the entire hundred and thirty-six acres;
Phantom Manor, the EuroDisney name for the
Haunted Mansion; Star Tours; Pirates of the
Caribbean; the Carrousel; and a trip on the
sternwheel steamboat *Mark Twain.*

"That's a two-hour schedule," Ben told him,
"but we've left a half-hour at each end in case
the princes persuade their mama to let them go
on something else."

Bond questioned him about the way security worked, learned about the underground tunnels which allowed maintenance and emergency access to any part of the park, while employees also kept a strict eye on each of the rides and experiences.

"There are people down there watching all the time—tending the TV monitors, the computers that run the main shows, and the Audio-Animatronics, the robot people and animals. The accent on everything down there is smooth and efficient running. The visitors and their safety come first."

As he talked, Ben pointed out the various routes and sights on the large plan. They went on for over two hours, after which Bond asked to be left alone with the chart.

"Now it starts," he thought, and for the next hour and a half he examined the map, thinking himself into David Dragonpol's mind, trying to follow the serial assassin's logic. What would *he* do? How would *he* go about something as calculated and cold-blooded as this particular killing?

When he had made certain decisions, he rang M's office. "I'm ready to put my suggestions to the whole team, sir."

"I'll get them in here. Some of them are probably asleep, but let's do it now."

As he entered the now crowded office, the first person he saw, waiting for him by the door, was the delectable Ann Reilly, assistant to the Armourer, Head of Q Branch, and therefore known to all as Q'ute. She was still as desirable as ever—a tall, elegant, leggy young woman with sleek and shining straw-colored hair which she wore in an immaculate, if severe, French pleat.

"M says I'm to give you anything you're going to need," she said, with her eyes wide and innocent.

"Chance, my darling Q'ute, would be a fine thing, as they say."

"Oh, you're hooked well and proper, James. I've met the lovely Flicka, and you might not escape from that one's clutches."

"Actually I might not want to."

"Good. Now what do you need?"

He had already prepared a small list which he handed over, telling her that Ben should take the stuff with him back to Paris. "I'll brief him before he goes."

She nodded and departed to search the Q Branch stores for the listed items.

As he turned back into the room, he found Flicka beside him. "That Q'ute person," she began. "You haven't been playing fast and loose with her, have you, darling James?"

"A little fast, but never loose."

"Well, forget it, my dear. I'll scratch her eyes out and rip the hair off her head if she ever makes a move."

"It's your subtle approach I love so much, Flick."

"Well, I do have one boon to crave."

"And?"

"M says I can't come with you. He's told me that EuroDisney is out-of-bounds to me. He's even suggesting that I should go and pamper myself in some health farm. A place called Shrublands."

"I'd try and talk him out of that, Flick. I went there once and it almost killed me."

"James, I want you to talk him out of keeping me away from EuroDisney."

He put his arms on her shoulders and looked into her face. "No, Flick. Nothing against your experience and training. Nothing against your sex. Nothing that's politically incorrect. But I'm going alone, and it's the only way. This is one of those times when we have to play it *mano a mano,* as they say."

She was about to protest when M called everyone to order. "Captain Bond has come to certain conclusions," he said, setting the stage for his agent to talk.

The plan of the EuroDisney complex was pinned to a board which Bill Tanner had placed on an easel. Bond walked over to it and began crisply—

"Please interrupt at any time. First, I believe that Dragonpol will spend Saturday night and Sunday morning inside EuroDisney, setting things up—"

"That's impossible, James. Nobody gets to stay inside. Our security—" Ben started.

"Just one minute, Ben." Bond silenced him with a look. "We're not talking about just anybody, we're talking about a very experienced serial assassin who can walk through walls. He has his own little theme park. I've seen it, and, believe me, he's forgotten everything your people know about Audio-Animatronics or optical illusions. I promise you that, however tight your security might be, Dragonpol will stay where he wants to stay, and be where he wants to be. If I'm right, he'll certainly be in the park over Saturday/Sunday night."

Ben went silent, allowing him to continue.

"What I've tried to do is put myself in Dragonpol's mind: tried to follow his logic; tried to think as he thinks, and plan as he plans."

"We understand all that, James," M cut in. "What we need to know is how *do* you think he'll go about it?"

"I think he'll use explosives, and I think he'll hit either here, or here." His finger stabbed at the chart, pointing to two of the main attractions of the park—Pirates of the Caribbean and the short trip on the riverboat *Mark Twain*.

"Why exactly?"

"Because there's water, and a certain amount of cover. One is enclosed, the other's on the surface. But in both cases he could detonate devices himself."

"So how and when would he get explosives into those areas?"

"I've already told you, sir. He'll bring them in either late on Saturday night or in the small hours of Sunday morning. Possibly only hours before the party arrives. That's how I'd do it if I were setting them up for a kill. To me these are the only two places, and I'm going to try and stop him—late on Saturday or, more likely, early on Sunday morning."

"And if you're wrong? If he has some other scheme?"

"Then either I'll be killed; or the royal party'll be killed; or you'll have to keep them a hundred miles away. You see, sir, there is one other remote—and that's the operative word—remote possibility."

"Which is?"

"That it's already set up. That he can kill them the moment they walk through the gates; and that he can do it without being there at all."

M gave a worried grunt. There were shuffles and murmurs from everybody else.

"You've chosen me for the White Knight." Bond actually smiled at them. "You either let me do it my way, and trust me, or you put someone else on the horse."

There was a long silence. Nobody looked either in his direction or at M. Finally it was M who spoke—

"All right. Good luck, James. You're the White Knight."

19

Death Among the Magic

Later, Smiling Ben told him that this was one of the best Saturdays EuroDisney had experienced in 1992: a year which had been, according to Ben, "a natural disaster on account of the weather." Today Disneyland was packed, and the sun shone, dancing off the turrets of the castle, glittering from the water around Big Thunder Mountain, and infecting the crowds with amiable good humor.

Most of the children, and some adults, wore mouse ears and carried balloons. The rides emptied as everyone took to the open spaces, crowded the sidewalks of Main Street USA, up through Adventureland and around Discoveryland, to see the afternoon's Grand Parade.

The Parade was one of the things he remembered clearly from his visit to the Magic Kingdom in Orlando. Here in France it seemed bigger and better than he recalled, but possibly this was a trick of memory and distance in time. It exploded onto the streets and walkways in a wonderfully choreographed snake of color, movement, and music. The marching bands swept by in celebration of the cheeky little mouse who had stolen the minds and hearts of the world for over six decades, their baton-twirlers leaping, hurling their sticks high, twisting, cartwheeling and seemingly doing impossible acts of juggling. Costumed young men and women dancers appeared to have walked straight out of a Hollywood movie—which was, after all, the general idea.

The bands and dancers were interspersed by a moving panorama of floats: Snow White stood by the Wishing Well, while the Dwarfs clowned; Cinderella's Pumpkin Coach was pulled by six decorated carrousel horses; Captain Hook's ship carried Peter Pan, Wendy, and the Lost Boys on a moving painted sea. There were Pooh Bear, Beauty and the Beast, Robin Hood and the foxy Sheriff, the animals from *The Jungle Book,* and all the rest, with some Disney characters walking and jumping along, miming with children in the crowd. In the place of honor, Mickey Mouse himself, in tailcoat and scarlet trousers, waved a white-gloved hand from his throne high above everyone. There was laughter, cheering and, for a time, everybody in this fabulous place became children again, caught up in the magic and wonder of it all.

Deep in the crowd, Bond was unrecognizable: gray-haired with thick horn-rimmed spectacles, looking much older and walking with a slight, stooping limp. He did not like having to resort to disguises, but in order to get Dragonpol he would have walked naked through fire—which he knew he even might be called upon to do before the next twenty-four hours were over.

Now, as he wandered around the park, he smiled with pleasure to see Chip and Dale, or Minnie, signing autograph books for clamoring children, while Pluto and Goofy played the fool with kids of all ages. Then the chill struck him. What if the man inside the hot stuffy Goofy suit was Dragonpol himself?

He banished the thought quickly. It was not impossible, but the idea smacked of paranoia, so he took himself off to pass the time on some of the rides. As on his last visit, in the United States, he enjoyed the Phantom Manor—as they called it here—with its incredible special effects: the ballroom full of twirling ghostly 18th-century dancers; the terrible time-wrecked dining room set for the wedding breakfast that never was, with the hapless bride's wraith appearing in the room; then another phantom seated, playing the organ; a glass bowl in which a pallid human woman's head talked endlessly of terrible portents, and the amazing moment on the way out when a mirror showed him seated between a pair of ghastly creatures. It was certainly value for money.

Coming out of Phantom Manor, he took a long and careful walk around the lake which was the main feature of Frontierland. Big Thunder Mountain reared up in the middle of the water and he watched as the rickety little train, with its open trucks full of screaming visitors, came spiraling down at top speed to sweep through the water splash at the base, then rise again in a dizzying turn that would take it back to the starting point.

He stood for a few minutes watching the hordes of people lining up to take a ride in one of the riverboats, *Molly Brown* or *Mark Twain*. These big replicas of the old steamboats from a more leisurely time plied constantly from their landing around the big reach of water that made the Rivers of the Far West and the lake surrounding both Big Thunder Mountain and Wilderness Island. Indian canoes and River Rogue keelboats also crossed and recrossed the water he had fingered as one of the possible locations Dragonpol might conceivably use as a final point of departure for the royal party.

Walking over to Discoveryland, he spent almost an hour in line for the Star Tours, watching R2D2 and C3PO preparing a craft for takeoff and finally entering the very realistic spaceship which was to take the passengers to the moon of Endor. Only when the doors slid into the closed position did he discover, like his fellow travelers, that the Robot, Rex, was also making his first space flight, taking their spacecraft in wrong and terrifying directions as they shook, bumped, and rattled at seemingly impossible speeds, straying right into a battle straight out of *Star Wars.*

Early in the evening he ate a pleasant salmon steak at the Blue Lagoon Restaurant, under what appeared to be a tropical night sky, with the sound of surf on the beaches. The lagoon itself was visible from where he sat, and every few minutes the boats full of visitors drifted past on their way to the adventure of the Pirates of the Caribbean which, he decided, would be his next experience.

Joining the line, he soon found himself floating in one of the boats, through a tunnel and then down a sickening lurch of a waterfall and into the quiet of the lagoon he had been watching during his meal. As he looked toward the diners, Bond had an overpowering sense that he himself was being watched by a malignant pair of eyes.

The smooth calm of the blue stretch of water changed as they appeared to round a headland to see a galleon under fire from cannon on the mainland. The explosions of the guns seemed very close, and great spouts of water leaped into the air as shot struck the sea close to his drifting craft. Then they were sailing slowly into the city under siege, full of pirates singing, pillaging, burning, drinking, chasing the local girls, and even selling off some of the more sturdy ones.

Once more he marveled at the incredibly lifelike figures and the consummate artistry of the experts—and the Imagineers—who produced such unbelievable effects, and the Audio-Animatronical beings.

Outside again Bond stood, sniffing the air. Suddenly, just as he had felt eyes upon him, he knew, as if by some extra sense, that he was here: that Dragonpol had penetrated this wonderland of illusion, pleasure, fun, excitement, and laughter. He had come to bring death among the magic.

Slowly the sky turned red and then darkened. The buildings became alive with light, the trees twinkled, and the park took on a new perspective. Soon he was jammed in among the crowds, watching the second big event of the day, the Main Street Electrical Parade, winding its way with its music and twenty-two twinkling floats from Fantasyland down Main Street.

Then the fireworks began to burst high above the castle and the wonder and sorcery of dreams and imagination were there to be carried away in the mind, a fairy tale held in the memories of all, from the smallest child to the oldest adult, forever.

As the crowds began to jostle happily toward the main gates, passing under the arches of the Main Street Station, Bond walked into the City Hall, showed his pass to one of the attendants, and went through a door that led down to the heartbeat of the park: the maze of tunnels, changing rooms, offices, computer stations, and banks of closed-circuit TV screens which monitored every area of the Disney kingdom.

Smiling Ben waited for him in a small office near the large banks of monitors.

"They'll all be gone in an hour," he said. "Then the boys'll be doing final tests on the rides, decorating the cars and boats to be used by the royals in the morning, and generally making sure all's well. After that things'll quiet down for the night."

A line from a half-remembered poem came into Bond's head—"And leave the world to darkness and to me." And to Dragonpol, he added almost aloud, too preoccupied to hear the rest of Ben's sentence.

"Sorry, Ben, what did you say?"

"I've put four extra men out there in Frontierland, watching the Riverboat Landing and the water around Rivers of the Far West. They'll be checking in every half-hour."

"Good. I hope they know their job."

"James, nobody's going to get past us tonight. You can sit with me and watch the screens. There's no way he's going to meddle with the rides without being spotted."

They drank coffee and sat talking, Bond's eyes never leaving the monitors. He saw the lead boat for Pirates of the Caribbean being decorated with velvet cushions and flowers, especially for the royal guests; and they were doing the same to one of the Doom Cars at Phantom Manor. As he watched, he came to the realization that his nerves were stretched almost to a taut breaking point.

"You really think he's going to organize something there?" Ben nodded toward the monitor.

Bond nodded, lips clamped shut.

"Which do you think it'll be, Pirates or the Riverboat?"

"I'd go for Pirates. Some kind of device near the galleon, where there's plenty of noise anyway. I'd put it right near the effect of the cannonball hitting the water. But what do I know?"

Just before two in the morning, Bond retired to the small changing room where Ben had left the bulky sports bag containing the equipment Q'ute had provided. It was all standard stuff—

a black wet suit, without a mask or air bottle, a waterproof holster containing his favorite weapon, the 9mm ASP automatic, with the guttersnipe sight, and two spare clips of Glaser slugs. While the weapon was technically out of production, Armaments Systems and Procedures still supplied his service with spare parts, and occasional new weapons: after all, this was a sophisticated remodeling of the Browning 9mm and *they* were certainly still being manufactured.

He also carried a Gerber fighting knife—a recent gift from the US Navy Seals—and a pack of four waterproof, hand-operated flares. There was nothing fancy here, and nothing that could really go wrong.

"Going for a swim?" Ben asked.

"Not if I can help it. Anything happened?" He picked up the spare radio that Ben had ready for him. "This all set?"

"It's tuned, and, yes, all quiet on the Western Front. Not a peep, and the boys out in Frontierland don't seem to have seen anything out of the ordinary."

They sat for the next ninety minutes, still scanning the monitors, with Ben checking in with his people around the lake every thirty minutes. The check-in consisted of a series of clicks on the radio, denoting each separate man, while Ben responded with a similar number of clicks.

When it happened, it came, as ever, suddenly and unexpectedly. Nothing showed on the monitors, and Ben kept glancing at his watch. The check-in clicks had not started on time. Number one should have begun at exactly three-thirty, and the others were due to follow in sequence.

"They're late." He did not yet sound alarmed, but Bond felt the hair bristle on the back of his neck.

"He's here," he said with absolute certainty. Then Ben's radio clamored—a series of rapid clicks which was the alarm signal.

"Jesus, you're right."

"I'm already there."

One of the little electric carts used by the staff to get around the underground tunnels had been placed in readiness just outside. Now Bond was held up for a moment as Ben argued, wanting to come with him.

"Stay where you are. If I need help, I'll call in." So he was off, whining away along the bare-walled tunnel lined with wiring and sanitation ducts. The underground passages were marked to show exactly where you were in relation to the world above, so navigation was a simple matter.

He reached Central Place and took a hard left, which brought him to the Riverboat Landing, leaping from the cart and climbing the metal ladder that would take him right onto the landing.

For a moment he closed his eyes to adjust to the darkness outside and waited by the door, which he softly pushed open.

He stood in the open air with all senses straining, looking up at the moored riverboats and hearing no unusual sound in the night. Slowly he inched forward until he reached the edge of the landing stage, moving sideways to get a view of the water. Darkness. Silence. Nothing. Time, he considered, for some light on the scene, so he unclipped the radio from his belt.

He was just lifting it to his mouth, the thumb of his right hand pressing the transmit button, when he felt the metal digging into the back of his neck and heard the throaty, soft whisper which sent a chill of ice down his spine.

"Thank you for coming, James Bond. I've only incapacitated the other watchers. For you, I have a special treat." Dragonpol's tone had altered to one of deep and desperate madness. This time he was not acting.

Dropping the radio, hoping that the touch of his thumb on the button would have already alerted Ben, Bond let his body go limp. It was an old trick, learned long ago. If the muscles seem to go inactive, the person threatening you will imagine he has complete dominance. "Okay, David." He spoke almost in a whisper so that Dragonpol would have to strain to hear him. "Where do you want me to go?"

"Shut up—" Dragonpol began, and Bond sagged at the knees, turning into the pistol touching his neck and bringing his right fist around in a piledriver which went wide, catching Dragonpol on the shoulder.

"Come in, the water's lovely," he shouted, reaching for the man's neck, his fingers connecting with a wet suit not unlike the one he was wearing, heaving and pulling his adversary off-balance.

As they fell from the landing stage, their bodies locked together, Dragonpol's pistol went off, and he felt a small burn in his left shoulder as a bullet tore at his wet suit.

They rolled into the water, with Dragonpol trying desperately to get an armlock on Bond, who was struggling to drag the ASP out of its holster, but his fingers were slipping on the waterproof material. Then he felt himself being pulled under with the actor's fingers clawing at his throat.

He was on his back now, the tall, heavy, muscular Dragonpol on top of him—fingers at his windpipe and the other arm across his chest pushing down. Bond tried to open his eyes, clamping his mouth shut as he was jammed further and further into the water.

He kicked and squirmed, putting every ounce of strength into moving his opponent from above him, but the man's grip simply tightened, and Bond was slowly thrust deeper under the water, lungs bursting and the strength fast leaving his body.

The redout came first. It was sudden and strange. In the brief tick of consciousness he thought something had happened to his eyes, then he realized that this was the moment before oblivion. He opened his mouth, felt the water rush in, choking him, darkness filtering into his brain.

As he gagged and choked, Bond was given a few seconds of clarity, allowing him to make a last, supreme effort. His muscles spasmed and he rolled to one side. For a moment Dragonpol lost his grip, slipping underneath Bond. The positions were reversed, but Bond did not have the strength left to maintain control.

With a shriek of rage, David Dragonpol pushed Bond away so that he floundered, all arms and thrashing legs, making the water foam around him. His adversary launched himself, screaming obscenities, straight in for a final kill.

In that flashing instant Bond saw him for what he was: a crazed killer of dreams, a weaver of nightmares, a destroyer of the beautiful fairy tales that this place gave to men, women, and children the world over. He made another grab for the ASP at his hip and this time pulled it free, his arm coming up, finger squeezing the trigger. The first shot caught Dragonpol in the shoulder, spinning him in a whirl of white water. The second shot went wide, flying out into the middle of the lake. Bond heard a sudden thump when the bullet found a resting place, and this seemed to terrify Dragonpol, who clutched at his shoulder but deliberately turned from Bond to look out into the lake.

"No!" he yelled. Then again, "No! You can't!" Nothing showed in his eyes as he glanced back, then splashed away, finally flinging himself forward, swimming out to where the sound had come from.

Bond stood in some four feet of water, puzzled, disinclined to finish off the mad killer who appeared to have found superhuman strength for some last battle only he could fight.

The second bullet had hit something very important to the man. That was obvious. But what? His hand reached down to his belt again, hauling out one of the flares. It was about the size of a small flashlight, with a ring pull at the top. Bond held it out at arm's length, pressing it next to the pistol in his right hand, grabbing at the ring with the other.

There was the usual pop and jerk in his fist, and the flare soared upward, arching away toward where Dragonpol still swam hard.

As the light seared the sky, David Dragonpol stopped swimming, turned, and began to shout, first in fury and then, as the flare dipped toward him, in terror. The flare touched the surface but did not go out.

Instead of a fizzle, a sudden gush of flame leaped into the air and then spread out in a great bowl of fire. In its midst was this tiny figure, engulfed by flame. There was the roar of burning chemicals, then loud above that noise, the sound of hideous screaming as the fire overwhelmed the man who had brought sudden, ingeniously planned death to so many.

20

Hints of Change

It says much for the Disney organization that they had the fire out long before any other local brigades arrived. They also had the lake dragged, a charred body and many small items removed, and the water relatively clean before eight in the morning.

The police were there as well, of course, though it was several weeks before their forensic conclusions were passed down to other authorities. It was perfectly clear that David Dragonpol had been determined to do away with the royal party at the expense of a large number of other innocent lives, though his mistake had been to incapacitate Ben's night watchers before he had set the trap and tethered it in the correct position—just under the surface in the direct path of the *Mark Twain*.

The trap, when all became clear, was an aluminum beer keg almost certainly filled with a deadly mixture of gasoline and thermite—a black powder of iron oxide mingled with aluminum granules. There had also been a simple remote-control device which would have proved very effective: an electrical detonator set into a small ball of plastique explosive.

If this revolting device had been exploded as the *Mark Twain* passed over it, the resultant fireball would have undoubtedly engulfed the paddle steamer. Very few people would have got out alive. The gasoline would have ignited, and in turn this would have set off the thermite.

Thermite burns rapidly, with a temperature in excess of $4,000°$ Fahrenheit and so fiercely that it was at one time used to cut and weld metal in shipyards.

Bond's one stray bullet had pierced the keg, spilling the contents, while the flare had ignited the gasoline, incinerating Dragonpol in the water. Happily, the fire did not spread onto Big Thunder Mountain or back to any of the other exhibits.

Later the French police learned that Dragonpol had bribed a truck driver to—as the driver said—"look the other way." Undoubtedly, the keg had been brought into the theme park with a normal delivery. Within forty-eight hours, the Disney security people had put new restrictions on all goods entering the facility.

By eight that Sunday morning, nobody would have known that there had even been an incident, though one look at Bond would have suggested that he was the loser in a barroom brawl.

The Disney emergency unit had patched him up, but there was no way short of makeup to hide the bruises.

Now he waited near the main entrance, surprised at the lack of police and local protection, which he had expected to be there in force ready to greet the royal party. So he was bewildered when he saw Ben, still in jeans and a T-shirt, wandering back to his office in the warren of tunnels beneath Disneyland.

"Nobody's told you?" Ben still wore his smile, but his eyebrows shot up in his own unique version of disbelief.

"Told me what?"

"It's off. She's not coming."

"Last night's little business did the trick, then?"

"No, James. This morning's little business did the trick."

"That's a question of semantics."

"No, I mean less than an hour ago."

"An hour—"

Ben explained that the royal party had been staying with friends on the outskirts of Paris, and the press had got wind of the location. The story was that they were there, cameras and notebooks at the ready, when she had emerged with her two children, at seven A.M., for the drive to EuroDisney would take at least an hour.

"It seems that one of your people was with the royal detectives. I haven't got the details, but she spotted Dragonpol's sister among the crowd. The lady in question had a very nasty hand grenade in her handbag. Your officer disarmed her. So it's all over. The princess made an immediate decision and called off the visit."

"Pity she didn't take notice earlier."

It was not until he arrived back in London, later in the day, that Bond learned the identity of the officer who had spotted Maeve Horton.

The taxi from Heathrow had dropped him in the King's Road and he walked, carrying his garment bag, to the Regency house. He was about to put his key in the lock when the door was opened by his elderly housekeeper, May, now returned from her jaunt up to Scotland.

May looked at him accusingly. "Mr. James, there's a young woman here who says she's a houseguest. She's a pleasant lass, and speaks English like a native, though she tells me she's foreign." To be "foreign," as far as May was concerned, was tantamount to being a carrier of what she called "that terrible Black Thing they had in the Middle Ages."

Flicka von Grüsse sat in the living room, wearing a very stylish pants suit in red, with a lot of military flair and gold buttons on the jacket.

"You didn't tell me about the Scotch dragon," she whispered after they got their breath back.

"Flick, the word is Scottish. I thought you spoke English. Scotch is a drink—though I'm always reading American novels which refer to Scottish people as Scotch. It's like calling citizens of Oporto winos."

"I know." She grinned. "I love you when you get all correctional. I hear there was a bonfire party out at EuroDisney."

"You've heard about Maeve—old Hort—as well, have you?"

"Heard about her? I nabbed her."

"You . . . ?"

It all came out over a light supper, served by May, who had begun to soften toward Flicka.

Fredericka von Grüsse had worked some kind of witchcraft on M and had been sent as the service representative among the Scotland Yard royal detectives.

When it came to leaving the house where the princess and her children had spent the night, Flicka had gone to take a look at the journalists before they brought the royal party out.

"Maeve was standing there, trying to look insignificant among the photographers," she told him. "So I took no notice, pretended I hadn't seen her. I walked around and chatted to some of the press people, then worked my way behind her, did a kind of mental frisk, and knew she was up to no good."

"So?" He liked the part about doing a mental frisk.

"So I jammed my gun in her ear and told her I'd blow her head off if she moved. The cops came down, searched her, and carted her away. She had this damned great grenade in her handbag, and there's no doubt she was going to use it."

Flicka had been allowed to sit in on the first interrogation, and it was immediately obvious that Maeve's love for brother David was of the unbalanced and unhealthy variety. "She said she'd have died for him, that he had more talent in his little finger than . . . Oh, you know how these obsessive people go on. The whole damned family was crazy if you ask me."

It also became clear that sister Maeve was the
true answer to one of the great Dragonpol con-
undrums. "She did the flowers," Flicka told him.
"Admitted it almost as soon as I asked. If anyone
had bothered to check her passport, they'd have
found she followed on David's heels, taking those
bloody roses with her and making sure that they
were delivered to the gravesides. Oh, by the way,
M wants us both in the office by nine tomorrow
morning."

"To congratulate us, no doubt." Bond cocked his
head and raised a quizzical eyebrow.

"Or to ask for a full explanation of two dead
bodies at Schloss Drache."

When it came to it, M asked no awkward
questions. He spoke for a long time about the
Dragonpol incident, getting quite serious about
it at one point. "Friend Dragonpol," he said, "is,
I believe, a symptom of the sick and dangerous
society in which we live."

From there he launched into the real reason he
had summoned them to his office.

"There are changes in the air." He seemed tense
and serious. "Changes that will affect this service
drastically. The job's changing with the world,
though I personally believe the world's a more
dangerous place than it was when we had a
cut-and-dried Cold War. A thousand times more
dangerous, which is probably why the powers-
that-be are demanding a complete reorganization.
It's going to affect me, and it's particularly going
to affect you two. You'll get the full details of
promotion and the new job within the week. I
simply wanted to warn you before it happens."

"I hope it's not playing detective again," Bond muttered. "That's *too* dangerous."

"Ah." M gave them an enigmatic look.

"Am I going to like the changes?" Bond asked.

"Probably. Almost certainly. You'll be doing some very different things in the future, James; and so will you, Fräulein von Grüsse." He picked up his old pipe and began to load it with the evil-smelling tobacco he had smoked since Bond first knew him. "They'll be bringing you in here for a briefing in a few days. Until then I suggest you take a short leave. If I'm right, it'll be the last one you'll get for a long time."

He dismissed them with an almost perfunctory gesture, but as they reached the door, he called Bond back.

"James, do I sense the possibility of wedding bells between you and Fräulein von Grüsse?"

"I don't know, sir. Maybe. Maybe not. Why do you ask?"

M made his familiar harrumphing noise. "I suppose that, contrary to your experience, I'm really just a sentimental old matchmaker."

"Really, sir?" He didn't believe a word of it.

"I'm just saying that you could do worse, James. You could do much worse."

"Well, sir, if it does happen, I'd ask only one thing of you."

"Oh yes? And what would that be?"

"Please, sir, don't send any flowers."